On Wings of Love

On Wings of Love

A Novel

by

Brenton G. Yorgason

Covenant Communications

Published by Covenant Communications, Inc.
American Fork, Utah

Copyright © 1995 by Brenton G. Yorgason
All rights reserved

Printed in the United States of America
First Printing: June 1995

01 00 99 98 97 96 95 94 10 9 8 7 6 5 4 3 2 1

ISBN 1-55503-853-0

Library of Congress Cataloging-in-Publication Data
Yorgason, Brenton G.
    On wings of love: a novel / Brenton G. Yorgason.
    ISBN 1-55503-853-0
    I. Title.
PS3575.05805   1995
813'.54—dc20   95-21904
                                         CIP

DEDICATION

This book is dedicated to Robert E. and Helen Wells, whose story and dream this is. They not only conceived it, but spent a lifetime recording Bob's experiences as a pilot, as well as their mutual interest in the increasingly popular aeronautics industry. They likewise drafted the early theme of this love/adventure story. Bob's professional life as a banker in Buenos Aires, Argentina, gave birth to the setting for this story, and to the romantic flavor that is included herein.

Elder Wells, a general authority for The Church of Jesus Christ of Latter-day Saints, has been a true friend for the past two decades, and always one to teach me about soaring above the mundane meanderings of the world. His and Helen's intimacy with the teachings of Jesus Christ and with the Savior Himself, have likewise provided motivation for the teachings of faith and hope that are contained within these pages.

ACKNOWLEDGEMENTS

My deepest thanks to Robert and Helen Wells and my wife, Margaret, and family, as well as to my editor, LuAnn B. Staheli, and the others at Covenant Communications who helped to prepare this work for publication.

AUTHOR'S NOTE

This novel, which is purely fictional, is placed in the historical setting of the famous Bendix Cup transcontinental air race of 1936. In this race, women were allowed—at last—to compete. The plane that Howard Hughes was to fly was, indeed, not ready for another two weeks. Thus his portrayal in the story is accurately stated.

The other two individuals who did in truth fly in the race were "Petite Laura" Ingalls and Amelia Earhart. Neither of these two women won the race, however, as two other little-known women placed first and second. Amelia Earhart flew in this race just one year before her untimely death as she attempted to cross the Pacific Ocean as she had done with the Atlantic.

In addition to these historical female characters, Roscoe Turner was a highly successful stunt and race pilot of the 1930s, even though he did not actually participate in the 1936 race. In addition to wining at least two Bendix Cup races during his career, he won many other close-circuit and cross-country races, competing against such prominent aviators as General Jimmy Dolittle of World Wars I and II fame.

The statement of Charles Lindbergh's whereabouts, in Wales, England, is also correct, as at this time he and his wife, Anne, were attempting to find anonymity after the tragic kidnapping and murder of their eldest son nearly five years earlier. Lindbergh made no attempt to fly in this race, but continued to serve as a spokesman for various blossoming airline manufacturers.

I have taken the liberty of using some of the names common to the air race community of the 1930s to give a sense of historicity to the novel. Most of the incidents described actually did happen to pilots and aircraft of that era, but for our purposes they have been fictitiously placed in the scenes of this novel for balance and intrigue.

Lastly, while enjoying research into the history of Argentina and North America in the 1930s, this novel is purely the workings of Robert Wells' and my imagination. Any resemblance to persons, living or dead, or to the airplanes they personally flew, is purely coincidental.

Chapter One

Early Spring 1936
Southern California

The sound of the giant palomino's hooves being sucked out of the recently prepared mud suddenly stopped. Maggie Rockwell, sitting astride her favorite stallion Pepper, whispered softly, calming her mount as best she could. A bead of perspiration worked its way slowly down her cheek, and, while squinting into the rising sun, she wiped it away. A bee buzzed harmlessly around the front of her saddle, trying futilely to find a suitable place upon which to light.

Maggie was suddenly aware of the spectacular beauty around her. The fog had not yet lifted and seemed to season the air with a musty, invigorating odor of its own. The picturesque valley, with its rolling, grassy hills and clumps of low trees, glowed in the early morning sunrise. She could see a large, sloping hill topped with huge boulders in the distance; on the other side of the valley, the mountains rose majestically with a stunning symmetry.

Taking in the immediate surroundings, Maggie examined the winding dirt road that snaked up from the fields below. It was along this road that the actual filming of her stunt would take place, and from her several rides over the terrain, Maggie knew it was an ideal location to shoot the rescue scene in the movie.

Suddenly she felt a chill go up her spine, and she became

instantly worried about the increasing wind. However, the director, who was climbing onto his platform a hundred yards away, seemed oblivious to her concerns and ordered the practice run to proceed posthaste.

Drawing in a deep breath and steeling her mind to the potential dangers of performing such a dangerous stunt, Maggie gripped tightly on the reins and waited. Almost immediately, a biplane flown by her close friend Roscoe Turner came into view. "Go, Pepper!" she shouted, while lighting into a full gallop. Glancing over her shoulder, she saw the plane tip its wings, signaling for her to proceed as planned. The rope ladder extended well below the plane and was flapping wildly in the wind.

At the last second, just as she stood in the saddle and extended her arms toward the plane, a great gust of wind arose. Leaping from the horse, Maggie's fingers swiped at the ladder, missing it by inches. After flying suspended in midair for what seemed forever, she finally plummeted to the ground beside the running horse. She landed hard into the prepared mud, face down in a gigantic bellyflop, and gradually slid to a horrifying stop.

Pepper, somehow sensing Maggie's miscalculation, rolled his eyes in fright. Laying back his ears, he bucked frantically and twisted—his hooves barely missing Maggie's head. The horse's left front hoof continued sinking into the puddle of mud and, as Maggie watched in horror, her beautiful stallion rolled end over end, coming to a stop in a final *kersplash*!

Muddy and bruised, but somehow still intact, Maggie worked her way to her feet and wiped the mud out of her eyes. She sloshed her way forward, fanning her arms as she made her way to her stunned and injured mount.

Pepper, seeing his master pressing forward, gathered courage and stumbled to his feet. Shaking violently, he sprayed mud and water everywhere, even onto the already mud-soaked Maggie. Finally, nodding his head as if to welcome Maggie to his side, he stood perfectly still. The two partners had survived a clear mishap, and, although Pepper would be out of commission for the next day's shoot, Maggie would be ready and would ride her other horse, Duncan. She determined silently that nothing would keep her from performing the stunt—not even a stubborn, inconsiderate German director.

Several miles away, Fernando Underwood gave the stablehands their designated chores around the buildings and grounds. He also directed the exercise program he had implemented for each horse boarded there.

After about an hour of work, he was just leaving for the university when a stablehand came running to Fernando to tell him of a sick horse in the stables. But when the two entered the horse's stall, Fernando sensed that the problem was more serious than previously indicated.

Without hesitating, Fernando directed the stablehand to notify Dr. William Bell, the veterinarian in charge of the university's horses. "She has a dangerously high temperature," he exclaimed, "and Doc will have to prescribe some medicine to bring it down. Oh—and while he is coming, bring me some eucalyptus bark. Be sure to pull it from the tree rather than picking it off the ground so there's no dirt on it."

Fernando also asked for the items needed to prepare and boil the liquid to produce a vapor that would fill the stall of the sick animal. Fernando knew what he should do, but he was also aware that a registered and licensed veterinarian was required to prescribe the medicine needed for the mare to survive.

An hour later, after the vet had arrived and administered to the horse, Fernando suddenly realized that he was hopelessly late for his exam.

"I have an emergency, Doc," he said hurriedly." I'm due on campus for an important exam. I have no transportation to get me there on time, and I was wondering if you could drop me off on your way back to your clinic."

Shortly, the two were speeding down the dirt road in the veterinarian's '34 Ford pickup. As they rode along, Dr. Bell considered the unusual young man seated beside him. He had often wanted to ask Fernando a few personal questions about his background, and he saw a chance to ask a question under the guise of professionalism.

Doc smiled at Fernando. "It seems that you know more about horses than I do. I am amazed at your practical knowledge in spotting that mare's problem and diagnosing it accurately. Where in the world did you learn so much?"

Fernando was instantly uncomfortable with the doctor's question about his past, and he intuitively deflected the question.

"Oh," he smiled nonchalantly. "I grew up around horses, and I guess I just kind of observed what others did to fix them up when they were sick."

Sensing that Fernando's response was purposely evasive, Dr. Bell determined to press further. "Fernando, just where did you grow up? How do you know so much about horses? You've either had a thorough education in veterinary science, or you have had the most extensive practical experience imaginable. You were able to diagnose a sick animal and prescribe the correct medicine as well as I could have."

Fernando accepted the compliment, but again he did not answer directly. "Actually, I've lived all over, and some of my friends are veterinarians who have loaned me books to read. Horses are just a hobby of mine, I suppose."

Recognizing the dangerous direction of the conversation, Fernando calmly but subtly turned the conversation back toward the veterinarian himself. "Where did you go to school, Doc?"

The doctor realized that he was not going to get any more personal information from this young man. He decided it best to just let it be and continue to work to build confidence and trust in their relationship.

"I went to a veterinary science school in Denver, Colorado. It has an enviable reputation and the tuition was tolerably low. My folks lived in the mountains on a ranch nearby, so I was close enough to home to make weekend visits possible."

Fernando saw that they had entered the campus and before the doctor could ask any more questions, he pointed toward a building—the engineering center—and gathered his books for a quick exit. Seconds later he jumped out of the truck, thanked the doctor for his kindness, and ran up the steps of the building.

Fernando's Strength of Materials class was one of the most important subjects required of all aspiring aeronautical engineers. He arrived to take the test just as the other students were settling in with their blue exam booklets. The test consisted of three questions, each focusing on an aspect of the history of aeronautics.

Fernando began writing, detailing how, in the beginning, aircraft had been built with bamboo, covered with linen cloth tightly stretched over the frame, and waterproofed and shrunk with dope, a special varnish. He elaborated on how subsequent progress was made with wooden frames still covered with linen cloth; eventually, plywood was tried as both part of the structure and part or all of the covering.

As he wrote, Fernando was suddenly conscious that he was very much out of place in the classroom. He was still wearing his red polo shirt and white polo riding breeches, sweat stained and smelly from the flanks of the horse he had ridden a couple of hours earlier while instructing a new hand on the fine points of working a polo horse. He was aware that his dark curly hair was tousled from the helmet he had worn while riding, but he hadn't noticed that the insteps of his tall black riding boots were carrying a smelly smear of manure from the stall of the sick horse.

Just at that instant of discovery, from the other side of the room appeared a beautiful, willowy young woman who was also late for the exam. Fernando noticed with great interest that she, too, was wearing riding gear consisting of a plaid shirt, western-cut trousers, and high-heeled western boots. She was tall, lithe, and obviously athletic, with an elegant grace in her walk. In spite of himself, Fernando was totally distracted.

Like Fernando, she was sweaty and dirty and showed the effects of having spent the morning in a corral around horses—and perhaps the results of a likely dumping in the dirt. Her waist was slender, but the tailored trousers revealed strong muscles in her hips and legs. In spite of his promise to himself three years earlier—after being summarily expelled from Cambridge, La Sorbonne, and then Harvard—he could not help being impressed with the girl who had just entered the room.

Unlike Fernando, the young woman was completely oblivious to the distinct strong odor of manure from the instep of her own boots. Fernando, however, noticed it and smiled as she gave her name to the exam assistant.

"Maggie—uh . . . Margaret Rockwell," she stammered, obviously out of breath and at the same time relieved that she had safely arrived for the exam. That was what happened when different classes take the exams together, Fernando grimaced, conscious that the only vacant desk in the room was directly to his left.

As she took her seat, Fernando became increasingly uncomfortable. While he could not help but appreciate her beauty and deportment, he was strongly aware that his attitude toward beautiful women had nearly been his downfall. Still, not wanting to appear rude, he glanced her way and attempted a weak, but cordial smile.

Perceiving that this stranger was obviously making an extremely feeble and ineffective pass, Maggie simply looked beyond him to the clock, opened her booklet, and began to write. She couldn't help but notice the other student's manure-laden boots, and the foul odor that had come from the same. "What an inconsiderate person," she whispered audibly, almost expecting a reply. But none came and she did her best to settle into her exam.

However, the more Maggie attempted to block the stranger and his boots from her mind, the more preoccupied she became with his presence next to her. Finally, after several minutes of haphazardly responding to the first exam question, her curiosity got the best of her. She just had to take a further look, and satisfy herself with a second glance that would tell her he wasn't as handsome as she had first thought.

Moving her head slightly to the right, Maggie allowed her eyes to glance casually at Fernando, hoping her glance would go undetected. To her surprise, Fernando was still smiling at her—a smile so captivating that it caught her clearly off guard and almost took her breath away.

"Your boots are smelly," Fernando whispered in spite of himself, smiling.

"As are yours!" she snapped back, both disturbed and pleased that she had caught him staring at her. "Why—"

"Quiet, please!" the assistant called as she stood and looked at both Maggie and Fernando.

"We've been caught," Fernando smiled sheepishly. "If you finish before I do, stick around, and I'll clean your boots for you."

Maggie didn't know whether to feel complimented, ashamed, angry, or simply sorry for the inappropriately familiar manner of the stranger's request. She decided that she was more angry than anything else, and for the next two hours she carried on a mental conversation with the man next to her—realizing that his brashness had caused her to lose her concentration completely. Yes, she consoled herself, he would certainly pay for the distraction and embarrassment he had caused her.

While Maggie's thoughts ran wild, Fernando tried to shake off thoughts of the young lady at his side. She was elegant and attractive, and even with mud-caked clothes and matted, water-soaked hair, she exuded an aura of self-confidence. But, most captivating of all, thought Fernand, were her freckles. Her Grecian nose was beautifully arrayed with freckles, obviously caused by so much time spent in the sun riding horses.

These thoughts sent Fernando on a mental search, and suddenly he was reliving the horror and shame of his former life. Although he had always been true to the promise he had made to his mother of not compromising the virtue of a young woman, his reckless need to impress them and find acceptance from them had nearly ruined him.

Enough of that. Fernando knew that he must concentrate on the exam.

Minutes passed as approximately fifty students wore down their pencil leads in frantic writing. The steady scratching on paper throughout the room created almost a monotonic symphony, with Fernando and Maggie, as well as everyone else, doing their level best to fulfill their professor's expectations.

After nearly three hours, Maggie was relieved beyond words when finally the attractive student beside her folded up his booklet, stood up, and handed it to the assistant. He glanced back at her, smiled awkwardly, and quietly exited the classroom. "Thank goodness," she thought to herself. "I hope I never see that arrogant, smelly man again."

However, although he had left the room, Maggie found herself consumed even more by thoughts of the handsome, though impudent, stranger. She reflected again on the melodic nature of his voice—the indisputable fact that he was broad shouldered, well-developed, and so . . . utterly handsome. Although she would never in the world admit it, she inwardly smiled at the interest he had shown in her.

Fernando, meanwhile, waited outside on the steps of the building, trying to convince himself that he was totally disinterested in this Maggie Rockwell as a woman, although he was intrigued with her obvious connection with animals and aviation. He had cleaned his boots on the grass below, and, although he wanted nothing more than to keep right on walking, he was duty-bound by his offer to clean the lady's boots. He would do so, and perhaps inquire about their shared interests before he bid her adieu and quietly excused himself from her life.

Remembering the consequences of his behavior that had devastated his life as he had formerly known it, Fernando told himself sternly. "You will avoid all entanglements."

"Are you saying that I'm an entanglement?"

Spinning around, Fernando felt his face flush with embarrassment. There, standing directly behind him, stood the woman who had occupied his thoughts since he had first laid eyes on her.

"Uh . . . er . . . I'm sorry, ma'am. It's just that . . . ."

"It's just that you're a lonely, egocentric polo jockey," Maggie countered, pleased that she could easily put this stranger in his place.

"You're right, of course," Fernando said politely, with a smile. "I'm sorry if I offended you, Miss . . . Miss Rockwell."

"Oh, and a touch of humility have you?" Maggie smiled, knowing that this conversation was going nowhere, and yet wishing that it would last indefinitely.

"Well," Fernando sighed honestly, "That was rude of me . . . especially since I was the first to smell up the testing center. Please allow me to apologize. My name is Fernando Underwood."

"Well, you already know mine," Maggie answered. "Shall we let bygones be bygones, so we can at least part friends?" She didn't know why she was speaking so foolishly, but the words had already been said. Extending her hand, she shook his, then quickly slipped off her boots.

She smiled innocently. "You offered to clean them."

Puzzled, yet somehow warmed by her request, Fernando wiped the boots off thoroughly and handed them back to her.

"For you, madam," he bowed genuinely. "I've never seen boots so muddy, but at least the first layer has disappeared."

"I had an accident this morning," Maggie admitted and without waiting for a reply, she positioned her boots under her arm, turned, and walked barefoot down the steps toward the parking lot.

Fernando suddenly felt alone. He knew that his misfortune with his family had led him into the dark and consuming world of alcohol and gambling. His increasing need to impress his peers—members of both sexes, really—had only fueled the fire

9

that had quite literally burned him out of their lives. The last thing he needed was a relationship with someone as beautiful and captivating as this Maggie Rockwell.

Chapter Two

The predawn hours of the following morning found Maggie Rockwell hastily preparing a serving of hot, steamy Quaker's Oats, a cereal that would give her the strength she needed for such an exhausting day ahead. She was stiff and sore from yesterday's fall, but other than that—and the hurt pride she had suffered at the whim of the callous and incautious director—she was fine.

Maggie, howbeit unlikely, was one of the top students in the aeronautical engineering department. That she was attending a university was unusual in and of itself. And that she was majoring in a hard science was even more improbable.

In addition to attending school, Maggie worked part-time for a motion picture studio. She was able to support herself and also send money home to her parents on a regular basis. She didn't mix much with the other students only partly because there was no time. In reality, she felt they might not accept her humble family background.

The students at the university came from prominent families, and so, Maggie concluded as she ate her cereal, Fernando Underwood also came, no doubt, from some elite and prominent family. Yet, he had seemed to distance himself from her with the way he had bid farewell to her the previous day, so why was she even thinking about him? From his attire, she guessed that he was merely a socially awkward polo player, and even though he obviously shared her interest in flying, he had definitely given her the signal that she served no purpose in his life, eliminating the need for her to think of him further.

Maggie's thoughts switched to her classmates in general in a conscious attempt to force the attractive stranger from her mind. The strategy worked only briefly before her thoughts returned to the puzzling Fernando Underwood. Their senior class was not large, having lost several members by attrition, so she knew that Fernando had to have seen her before, even though she had not been aware of his presence until the day before at their exam. She had to admit that he was ruggedly handsome, and there was something attractively different about his way of speaking, a hint of a British accent. Still, his reclusive manner seemed oddly out of character, and she reasoned that something, somehow, was causing him to behave the way he had.

As she drove her newly leased '33 Chevrolet Convertible Roadster into the awakening morning, she found herself thinking again about Fernando. Shifting the car into third gear, she wondered what he would think if he knew that she was on her way to participate in a very difficult and dangerous movie scene for a major Hollywood studio. Maggie was a part-time stunt rider standing in for the leading lady—the famous movie star Greta Garbo—whose name appeared almost daily in the gossip columns of Hollywood's newspapers.

In addition to her education in a male-dominated field, Maggie was proud to have obtained needed employment in movie stunt riding. Her father had given her two palomino stallions before leaving northern Arizona, and each was now stabled, free of charge, at the movie location.

Not only had Maggie's beautiful horses and riding abilities given her an income and a leased automobile for transportation, she had also consequently developed a keen interest in flying and the finances with which to pursue her aeronautical education. Many of her scenes were closely related to airplanes, parachuting, and horse stunts—all three of which were now very much in vogue in Hollywood. She had specialized in both horseback stunts and flying stunts so she could get more jobs; the major studios hired her, since they could get twice the skill at the same price.

In her mind, Maggie unwittingly began an imaginative conversation with an absent Fernando Underwood. "You should know," she justified herself aloud, "I have been repeatedly called upon because I am dependable and capable, and I create a good impression because of my professionalism."

Finishing her sentence, staring into the vacant seat at her right, Maggie suddenly realized she was thinking about and speaking to someone she would probably never again lay eyes upon. But, as she was not at all interested in him, that was completely irrelevant.

A half hour later, when a still-very-sore Maggie Rockwell arrived at the location for the movie filming, the sun was just peeking over the horizon. Not even a slight breeze interrupted the absolute calm. Maggie opened her door, stepped slowly and stiffly down, and looked around. The vast array of blooming flowers cascaded wildly around her—white marguerites, Santa Barbara daisies, snapdragons, achillea, and pink Bonica roses. Their fragrance, subtly changing with each breath that she took, was surprisingly intoxicating. She offered a silent prayer of thanks, expressing gratitude for the natural beauty of God's garden.

Upon completing her quiet reverie, Maggie returned her thoughts to the task at hand. She could now see several small groups of men setting up tripods, cameras, and reflector equipment at various locations. Trailers were parked close by, where men were saddling horses and adjusting their western attire.

These thoughts spun into others as she walked toward the spot where the final shooting was to take place. She cleared her mind and mentally completed her test run of the stunt that had caused her such a mishap yesterday, which they would film today. Her favorite mount, Pepper, had sprained his ankle yesterday during her fall, and the veterinarian was supposed to be out to examine him—hopefully, within the hour.

She nestled in the comfortable saddle astride her second stallion, Duncan. Maggie knew that this time she was ready. Patting Duncan on the neck, she was, as always, appreciative of his beauty. Both Duncan and Pepper were tame and obedient, yet very photogenic, and she was thankful for the sacrifice her parents had made to haul them to California for her stunt work.

Again, the stunt involved jumping from a running horse to a rope ladder hanging from a low passing biplane. Maggie noticed that several high cirrus clouds hung suspended in the skies, and the day's weather was perfectly calm, almost balmy, in contrast to the weather on the day of her unsuccessful practice run. Maggie drew a deep breath, savoring the stillness.

At that instant, a voice spoke from behind her, breaking the silence. It was a soft, deep voice, and strangely familiar to Maggie. Glancing quickly over her shoulder, she was startled to see Fernando Underwood approach quietly and take Duncan's reins in his hands.

Sensing that for the second time in two days her face was flushed with embarrassment, she stammered, "What on earth are you doing here?"

"Well," Fernando coughed, feeling suddenly on the spot himself. "I . . . uh . . . actually a veterinarian friend, Doc Bell, asked me to come out and help him with a horse's sprained foot. He's a palomino stallion—looks a lot like this one in fact. After working with him, I thought I'd stick around to see how movies were made."

Not knowing how to respond, Maggie asked, "But . . . how did you know I was out here?"

"You'll have to believe me, Miss Rockwell, when I tell you that I had no idea. The last thing I need right now is a relationship."

Maggie stared at Fernando. "Well, Mr. Polo Jockey," she said haughtily. "I've got news for you. You're pursuing a relationship all right, but it's with my palomino, Pepper, not with me. The horse you've just taken care of is mine, and is the twin to Duncan here."

Although she didn't want to acknowledge her appreciation for this man's interest in Pepper's sprain, Maggie was acutely aware that he had helped her twice without even knowing it was her. Yet his presence there seemed too coincidental to have just happened.

Fernando, seeing that he had offended Maggie, fervently wished that he hadn't come to the set to assist Dr. Bell. "I'm really quite harmless, ma'am. Even so, I have great admiration for anyone—let alone a lady of your beauty and grace—who can ride a horse like you seem to. I'm not attempting to patronize you, either. I simply want you to know of my admiration for your horses . . . and your ability to ride."

Maggie suddenly felt her heart softening. "I appreciate your concern for Pepper. . . . I truly do. Excuse me now. I must prepare for the shoot."

As she turned, Fernando surprised himself by blurting, "Miss Rockwell, while I would be blind not to appreciate your beauty, I would sincerely like to get to know you . . . as a friend and a horse lover." He smiled at the memory of their meeting and added, "And, I must admit, I'm curious why someone of your riding talents is enrolled in an aeronautical engineering class."

Maggie realized that his disarming words were to her liking because she could now become acquainted with this handsome stranger without any expectations between them. "Very well," she acquiesced. "If you'll take a position behind the camera over there until I've finished the shoot, perhaps you will accompany me to the stalls and give me an update on Pepper's ankle."

The sound of the approaching airplane interrupted their conversation. Having made a wide circle after arriving at the filming location, it was now coming in for a brief landing and final instructions. Maggie and Fernando watched the plane draw closer and lower, seeing that the pilot was going to land on the part of the dirt road that was straight with no trees close by. They heard the pilot reduce his power, saw him increase the pitch of the propeller, and noticed him slip slightly in order to see over the round nose of the aircraft. They admired the perfect three-point landing after straightening out of the slip. The plane taxied towards them, trailing a plume of dust. Fernando saw that it was a Waco biplane with wheel-pants to increase the speed and a bigger engine and propeller than normal—at least bigger than any he had seen previously.

The pilot shut off the engine. A few of the men who had helped Maggie yesterday after her fall now ran over and helped the pilot turn the plane around so that it pointed back the way it had landed. Fernando loved everything associated with aviation and looked wistfully at the Waco and its pilot while he savored the distinct oil-gas smell of the engine. It had been over three years since he had been at the controls of an airplane, and he had deeply missed flying.

Still seated in the cockpit, the pilot pulled off his helmet and goggles, revealing wavy greying hair and a rather weather-beaten face. He had a wide bushy moustache, typical of many pilots of the post-war era. The epitome of the adventurous, competent aviator of the middle 1930s, the pilot wore a leather jacket and a long white silk scarf around his neck.

Everyone was assembled for the shoot except the director. "Herr Direktor is coming," one of the assistant directors announced discreetly, although with an exaggerated accent. Fernando smiled when another man laughingly referred to the director as "Herr Diktator."

When the director finally stepped out of the car in which he had been sitting, Fernando could see that this great director looked the part—short and stout, with a monocle over his right eye. In addition, he had brightly polished boots, a waxed moustache, and a florid-red face. And now he was irritated, convinced that Maggie had been in total error with her fall yesterday.

Shouting to no one in particular, the director exclaimed, "Ver ees dat gurl? She ees eempossible! Vee are behind schedule, und vit anuser fall like yesterday, she vill only make tings vorse!"

He turned to an assistant and angrily demanded, "Are zee bad men ready on zee horses? Are zee kameramen in zer positions? Is zee film loaded und ready?"

The aide calmly assured him that everyone was now ready, including Maggie, who was sitting astride her palomino some fifty yards in the distance.

Looking in her direction, the director insisted on more details. "And zee aeroplane? Ees it ready to take off for zee shoot?"

His assistant again reassured the impatient director that the plane was ready for takeoff, and that the cameras were loaded and ready to roll.

Herr Direktor yelled at Maggie, reprimanding her again for making such an unforgivable riding mistake in the previous day's trial run.

Maggie did not even attempt a reply, which she had done immediately following her accident, because she knew that her problem was simply a gust of wind and nothing else. She gritted her teeth in anger as she wheeled her palomino around and galloped to where Roscoe was waiting inside his plane. Maggie liked and trusted this pilot. He was one of the finest professional pilots in the movie business.

"Nothing like a happy director is there, Roscoe?" she yelled, only a few of her words reaching the pilot who had started his engine back up seconds before.

Maggie had one last comment for him before she rode off. "Roscoe, your timing was perfect. I'll get it right this morning and see you in the cockpit."

Roscoe gave her a thumbs-up, winked through his goggles, and started down the makeshift runway.

Maggie unexpectedly rode over to where Fernando was observing and exclaimed, "I'm not as upset as I may sound, but I have a present for the diktator today. When the plane comes back following the stunt, be sure to duck." She smiled and winked at Fernando, who didn't quite grasp what she was trying to say.

Without waiting for a reply, Maggie turned her horse and galloped confidently down the dirt road to her starting point. Once there, she waved in readiness and moved to sit sideways in the saddle like a resting cowboy, very much at ease on her obedient palomino. Unlike the trial run twenty-four hours ago, she could now see the "bad guys" in their black hats down the road. They were the villains who were after her, and her hero would provide her escape by dropping a rope ladder from the cockpit. It was her responsibility to jump from her horse to the ladder at full gallop—in a completely synchronized motion—before the main cameras.

Chapter Three

The seconds turned into minutes, and Maggie felt her confidence grow—in spite of her previous spill and the danger that awaited her now. She was well-trained from many years of riding the range like one of her father's cowboys and from her years in rodeo and circus riding. She had grown up on a western cattle ranch near Fredonia, just a few miles north of the famous Grand Canyon. She and her only brother, William, had left northern Arizona to perform trick circus riding and rodeo stunts. When a riding accident in nearby Kanab, Utah, had put William temporarily out of commission, Maggie had found that there was a demand for her alone. She had developed a rodeo following that had allowed her to make good money, but with the change to the movie stunts, she had been able to attend one of the most exclusive universities in the country, with money left over to send home to help pay the mortgage on her parents' ranch.

Roscoe, meanwhile, had gunned his engine the minute Maggie had left him. The engine was still warm from his recent arrival; therefore, he took off quickly and climbed for altitude. Directly over the prearranged starting point, he rocked his wings to signal the cameramen before he began his descent.

The director, noting the rocked wing signal, waved a flag for attention and brought it down smartly in a starting motion. Simultaneously, his assistant fired a red flare from a Marine pistol. The brightly burning flare arched high, glowing clearly against the blue morning sky, and the action began to unfold.

Maggie adjusted her long yellow scarf over her blonde platinum wig—a wig she was consigned to wear to coincide with the appearance of the heroine she was impersonating. When she saw the flare, she dug her heels into the flanks of her horse, and was immediately at a full gallop toward the cameramen. The villains in their black hats began their pursuit of the fleeing heroine. Upon a given signal, they pulled their six-shooters and fired blank smoke cartridges at her. These blanks would show up on film and would punctuate the fact that she had discovered their nefarious and dastardly plan to rob her father's bank.

The mean-spirited and unshaven villains were gaining on the lady in distress when the airplane appeared, diving directly toward her from behind. Maggie and Roscoe, with the help of Herr Direktor, had timed their convergence to coincide at a wide point in the dirt road. Within seconds, Roscoe could be seen looking down over the left side of the leather cowl surrounding the open cockpit. He threw out the rope ladder, allowing it to whip in the rushing wind of the slip stream.

Maggie felt the throb of the spinning propeller above her head and knew that the rope was just behind it. She turned her head and saw, to her relief, the streamlined wheel pass over her with the rope ladder twisting behind the near side of the plane. Urging her palomino on, she knew that this was her moment of truth.

Roscoe had flown the plane into perfect position, and at just the right second, Maggie grabbed the bottom rung of the ladder with her gloved right hand. She turned in the saddle, dropping the knotted reins on the neck of the horse. With her free left hand, she reached higher for the second rung. With both hands holding the ladder firmly, she kicked her feet loose from the stirrups and started to climb hand over hand. Her well-trained horse, with saddle empty and stirrups flopping, ran straight ahead according to plan, veering away from the low-flying plane.

Roscoe pulled slowly back on the controls, allowing the plane to gradually begin its ascent with wings level. Maggie, at the same instant, found herself struggling against the force of the wind as she flapped around like a small rag doll. Soon, however, she felt her foot touch the bottom rung of the plane's ladder. Slowly and carefully, she scaled the side of the plane, fully aware that, because she wasn't wearing a parachute, any slip meant certain death.

Within minutes she was strapped securely into her seat in front of the pilot, where she breathed a sigh of relief and pulled in the ladder. Removing the platinum wig, she located the helmet and goggles she had placed there earlier, and put them on. After taking a second deep breath, she tapped the top of her helmet three times, signaling for Roscoe to give her control of the plane.

Roscoe, from behind, had been waiting for this signal and immediately lifted his hands from the stick and throttle. He removed his boots from the rudder pedals and relaxed, feeling gratified at another job well done.

You've got it, girl, he thought gleefully as he watched Maggie. *After that stunt, you deserve your victory roll!*

Maggie was now in another of her favorite elements. She reflected how quickly she could change from loving her palomino, galloping at the touch of her reins, to being in the air at the controls of a large, beautiful acrobatic biplane—and of course she loved flying the plane as much as she loved riding her horses.

They were by now some distance from the camera crews and the director on the ground. Maggie made a climbing turn to the right, arching the plane back toward her audience on the ground. She knew instinctively that she had enough altitude by the time she was directly over them and grinned mischievously as she determined her next move. Checking her belts a second time before she rolled upside down for a few seconds, she pulled through into a power dive directly toward the crew below.

At just the right instant, she reversed the controls, initiating a high speed pullout while going literally straight into the air. With this maximum gravitation pull, the wires of the wings began to vibrate in the wind as the engine screamed. Here, with an elegance born of years of flying, she began her victory roll.

Fernando had no idea that Maggie was at the controls, but he did know professional aerobatics. What he saw was a perfect four-point vertical roll with a pullover to inverted flight at the top. This time, he mentally noted that the plane went farther away than before, prior to beginning a second dive. From where he stood, it looked like the pilot, Roscoe, was making a classic military strafing run on some target. Fernando had practiced the same maneuver, and, although he was standing quietly on the ground, in his mind he was experiencing the sensation as though he were in the plane itself.

Back in the cockpit, Maggie looked over the long nose of the diving biplane and spotted her target—Herr Direktor—who was still standing at his command position. She smiled as she pointed the prop spinner squarely toward him. Everyone else had been tipped off, including the assistant, and they had all run for cover. The director stood alone and unwittingly on his high perch.

By the time he correctly guessed that the yellow-scarfed Maggie was piloting the plane and was not going to pull up like she had done the first time, it was too late for him to run. He saw the shining chrome spinner of the prop pointed at him, and it was obvious that Maggie would drill him if he didn't hit the ground.

The man threw himself headfirst into the dust, and the prop went by overhead with just a few feet to spare. He jumped to his feet after the plane sped past, and he began shouting obscenities in German, while shaking his fist wildly. He was determined to tell the studio bosses that this was a crazy woman whose contract must be canceled before she killed them all.

Feeling no remorse whatsoever, Maggie brought the plane back and around to a perfect landing. She taxied to where the men were waiting, followed by billowing clouds of dust.

The director had driven off in a huff toward his trailer. Maggie pulled the throttle back, and as the engine clanked to a stop, she cut the switches, unstrapped her seat and shoulder harness, and stood on the seat to swing out on the wing. To her surprise, Fernando was the first to arrive at the side of the plane, and he offered a hand so she could make the long step to the ground.

Roscoe, standing up and sweeping his arm in an arc-like movement in front of Maggie with a "Sir Walter Raleigh" gesture of courtesy, remarked, "My dear, you treat my plane real sweet like that, and you can take over the controls anytime you like."

An idol in the flying community, Roscoe had flown in France at the end of the war, and in the last two decades had flown for— or against—various governments around the world. He had flown for goldminers, bankers, smugglers, and anyone else who wanted to hire the best pilot in the world to get an important job done. Roscoe had been a circus lion tamer in his younger days, and he always kept one or more lions at his hangar in place of watch dogs; no one ever entered his hangars when the lions were loose. He was the flying fraternity's best friend and their soft touch when they were in need.

"You were marvelous!" Maggie smiled at her friend. "Thanks for pulling off a perfect stunt."

"Don't thank me," Roscoe responded admiringly. "You did the hard part. No way could I ever grab a rope ladder coming at me at sixty miles an hour and climb up hand-over-hand in the slip stream. You were absolutely magnificent!"

At Roscoe's questioning look toward Fernando, Maggie performed the necessary introductions. "Roscoe, this is Fernando Underwood. He is a future aeronautical engineer, and . . . uh . . . is in my class at the university. He's also acting as veterinarian to my horse."

Maggie turned back to Roscoe."Fernando, I'd like you to meet Roscoe Turner. He's been my flying instructor and is the best pilot and friend anyone could hope to have."

Roscoe graciously accepted the compliment and laughed while he asked, "Fernando, what did you think of Maggie's buzz job on the director? She sure made him eat the same dust she ate yesterday."

For the first time it dawned on Fernando that it was Maggie at the controls of the biplane. He understood her suggestion that he watch what she was going to do and specifically why he had been warned to stay away from the director. An unexpected wave of admiration swept over him as he realized that this young lady was not only an expert rider and acrobat, but also an accomplished stunt pilot. Her vertical victory roll was very impressive.

Digesting these feelings, Fernando evaluated Maggie's actions. In her anger, she had piloted the biplane dangerously close to the director and the ground. In fact, she had clipped the top off a small tree just behind the director's raised platform, and the branch was still protruding from her landing gear.

Sensing Fernando's concern for what she had done and considering that perhaps her anger had taken her a little too far, Maggie explained, "I just had to get back at him for what he did to me yesterday. He insisted that we practice the stunt in a gusty wind storm, and that was wrong." She paused and added, "In fact, in the future, I think I'll have a clause in my contract stating that those at risk will decide if conditions are safe for the stunt or we won't do it. Anyway, I feel better now. I made sure I could see him, so I knew he wasn't really in any danger."

Without allowing Fernando an opportunity to respond, Maggie waved to the other horsemen—the bad guys—who were guiding their horses into the temporary stalls. Shouting into the wind, she exclaimed, "Great ride, gentlemen. Thanks for the help and support. I thought you were going to catch up with me too soon, but your timing was perfect."

Maggie turned back to Roscoe. "I need to talk to you about getting a plane to fly in the Bendix Cup cross-country race this coming September. I understand the officials are finally letting women back into the race. When can I come to see you at the hangar?"

Fernando, feeling somewhat left out of the conversation, was totally surprised by Maggie's inquiry into piloting in the most dangerous air race of the day. He wanted to interject his feelings

24

of caution and warning, but since he hardly even knew this girl, he decided to bite his tongue and remain silent. Instead, he smiled at Roscoe.

"It's been a pleasure to meet you," he said, tipping his jockey cap. "Maggie, I'll be at the stall when you're ready to see how Pepper is doing." He excused himself and strode away, anxious to be alone with his thoughts.

As Fernando retreated across the field toward the cameramen, Maggie gazed in astonishment after him. She had never experienced such unexpected ambivalence in her emotions. Even then, she sensed a feeling of embarrassment for her dangerous stunt and hoped she hadn't blown it with this man she had met only yesterday.

They learned that the filming of the stunt had been successful and that the German director had returned, acting as if nothing out of the ordinary had transpired. Sensing the man's willingness to let the incident pass, Maggie put her own pride aside. She waited until he was alone, then approached him and apologized.

The director's only response was a grunt and a wave of the arm, but Maggie knew that this signaled a truce between them.

Maggie soon found herself driving back toward town in her rented convertible with Fernando Underwood sitting at her side. They had talked about Pepper's injury, and then, because Doc Bell had earlier returned to town without him, Fernando had reluctantly accepted a ride from Maggie.

Fernando sat quietly, still sobered by Maggie's lack of caution with the director. *But*, he reasoned, *they've worked things out, and it should perhaps be dropped.* After all, the matter was between Maggie and her director; it was none of Fernando's business.

Having put aside his concerns, Fernando began to enjoy the feeling of comfort—even excitement—in being with this unusual young woman. Her car had wire spoke-wheels with two spares embedded in the front fenders, and a rumble seat in back.

He would have to be cautious not to get carried away with the car because it caused him to reflect on the many cars he had nurtured in his early teenage life.

The previous three years suddenly seemed very long and lonely to Fernando, and his mind at once left the car and his memories, while he inwardly rejoiced in this new friendship. Still, he knew he must proceed without entanglements, working through the complications of his past, while hopefully redeeming himself in the eyes of his family back home.

Maggie was the first to speak. "Fernando, you say you're a horse expert and a polo jockey, but somehow I think there's much more to you than you're letting on."

Intrigued with Maggie's intuition, yet knowing that he couldn't disclose his past to anyone—let alone this remarkably beautiful woman—he smiled and said, "I'll tell you about me, but first I need to know about you. Would that be asking too much?"

Maggie, in spite of feeling vulnerable, decided to respond to his request. This man, she reasoned, was obviously uneasy with talking about himself.

"That's a deal," she smiled, her hands graceful on the large steering wheel. "I'm actually from a place you've probably never heard of—unless, that is, you know where the best cowboy movies are filmed."

Fernando was intrigued. "I'm afraid that if it's somewhere outside of Hollywood, you've stumped me."

"Fredonia, Arizona . . . a few miles from the north rim of the Grand Canyon."

At Fernando's look of interest, Maggie smiled excitedly and continued, "It's the most beautiful place on earth—red cliffs, pine-tree forests, snow-covered blue mountains, and desert with cactus and sand dunes. In fact," she continued, glancing over at Fernando, "nearby are old mining towns that are perfect for movie sets. Local cowboys from the ranches can do the cowboy parts. The Navajo reservation is just a few miles away."

It was evident that Maggie was proud of her heritage and home, and in spite of himself, Fernando felt a desire to visit the area she had described.

"Fernando, what about you?" she asked, pressing to change the direction of the conversation. "Where are you from?"

"I'm embarrassed to go into it, Maggie," Fernando hedged, "but I can tell you where I live now . . . right behind that stable, around the corner we're approaching."

Sensing that she would have to wait for another time, if ever, to learn about this Fernando Underwood, Maggie replied without thinking, "You live in these stables?" As soon as the words were out of her mouth, she knew that she had spoken condescendingly and wished with all her heart that she could retract the tone of her question.

"Yes," Fernando laughed, obviously unoffended by her question. "Actually, I live in that apartment over there, next to the main stables. For some reason, they've put me in charge of this place, which actually makes my living conditions ideal."

Maggie was astonished at the appearance of an entirely different Fernando Underwood that she had expected.

"I must say, Fernando," she countered, smiling, "you do have a way of throwing a person off. I could have sworn that you were . . ."

" . . . A stuck-up snob?" Fernando finished for her. "I admit I was a bit high handed, and I apologize. Meanwhile, I would definitely like to continue our conversation . . . perhaps some day at the stables where you permanently keep your horses."

This man was throwing her one left curve after another, and she was totally unprepared to answer. "Actually," she began hesitantly, "I was wondering what you were doing for dinner tonight. My folks just shipped me a large package of half-frozen steak, and I'm going to have to cook it right away, before it spoils."

Fernando was alert to the risk of disclosure that such a setting might bring. Still, it had been too long since he had socialized with anyone, let alone a member of the opposite sex. "I suppose

I could help you eat it," he answered slowly. "What time would be good for you?"

"Aren't you going to ask where I live?" Maggie teased, happy at last to be on top of the concluding conversation.

Fernando looked surprised. "Oh, yes . . . how silly of me."

Maggie gave him her address, put the Chevrolet into gear, and said, "Seven o'clock would be fine, Mr. Underwood. But please don't be late. The steaks will burn."

Climbing out of the car and closing the door, Fernando waved weakly before he turned and walked into the stables.

For a brief instant, Maggie simply sat there, sorting through the unusual conversation and experience she had just shared with Fernando. She came to the conclusion that not only were her emotions and impressions becoming increasingly unstable, the male species was truly unpredictable. *Except,* she smiled, *when an experienced lady decides to take the bull by the horns and tame him.* And Fernando, she decided, definitely needed taming.

Chapter Four

Later That Morning
The British Consulate, Los Angeles, California

The very distinguished British diplomat, Lord Jockham, the Earl of Wittingham, scanned the morning mail from England. Giving a deep sigh, he began the laborious task of reading each letter that had just arrived. His secretary had left the correspondence in a neat stack, all opened and ready for his reading. After digesting each item, he dictated a short set of instructions to be given to the staff member who would follow through with his directives.

"Please tell Mr. Samuelson to check this insurance claim from Lloyd's through the Los Angeles Port Authority. There is a man there by the name of William Josephson who can help us immeasurably. Terrible tragedy to lose that ship, but at least there was no loss of life."

He went on to the next item in the stack of correspondence.

"Telephone MGM film company and tell them that London approves their request to film His Majesty's visit to Australia this fall. They want a special permit so they can get their news camera closer than usual. We see no security risk. Please give them the names of whom to contact after they arrive in Australia."

He looked at the next set of papers in front of him. "What's all this?" he asked himself. "Hmmmm . . . most fascinating."

He turned to his secretary who was sitting poised and ready to write. "By jove, old Douglas is really onto something hot. Please give him a call at once and set up a luncheon at his earliest convenience."

Lord Jockham's secretary exited immediately to make the phone call. The Earl reread the pages of background information that had just arrived from the home office in London. He underlined some parts for emphasis, then called his Vice-Consul, Sir Charles.

"Charles, you remember our friend, Douglas, and his request that we run an identification check on that young polo player? . . . Yes, yes . . . Well, I've just received a reply from London. Why don't you come over and look at this stack of material . . . We have ourselves one beauty of a puzzle to piece together."

Lord Jockham hung up the phone just as his secretary reentered his office.

"I am extremely sorry, sir, but your friend Douglas is at the studio and can't be interrupted."

"Nonsense!" Lord Jockham exclaimed, his military bearing still with him. "Tell them that the King of England's representative demands that the call be put through . . . We are on his errand, and he'll want an update, I'm sure."

Shortly, his secretary returned with the news that the actor named Douglas was, in fact, on the line. Although he was on location filming a demanding fencing episode, he had interrupted the shoot to take the call.

"Yes, Jock, this is Douglas. How in the King's good name did you find me over here at the gymnasium?"

"I called the studio on the hunch you might be filming. I threatened that His Highness might take back his colonies if they didn't tell me your number. It seemed to work, old chap," he concluded, chuckling at his own humor and feeling a bit more relaxed.

Douglas was happy that his friend had called. "No problem on this end, Jock. I had just about worn out my antagonists here, so they're happy for the time out. What is so urgent that I deserve this privilege of speaking with Your Excellency?" His formality was exaggerated; Douglas was not above small talk with his good friend, Jock.

"Are you interested in learning about your mysterious young polo player, Fernando Underwood?"

Douglas was instantly alert. He had wondered what news might come from his inquiry. It had been several weeks since his request had first been made.

"Most certainly!" he replied.

"I have here a full dossier on Underwood's family and several other related matters. When can we meet? I think you should see what we have found. We do have positive identification, and as you suspected, it is all very sensitive."

Douglas was intrigued with the news. "I can change my luncheon today and meet you at our usual place in a couple of hours. What do you say?"

"I am free, old chap, but I would not want to inconvenience so important a movie star."

Douglas was equal to the banter. "Jocko, dear friend, you are much more important than the studio people who have invited me to lunch. They only want to talk money—and that can wait."

"Douglas is in for a real surprise," whispered the consul, as he replaced the receiver in its cradle.

At precisely one o'clock, two flamboyant Rolls Royces pulled into the parking lot of the fashionable Polo Lounge in downtown Beverly Hills.

The two friends exited their respective automobiles, met at the door, and embraced warmly. They were ushered inside the lounge by a doorman who instantly recognized them both. Immediately, they were led by the maitre d' to a secluded booth. Sitting down in the dimly lit area, they placed an order for "the usual" and Jock asked for more light, explaining that they had several documents to review. Turning to Douglas, Jock whispered, "Laddie, you have no idea what a goldmine of fascinating problems you have dug up."

Immediately, the consul opened his briefcase and extracted the file. Still speaking softly, he asked, "Do you remember who the Underwood family is?"

Douglas, reflecting briefly, answered, "Not in detail, Jock, but I have the impression that they own a major bank and some insurance company—oh, and a shipping line, I believe. Seems like they have holdings in India and South America. At least there were multiple interests and a lot of wealth, if my memory serves me correctly. Is that what you mean?"

The consul nodded silently. Douglas remembered something else.

"I do say, I think I remember that they contributed substantially to the Shakespearean arts. Is this one and the same family?"

Peering over the spectacles he had taken out to better read the papers, the consul replied, "Yes, it's Fernando's mother's family. Have you ever heard of the San Martin family from Argentina?"

Douglas, stirring his memory briefly, finally asked, "Wasn't there a world class polo player by that name? I think I lost track of him years ago. Seems he returned to some place in South America to look after his family interests down there. Guess I never paid much attention to which country. What are you leading up to, Jock?"

Jock was hardly able to contain his excitement. "This is a most intriguing situation you have stumbled onto, Douglas. And, you are correct about the Underwood fortunes. I have the file from our office covering all the interests you mentioned and many more that are not as well known. Very large . . . very large! And the polo player, Don Hugo San Martin Braun, whose Argentine holdings are even greater than those of the Underwoods of England, married Helen Underwood—thus uniting these two immense dynasties. These two newlyweds disappeared straightway to Argentina—to rear a family, I'm sure.

"Helen and Hugo," he continued, obviously enjoying his

detective work, "have been married now for approximately thirty years. I suppose Hugo is in his mid-50s, and she must be close to that age herself. She was especially attractive, apparently still is. Hugo, if you remember, was of the same build as the young Fernando whom we recently observed on the polo field. According to press releases, Hugo has continued playing polo and is an eight-goal handicap. He happens to have a son named Fernando, which makes us sure we have the right man. Would you like to hear more about the San Martin family?"

Douglas nodded, although Lord Jockham was forced to wait while the waiter delivered their iced beverages. When he had finished, Jock took a deep breath and glanced around him to ensure once again the privacy of the conversation.

"Let me go back to the beginning, Douglas," he began. "You won't believe what we have here. The San Martin family are old-time Argentines, but have a long tradition of marrying into British or German families of wealth. If there were royalty in Argentina, or at least in Buenos Aires, it would be this family. There is no one more prominent or more important. Our sources say they own half the country, and that is not an exaggeration."

Seeing that he had his friend's total attention, Jock continued, "The San Martin wealth dates back to the Spanish Crown land-grant days. Their land deeds go back to when the King of Spain gave them tremendous tracts of land the size of the British isles—and all for services rendered. Their progenitor must have saved the life of the king, or perhaps even his entire kingdom.

"Over the centuries—and this family goes back to the very beginning of the Spanish occupation of Latin America—they have learned to protect their land and their kingdom. It truly is that—a veritable kingdom. They marry well, then divide parts and pieces of land and holding companies among the descendants to make it look diversified, but the real power continues in the hands of whomever the family chooses to head up everything, the one genius who keeps the increasingly complex family working together. This is all done legally, of course.

"This report," he continued, "says that Don Hugo is the top man of the family—the reigning genius. He is a financial wizard and a polished diplomat. And, as I just said, he's a great polo player. His conglomerate is a trust—owned and managed by his brothers, uncles, and their descendants. Don Hugo is respectfully referred to as "the King of the Gauchos." And, before his disgrace, our young Fernando was "the Prince.""

Douglas had been following the story very intently up until now, but at this point he had to interrupt. "Just a minute, Jock. The disgrace? What disgrace? Come on, man, you're keeping me dangling out there. What on earth happened?"

Jock paused deliberately. "I am getting to that, but please be patient. First, I have to tell you the rest of the information about their "empire." They have huge *estancias*, great working ranches, several with over one million acres each. These are divided into stock companies with family members holding shares in the companies. Some of them live overseas, so it looks like an international holding company.

"The same thing goes for the sheep ranches down south in the Patagonia of Argentina, with literally hundreds of thousands of sheep. In addition, they have wool-buying companies, wool warehouses, and facilities for washing and weaving woolen goods equal to the finest in England. Moreover, their holdings include refrigerated packing plants to handle their meat, where it is canned for export or shipped as cold-frozen beef in their own ships. They also have interests in sugar plantations with sugar mills, and—shall I go on?"

Douglas could hardly believe what he was hearing. But, just at that moment, the waiter arrived with their entrees. The minute the waiter left, Jock continued. "The San Martin family has a kingdom that could appear to evolve right out of a book of fiction. They live like royalty, but have avoided the limelight. Nor are they ostentatious. They try very hard to avoid spoiling their children, rearing them instead to be productive in society.

"Furthermore," he continued, taking a deep breath, "those

who get to the top positions in the family infrastructure seem to earn it. They are very close-mouthed about themselves and avoid any kind of publicity. From what we have learned, they are afraid of kidnapping threats, like the Charles Lindberg case here in the United States.

"As breeders of fine cattle and sheep and horses—oh, I forgot to mention the race horses and polo ponies and thousands of good horses for their properties—the San Martin dynasty tries to constantly improve the lineage of their family. Of course, it doesn't always work like those of the older generation in the family want it to . . . ."

Douglas was less interested in his friend's venturing into this family's history than in the fascinating mystery he had turned up. He was intrigued by this "Gaucho Prince" named Fernando Underwood. The pieces seemed to fit, but still there were major gaps. He had sensed that Fernando was from some kind of elite background, no matter how poor he was trying to act. He had the refinement of a wealthy family and played polo like an international champion. But none of what Jock had just brought to light explained the mystery that surrounded him. Impatiently Douglas interrupted Jock's lengthy account of family pedigree. "Come now, Jock. You said there was a disgrace related to young Fernando. What happened?"

"Here are some newspaper clippings, Douglas," replied the consul, almost casually. "I will let you read them, but only on one condition. I have been warned by London not to get involved in the wrong way, or it could affect my career. I am too close to retirement to go against instructions from higher up. London wants this handled in whatever way the father, Don Hugo, down in Buenos Aires, wants it handled."

"But of course," Douglas snapped, eager for the consul to continue.

"There is a great deal at stake, Douglas," Jock continued. "Fernando was the heir apparent to lead the entire family dynasty . . . and, of course, their fortune. He was to take his father's place once he settled down, married, and proved himself. Unfortunately, this disaster broke open. Maybe there was a gene flaw or an environmental weakness in the way he was reared. I'll let you read about it—but the bottom line is that after scandals in France and England, and especially after a devastating scandal and accident in Boston, Don Hugo ordered Fernando to never return home to Argentina."

"But, please . . . " pressed Douglas. "What scandals?"

Expecting the request, Jock continued. "There was a party with drinking, a car accident . . . how messy the tabloids make these society escapades seem. And Fernando's lady friend, or rather, fiancé . . . what a tragedy. At any rate, Fernando became an instant disgrace to his family. You will read the details in the clippings I have here. There was a subsequent police investigation of the accident, which exonerated Fernando. Even so, at that time, he simply disappeared from sight. That was about three years ago.

"The family in Argentina has had private investigators trying to locate him without letting him know they are interested. Twice a year Fernando writes home, but the letters are mailed from different cities throughout the country and so they have been unable to trace him.

"Extraordinary as it may appear, Fernando Underwood is a brilliant student, an outstanding polo player, and a winning yachtsman, in addition to being a renowned pilot. However, we have also learned that he has a few problems. These deficiencies, shall we call them, seem to cause his difficulties—unless, of course, he has outgrown them through this last fracas."

The consul paused to get his breath before he added one last point. "I have orders—mind you, orders—not to intervene until the father gets in touch with me. The family in England is contacting the family in Argentina who will let us know how they wish for us to proceed.

"Now, my friend," he concluded finally, rubbing his temples with his fingers, "do you see what you have stirred up? What if

36

the young man really doesn't want to return to his family? What if he is better off without all that money and responsibility? What if the family still does not want to have anything to do with him? Then what?"

Douglas remained silent, trance-like, so Jock continued. "My friend, what do you make of all you have started?"

Returning to reality, Douglas asked, "What in the world are these scandals all about? Is he some Jack the Ripper?"

"Good heavens, no! Not that bad at all. Just the kind of thing that this very conservative and secretive family will not tolerate. Drinking, gambling, apparent womanizing, and brawls. Just read the clippings and letters. To me it is simply a matter of an authoritarian father applying uncompromising control on his son, and it backfired—not just on Fernando, but on everyone—the parents, the young man, and of course the family. In some way or another, the lad felt it was unjust, and he rebelled. He is more than likely trying to make it now on his own."

"I would suspect," Douglas interrupted, "that Fernando has a healthy dose of pride and does not want his family involved in what he is doing." His face lit up. "I owe him something for repairing my car that day. . . . Extremely fortunate that he happened to come by. He certainly got me out of a fix. This is my plan. I'm taking my yacht out to the Catalina Island this next weekend. Perhaps if I invite him, he will reveal more of himself and I can keep you out of trouble while we continue to gather information."

Nodding agreeably, Jock allowed him to outline his plan. The two friends finished their dessert, all the while arguing jovially about who would pay the bill. They walked out into the California afternoon sunshine, totally unaware of how their scheme was presently unraveling beyond repair.

Chapter Five

That evening, in an effort to put her new friend at ease, Maggie borrowed two candles from her neighbor next door, placed the candles on her small ornate tablecloth and lit them. She had no sooner done so, when Fernando arrived, carrying a heavy, mysterious cardboard box. She welcomed him in, and after the normal pleasantries, invited him to sit down for an already dished-up meal. The distinct aroma of sizzling steaks permeated her entire apartment, and Maggie sensed Fernando's anticipation, as he licked his lips while glancing toward the burner where the steaks were cooking.

It had been months since Maggie had entertained anyone, let alone a man, and the thought caused her heart to stir wistfully. If only she didn't burn the steaks, she said to herself, perhaps their friendship would extend to another day.

Almost immediately they were seated, dinner was served, and at Maggie's suggestion, she offered a brief blessing on the food. Maggie's spiritual inclination caught Fernando completely off guard, although he made every effort to not judge her harshly or to consider her behavior extreme. After all, when he was a small child, he and his brother, Ricardo, were taught by their mother to "say grace." It was just that as an adult, he had never participated in the same youth-oriented ritual.

While Maggie bowed her head and spoke, Fernando watched her face. Her facial features, almost dancing in the candlelight between them, were classic. Her lips were full, and her jawline square although feminine, showing character and determination. Her eyebrows, he noted, were well arched.

Maggie concluded, and when she opened her eyes, Fernando saw that they were brilliantly clear green and sparkled with excitement.

As they ate, they discussed their classes at the university. Neither ventured into personal references, yet both found themselves wanting to become better acquainted with the other. The only personal comments were made by Fernando when he complimented Maggie on the delicious steak—the best he had eaten in several years.

Following dinner, Fernando was helping with the dishes when Maggie, determined to risk becoming a bit more personal, began telling Fernando a little more of her background. She hoped that by sharing some of her life, it would help Fernando to reveal more of his past.

"My family, the Rockwells," she said, "actually tie into Abraham Lincoln and Ulysses S. Grant, two of our former presidents. They were distant cousins to my great-great-grandparents who came to the United States from Dorchester, England. My great-grandfather, Seymore Rockwell, was born in the state of Connecticut in 1813. They say he was quite a rabble-rouser, but also a most adventurous man."

"You seem to know quite a bit about your progenitors, Maggie. I am duly impressed."

Maggie shrugged. "What about your roots, Fernando? You certainly seem the adventuresome sort. Taking up your earlier offer, I really would enjoy learning more about you."

As if he had prepared a ready defense against such questions, Fernando changed the subject smoothly. "Would you be interested in hearing the music of my country?"

"Yes, I would," Maggie replied, completely taken by surprise.

"Permit me to open the box I brought over." With that, Fernando retrieved the box from where he had placed it near the front door. Opening the four flaps, he slowly extracted several paper-wrapped phonograph records.

"This is tango music," he continued, placing the first record on Maggie's phonograph. "It is the most popular music of my country."

Maggie wanted desperately to ask about his country because she had no idea where the tango came from. It sounded kind of French, yet she thought he had mentioned Argentina at one time. What she did know, however, were the basic tango steps. She had learned them several years earlier while attending a dance class in nearby Kanab, Utah. Since she didn't want to appear a know-it-all, she said nothing as he explained the basic steps.

"This is a romantic-type of dance music," Fernando said, and added, laughing, "It was so romantic, that for a time, it was banned. But that attitude has changed, and the music is now socially acceptable all over the world."

"Is the tango anything like the Cuban rumba?" she asked, reaching into her own love for music. She had only learned a few steps of the rumba during the same early instructions, but had loved its fascinating new rhythms.

"Yes, and no, " Fernando replied. "The tango borrowed some of the accentuation from the rumba, or maybe the rumba borrowed it from the tango. I don't really know which came first. What I do know is that our tango has been very popular in Paris, London, and Europe in general because it is so sensuous."

"My goodness, Mr. Underwood, you don't say . . . ." Maggie smiled, surprised by Fernando's directness.

Fernando swallowed uncomfortably, sensing Maggie's emotional response to what he had intended to be an academic reference. He forced himself to continue, "Your dancers, Vernon and Irene Castle, have made the tango quite popular here in the States. The tango has long, slow steps punctuated with short, quick steps, and is really not too hard to learn, especially when the woman has long legs like you do."

At the look in Maggie's eyes, Fernando saw that he had

revealed his awareness of her figure. He certainly didn't want her
to be offended that he had noticed this part of her attractive
anatomy. Nor did he want her to think that he was making a
romantic pitch.

Sensing his discomfort, Maggie lowered her head to hide a
self-conscious smile. She was properly demure, but inside she was
pleased that he had really noticed that she was a woman—and
with attractive legs, no less. She was also pleased with his increasing comfort in speaking with her.

Fernando, at a loss for words, and seeing that Maggie
remained quiet, quickly turned back to the record player and put
on the first record—Carlos Gardel, the Bing Crosby of
Argentina. The unusual beat of the music had a stirring effect on
both of them, and in spite of herself, Maggie looked up from
where she was sitting. Fernando stood tall, towering over her, and
without speaking, invited her to dance. "Don't mind if I do, Mr.
Underwood," she smiled, standing up and allowing Fernando to
take her hand in his. "Show me the basic step, and if I don't have
two left feet, maybe I can catch on."

Fernando waited to be in rhythm with the music, then started
dancing, moving slowly so that Maggie could follow his lead. He
began by doing the long, stretching, slow steps and eventually the
intricate, short, twisting steps. Fernando knew that, although he
could dance alone, two partners in perfect synchronization was
even more spectacular—a real showstopper. Becoming increasingly bold, he did a full pivot, which caused Maggie's head to
whirl. He stopped dead in his tracks, throwing her briefly off balance.

"Now," he smiled encouragingly, "when I say 'Go,' step backwards three long steps." He waited for the right place in the
music. "Go!"

Maggie stepped backwards to the strong pulse of the music,
anticipating Fernando's next verbal command. Instead of talking
her through the next part, he gently pushed her left hip back with
his right hand. With his left hand in hers, he pulled her right

shoulder forward. The twisting movement caused her feet to reverse, and to her surprise his feet entwined with hers in a perfect dance-step turn of the tango.

He stopped right there, smiling proudly at his successful efforts at teaching her to tango. "Bravo, Miss Rockwell! You're a natural. Now let's do it again, but this time, we won't quit."

Fernando thought he was teaching her to tango, but Maggie felt it was some kind of romantic enchantment. She sensed that the underlying beat of the music combined with the romantic words, even though she could not understand the Spanish. The music and words, coupled with the growing pleasure of being held closely by a tall, dark, and handsome man—were all making her feet and soul react in a magical way that was increasingly disconcerting to her. No dance before had affected her in quite this way.

"Maggie, you are a marvelous dancer. You move like you had danced the tango many times before. Are you sure that you haven't?" His question was very sincere. "I've never had a better partner. This can't be your first time."

Secretly Maggie was thrilled. Never in her life had anyone complimented her on dancing so well, and here she was dancing with a stranger . . . a new friend who danced with a flare she had never before seen. Maggie reassured him that she had never heard that particular music, but she revealed the fact that she had received some basic instructions in the tango while in high school. Such a revelation momentarily threw Fernando off-guard, but he recovered, thinking that he could now move quickly into advanced movements.

Without speaking, Fernando turned the record over and they danced to the music on the other side. The steps became more and more elaborate as Maggie became more comfortable. She felt that her cowboy boots were like Cinderella slippers with fairy godmother dust on them, and even though she knew there were no romantic notions between herself and Fernando, she was beginning to feel very much at ease in his arms.

Fernando was likewise under the spell of the music. He marveled that in all his years of dancing with attractive women in the world's great cities, he had only once previously allowed himself to be totally swept away with the experience. He could feel the grace and strength of Maggie's body as she moved smoothly with his lead. She was responsive and even eager for his leadership in the dance, allowing him to initiate every step as closely as if they were tied together by an invisible cord. His mind was becoming quite blurred; he began to think more and more about the woman he was dancing with rather than the dance itself.

Maggie, equally unsure of what was happening to her emotions, followed his lead with increasing ease. What was happening was not only with her feet—because, in spite of her resolve to contain her thoughts and feelings, she was being swept away by Fernando. And all this without speaking a word to this . . . this puzzle from somewhere in South America.

Finally, after a lengthy statue-like pause where Fernando held Maggie close to him for several seconds, he lowered her gracefully until her long ponytail almost touched the floor. Looking deeply into her eyes, he brought her instantly back to a standing position.

Bowing with a sweeping gesture, Fernando released her, turned, and removed the final record. Placing it in its paper sheath, he immediately began searching for what to say or do next.

Maggie was deep into her own thoughts. Taking two clean glasses from her cupboard, she filled them with water before returning to where Fernando was repacking the records.

"Care for a drink, kind sir?"

The sound of Maggie's melodic voice caught Fernando off-guard. The music had been the only sound for some time and just hearing her words once again sent his emotions on a search for understanding.

"Why, thank you, ma'am," he answered in a contrived western drawl before taking the glass and drinking the water in one long gulp. "I'm afraid I haven't danced like that for years."

"I'm afraid I haven't danced like that *ever,*" Maggie quipped.

"You're a natural, Maggie, just like you are with riding and flying. In fact," Fernando laughed gently, "I'm not sure there's anything you can't do."

Enjoying the words of genuine praise, yet suddenly becoming uncomfortable with how personal the conversation was becoming, Maggie searched in her mind for a way to redirect without seeming unappreciative.

Similar to her thoughts, Fernando, too, knew he must leave immediately. He was certain of only one thing—Maggie Rockwell from somewhere in northern Arizona, was one of the two most unusual ladies he had ever known. He certainly didn't want to send out any signal of what he was feeling. Or did he? Only once before had he experienced such a flood of emotions, and that was with his former fiancée—prior to her tragic death in the chain reaction auto accident that had nearly claimed his own life.

These thoughts blurred into others, and, within seconds, Fernando abruptly picked up the heavy box of records and adjusted it in his arms.

"I really must be going, Maggie," he said hoarsely, at the same time feeling tears forming uncontrollably in his eyes. "The evening has been most enjoyable . . . one that I'll remember for a long, long time."

Bowing slightly, without so much as taking her hand, he turned and opened the door. Not looking back, he walked quickly and quietly out into the night.

"But . . . Fernando, can I give you a lift home?"

Spinning around and walking backward, he smiled slightly and called out, "No, thank you, Maggie . . . It's only a few blocks, and the walk will do me good. Now, you take care of your horses, you hear?"

As Fernando turned a final time and quickly disappeared into the blackness of the night, Maggie found herself at a loss for words. Her feelings—the bedrock of her resolve to remain emotionally unattached—were suddenly crumbling in her mind. At the same time, an unexpected fear was creeping in—fear that she would never again spend an evening with the unusual Fernando Underwood.

"Goodnight, Fernando," she called, waving into the blackness. "I will take care of my horses."

Chapter Six

The growing darkness cast longer and longer shadows across the equestrian training track. Fernando and Maggie, seated leisurely on the grass in front of Fernando's apartment, gazed into each other's eyes. Fernando, trying to be understood, searched for understanding and empathy. Maggie, on the other hand, put all of her mental resources to work, attempting to make sense out of what she was hearing. It had been a full week since the steak dinner and dancing at her apartment, and, although she and Fernando had accidentally bumped into each other twice since, not until now had they been able to speak frankly. Fernando had invited her to the stables for a quick workout with his horses, and, with the horses eating contentedly in their separate stalls, he wasted no time in disclosing what had been such a mystery—his background and rationale for having been so private.

"I am from Buenos Aires, Argentina. For the time being, I do not want anyone to connect me with the past. I must graduate on my own, then do all within my power to mend some pretty tall fences with my family there. I have made serious mistakes which not even time may be able to correct. After I have graduated and have done what I can to erase the disappointment I have caused my parents and family, someday perhaps I can tell you more . . ."

Sensing that his statement had cast its intended shadow in Maggie's mind, Fernando continued, "I have lived and studied in England, France, the eastern states, and of course, in Argentina.

I have attended a number of prestigious universities, but I must make it through AeroTec on my own. After presenting documentation to my father, I hope that he, my mother, and the rest of my family will again accept me."

"But, Fernando," Maggie interrupted, "You surely can't have—"

Not waiting for her to complete her thought, Fernando continued with his own. "I am just a semester from graduation, Maggie. Please allow my past to remain where it is until then. I haven't broken the law or anything like that. It is just a family situation that I can't explain right now. Do you understand?"

"Will I see you again, Fernando?" Without knowing why, Maggie immediately found herself blushing, even though it was too dark for him to see her clearly. "As friends, I mean."

"Of course—that is, if you would like to," Fernando answered, sensing her embarrassment. "But you see," he added apologetically, "I'm afraid that you find me at a disadvantage because I can't even drive you home. Some friend that will be . . ."

In spite of her efforts to control the direction of her emotions, Maggie knew she was hopelessly falling for this private, yet transparent man. He was strong, to be sure, but reticent in a little boy kind of way. His relationship with his family had been deeply scarred, and, because of his further need to heal and prove himself, she could understand his need for privacy.

"Fernando, I do trust you and very much appreciate your honesty. Because of our . . . uh . . . friendship, I will be here when you need me. Anyway, my horse still needs to be checked on, and I definitely want to watch you play polo. I would like you to train my ponies so they won't spook from the mallets, too.

"Besides all that," she continued, feeling very glib and loose with her thoughts, "I do need help preparing for my aeronautical exams."

"Whoa, young lady! I'm not going anywhere. It's been some time since I have enjoyed a true friendship, and I certainly don't want that to end."

Again Maggie was embarrassed. Why was this man affecting her as he was? He had sent no romantic signals, yet her heart was beating wildly, just being with him.

Fernando, also, was attempting to sort out his own feelings. True, he and Maggie had agreed to be just friends, but he was feeling emotions for her that went far beyond that. In truth, they were becoming similar to those he had felt for his fiancée, Rachel Cummings—both before and after her tragic and untimely death. Even so, he reasoned silently, he could not allow such involvement. He and Maggie must remain simply friends, without complications. The risks of romantic involvement were simply too great for him to consider.

Climbing to his feet, Fernando assisted Maggie to hers. Without speaking, he slowly walked over to her roadster and opened the door.

"Good-night, Maggie," he sighed almost inaudibly. "I'm sure I'll be the one to benefit while we prepare for our final. Besides, we've got to get your horse healed so you can take me into the canyons like you promised. A good day on a horse will do this polo jockey one world of good."

Smiling awkwardly, Maggie briefly placed her hand on his before speaking. "I'm sorry about your family, Fernando. If I can be of any help, please let me." She slipped into the driver's seat, started the engine, and drove off in a daze, wondering what had just transpired. It was the most abrupt, yet cordial conclusion to an evening she had ever experienced, yet she knew she couldn't put a lasso around these final moments.

As Maggie drove away, Fernando stood watching the little roadster's tail lights disappear down the lane. He knew exactly what had just taken place, but he hoped he hadn't given Maggie any false hopes. She was too fine a lady for that, and besides, he had no inclination to make any more of their relationship than what it was. *Still,* he reasoned, *if things were different, perhaps . . .*

Fernando's mind, along with the sound of the roadster's engine, began to blur, and before too many minutes had passed, he found himself leaning against a fence and staring blankly into the star-filled galaxies above. In his mind's eye, Fernando was suddenly far away in beautiful Buenos Aires. The stars seemed to beckon him southward, and, within seconds, he was alone at the large country home north of their main Argentine ranch. His thoughts centered on his family—his intensely controlling, though well-meaning father and his beautiful, compassionate mother. They were the finest parents a child could hope for, and somehow . . . somewhere . . . he would be welcomed back into their arms and their hearts. Such a thought, a hope, seemed impossible at best, but to Fernando, the slim chance of redeeming himself was all he needed to make it through the final few months of college.

The next two days were anything but settling for Fernando. His thoughts were consumed with varying emotions—vacillating back and forth between his estranged family in Argentina, his former fiancée, Rachel, and the extraordinary Maggie Rockwell. Not only could he not concentrate on his studies, but he found himself simply going through the motions with his polo students.

Finally, by mid-Saturday afternoon, Fernando reached the breaking point. Nothing could be resolved in his mind, so, after tending to his chores at the stables, he set out on foot, determined to get away from campus and the noises of the city. He had turned down an offer to visit Catalina Island with a man whose auto he had repaired, wanting to be by himself.

After walking for almost an hour, Fernando noticed a small stream running alongside the road. Almost without thinking, he walked over to the stream, sat down and removed his boots and socks, then rolled up his pant legs and submerged his feet in the cool, refreshing water. Leaning back, he closed his eyes, cupped his head in his hands, and nestled into the tall grass beneath him. Immediately his mind relaxed, as he slowly slid into a state of near-sleep. A large bumblebee buzzed menacingly to his right, then left the area in search of new pollen-laden flowers. In the distance, he could hear the whine of an automobile engine. His mind shifted to the stream and the absolute serenity of the moment. Oh, if only life could be this simple, he considered, I could—

"Excuse me, stranger. Going my way?"

Startled back to reality, Fernando jerked his head around, only to find himself staring up into the eyes of Maggie Rockwell. She was sitting in her idling car and had slid over to the passenger side.

Fernando hurried to his feet and dusted himself off. "Maggie? How on earth did you—?"

" . . . Find you? Why, Mr. Underwood, how in the world could you suppose that I was even searching for you?"

"Well, I don't know, I . . ."

Fernando noticed a slight wink; Maggie smiled teasingly.

"Actually, Fernando," she again interrupted, "I have been hunting for you. One of your stablehands pointed in this direction, saying that you had gone for a long walk. Therefore, given my circumstance, I thought it worth my while to try to locate you."

"I'm afraid I don't understand," Fernando questioned. "What's the matter?"

"Well, kind sir, it's about the Bendix Cup cross-country air-race . . . My friend Roscoe and I are deeply committed to it, and he and I were thinking that perhaps you could give us your perspective."

"So, you want me to—"

"Just climb in, hang on, and come with me to the airport. Roscoe is waiting at his office. I told him I would try to find you and invite you along. He thought that was a capital idea."

Without replying, Fernando reached down and unrolled pant legs. Picking up his boots and socks, he opened the car door and climbed inside. As he began working his socks back onto his drying feet, Maggie put the roadster into gear, popped the clutch, and sped quickly in the same direction Fernando had been walking.

Within minutes, the car crested a hill and came to a stop at the nearest private hangar of the nearby expanding airport. Outside the hangar, they noticed a number of planes parked and tethered in neatly marked rows. Fernando thought it curious that each of the planes in the first row was painted similarly to the others and asked about them. "They're Roscoe's fleet of planes—for charter or rent," she exclaimed, as excited as a young school girl. "The second row are planes for sale, and the third are planes belonging to Roscoe's clients. They park them here so that Roscoe's mechanics can do regular maintenance on them. Inside the hangar, he has his own race planes—the ones he has used before, plus the new one they are putting together for the big race."

Maggie continued, explaining further. "Everyone thinks that Roscoe is wealthy because he has such a large fleet and it looks like a successful operation. The truth is, he is deeply in debt and in trouble with the banks. He has been too generous with his friends—you know, other pilots who have gotten down on their luck. These pilots may have wrecked their plane, flunked their flight physical, be out of work, or whatever. . . . The point is, Roscoe's caring nature has placed him in dire straits."

Fernando didn't quite know how to respond, so instead of speaking, he just nodded and exited the now-parked car. Following Maggie into Roscoe's office, Fernando noticed the impressive trophies on stands, the pictures on the walls, and framed newspaper clippings recounting Roscoe's rescue flights and race exploits. In addition, there were autographed pictures of famous movie actors and other celebrities Roscoe had flown in his planes. At a large rolltop desk covered with scattered papers, sat Roscoe.

"Hello, kids," he greeted. "Don't mind Gertrude . . . she won't bite. Even so, it's best to never turn your back on her."

Roscoe was looking down at a large lioness lying on the floor beside him. When he stood up, the lioness followed, so Fernando and Maggie backed cautiously away. Sensing their discomfort, Roscoe gave a signal to the beautiful animal. She immediately lay back down on the floor.

"Best watchdog I have ever had," he stated proudly. "Come with me, kids. I want to show you my new Ryan Sportster. Maggie tells me you are an accomplished pilot in your own right, Fernando, so you'll appreciate this beauty of the sky."

As the three walked out into the hangar, Roscoe couldn't help but think of the couple at his side. Maggie had insisted that the two were merely friends, but Roscoe sensed otherwise. Smiling to himself, he wondered how long it would take for them to cross over that invisible barrier that propelled couples toward the altar.

Walking past several exotic race planes sheltered from the weather, Fernando noticed the spotless floor—certainly unusual for a typical flight operation. Normally, there was grease and oil dripping from the planes, with dirt ground into the floor. But not here. In Roscoe's hangar, everything was almost spitshined. The cement floor was perhaps the most telling, painted a military gray, and shined from frequent sweepings and cleanings. Roscoe obviously ran a tight operation, which meant that the planes were likely in shipshape, also.

The three of them walked through a smaller door within the hangar door and outside into the late afternoon sunlight. In front of them was a shiny, polished low-wing monoplane.

"Just look at that little beauty," exclaimed Roscoe, suddenly breaking the silence. "Ryan's has produced a real winner again, don't you think? Ryan's is a fine little factory down in San Diego. The price is a bit high, but I have it on consignment, to show my clients. Why don't you both take it up for a spin? Over there are the parachutes that I packed myself and two sets of helmets and goggles. I think they will fit famously."

Maggie and Fernando stared at each other, not believing the generous offer. It had been over three years since Fernando had been in the air, and to be trusted with such a plane was something he was altogether unprepared for.

Without waiting for a reply, Roscoe led them over to the bright silver plane. On the leading edge of the wing were two parachutes with their harnesses hanging down. On top of each parachute was a canvas summerweight helmet with the newest-style goggles. Roscoe sensed with pleasure that both Fernando and Maggie knew exactly what to do.

"You really mean it, Roscoe?" Maggie exclaimed excitedly.

"Of course! After the beating you took from Herr Direktor a couple of weeks ago, you deserve a bit of heaven."

"What about me?" Fernando asked, smiling widely. "I haven't done anything to warrant such a gift . . . ."

"Oh, yes you have " Roscoe laughed. "You cured a beautiful palomino stallion, along with an empty heart. So you've earned many such flights."

Maggie and Fernando glanced uncomfortably at each other. Neither knew who should go first, and at last Fernando motioned for Maggie to follow his lead. Turning away from the plane, they picked up the straps, slipped their arms into the right places, and stepped forward so that the parachute packs dropped from the wing, hitting them simultaneously in the back of the knees. Each quickly reached down to pull the bottom straps up between their legs, buckling up.

Maggie tried a helmet first before handing it to Fernando. "I think this is more your size," she laughed. She was right, and soon both were ready—Fernando still in his polo clothes and Maggie in her western attire—but now both looking like seasoned acrobatic pilots.

Even though Roscoe knew they were experienced pilots, he gave them a series of instructions specific to this aircraft.

"Sorry, folks, but there is no way for you to communicate between each other, except by the usual hand signals and wiggling of the stick. Stalling speed is 65, red line is 200. It's stressed for six G's positive and three G's negative, so it will take any wringing-out you want to try . . . except, of course, for an inverted spin. It will take that, I'm sure, but no one has attempted such a maneuver; therefore, we don't know how it will behave. Be sure you stay above 3,000 feet."

Fernando's mind reached back frantically to the years in his life that were so filled with flying new aircraft. It seemed long ago, almost in another lifetime—and yet the memories came rushing back, as though it had been only yesterday. He could do it, he was sure, especially with Maggie at his side.

"It has gas for a full ninety minutes," Roscoe added, "and you've got about one hour of sunshine left. The electric starter is on the left of the panel and the master switch and magnetos are right beside it. Primer and fuel selector are on the floor to your left. Trim tabs are in the usual place and set for takeoff. I just flew it myself and left it set correctly for you.

"Now," he concluded, patting both Maggie and Fernando on the shoulder, "go have some fun, but don't wreck it. Maggie knows where the restricted aerobatics practice area is, between the airport and the river. I'll drive over there and watch you do your stuff."

As the two pilots climbed into the smart, sporty aircraft, Roscoe called, "Oh, I almost forgot. Check the mags at 1,800 r.p.m.'s. I'll pull your wheel chocks when you give me the signal." He walked out to the end of the wing. While the pair of pilots were getting situated—Maggie up front and Fernando in back— Maggie said softly so Roscoe could not hear, "Fernando, you do have a pilot's license, don't you?" He nodded affirmatively, without answering.

"Any aerobatics experience?"

He nodded, smiling.

"How many hours do you have?" she asked, expecting him to say perhaps two hundred or so.

"Over two thousand, with single-engine, multi-engined, commercial and instructor carnets."

His reply was not stated with arrogance, but matter-of-factly, and Maggie was impressed. As far as she knew, very few pilots had that many hours—unless they were fully immersed in aviation on a daily basis.

The next hour was one of sheer delight for both of them. Neither had previously had so much fun wringing out a new plane. Each was respectful of the other, sharing equal time performing stunts. No other planes were in the air on this particular day, so there was no traffic at the airport. Because of this, when the mechanics and line boys from Roscoe's hangar heard the engine laboring in climbs and dives, they came outside to watch, sensing something unusual was happening. A few of them lay down on the grass, giving them a better view of this display in the sky without getting a crick in their necks.

Finally, resigning herself to the lateness of the evening, Maggie pointed to her watch, signaling that the hour was over. She was exhausted, her emotions at a fever pitch. To her memory, she had never experienced such an emotional high.

Fernando had likewise noted that the sun had just dipped below the horizon, so he was expecting Maggie's signal. He had never gotten over the euphoria that came with flying, and to be maneuvering with such an advanced plane was an experience he had not even remotely anticipated. Wiggling the stick from the back cockpit, he signalled to Maggie that he would like to take the last turn and make the landing. Smiling to herself, while sensing his little boy excitement, Maggie let go and sat back. She placed her hands on the cockpit edge, waiting for whatever he might have in mind.

Feeling a rush of adrenaline, Fernando made the traffic circuit at higher-than-normal altitude. Instead of lowering the nose toward the runway, he remained high and level—flying in the right direction yet showing no intention of landing.

Maggie, suddenly concerned that something might be wrong, began to consider her options. She had never seen a landing approach like this and tensed up, wondering how she would respond if needed.

She had had no need for concern because, when the plane was almost over the end of the pavement, Fernando pulled the nose up into a full stall. He kicked hard rudder and put the plane into an intentional spin—one turn, two turns, full recovery followed by a violent slip toward the runway, first on one side and then the other. He smoothly bled off the excess speed and kicked the plane straight for a perfect landing.

Maggie was speechless. Never in her entire flying career had she participated in such a feat, and her heart beat wildly. This man was the most exciting, impulsive person she had ever met, yet she sensed that she had barely begun to scratch the surface in knowing who he was.

When Fernando and Maggie pulled up on the apron in front of the hangar, Roscoe and the other spectators came running toward them. Fernando cut the mixture, allowing the prop to wind down to a stop. When the engine became silent, the crowd burst into applause. Grinning widely, Fernando finished the shutdown procedure by putting everything in place for the next pilot to start up.

Maggie was already out of the plane, removing her chute, when Fernando stepped down. Without acknowledging the others, he unbuckled his chute straps and flipped the chute over his right shoulder, holding the pack by the crotch straps.

Roscoe, slapping Fernando on the back, said, "Sorry you quit, kids. That was quite a show. We haven't seen anything like that for a long time. Tell me, who did that two-turn spin as you came in?"

Maggie quickly spoke up, "That was Fernando. I've heard of that kind of maneuver, but I've never seen it or experienced it. For a minute there, the ground looked awfully close over that nose."

"And, the eight-point hesitation rolls?"

While Fernando fidgeted nervously, Maggie again responded.

"Fernando did those, also."

Roscoe's suspicions were being confirmed. " . . . And, who did that perfect tail slide?"

Maggie started to reply, but Roscoe himself answered his own question, "I'll bet it was you, right, Fernando?"

Fernando shrugged his shoulders and smiled modestly, but remained silent.

"Fernando," Roscoe pressed, "just what kind of aerobatics plane do you usually fly?"

"Uh . . . actually, a German Jungmeister with 240 horsepower."

Roscoe whistled knowingly. "I hear that's the best aerobatics plane ever built—perfect balance, perfect response. How do you think it compares with the Ryan?"

Fernando didn't want to offend the plane's owner since he had enjoyed the flight tremendously. Still, he had to respond honestly, "Well, for pure aerobatics, the Jungmeister is the better of the two, but the Ryan, with an experienced pilot, can do everything the Jungmeister is capable of. I prefer the looks of the Ryan—the aluminum fuselage is perfectly molded, and the monoplane picks up speed faster than the biplane. On the other hand, the Ryan needs more horsepower to compete directly with the German plane."

There was a new respect in Roscoe's tone of voice, as though he were talking to an equal, not just another young pilot. Where did Maggie find this young man? Roscoe knew the Jungmeister was a precision and custom-made plane, and there were only two such airplanes in the United States. They were incredibly expensive, and very hard to come by. And . . . that spin to a landing . . . . Roscoe admitted to himself that he had never tried that.

After the trio rolled the Ryan into the hangar, Fernando did the unexpected. He pulled Roscoe aside and whispered, "Why don't we get a plane for Maggie to fly in the Bendix Cup cross-country race?" Roscoe smiled widely, giving an okay sign. Fernando returned the acknowledgement with a wink, after which the two men spent time discussing the various aspects of the newly manufactured Ryan.

Maggie remained silent. Her thoughts were in another direction, trying to come to grips with the unusual Fernando Underwood. The mystery of his past haunted her mind, but it was not nearly equal to the mystery of his smile. Something was happening inside her that was growing uncontrollably, and she resigned herself to be entirely at the mercy of these emotions.

Finally, seeing that the hour was late, Maggie thanked Roscoe for the ride, said goodbye, and beckoned Fernando to follow her to the auto. The sun had set, and the evening was mild. Fernando insisted they leave the top down.

With the evening winds blowing through their hair, Maggie and Fernando drove back toward the polo stables. After agonizing over how to proceed, Maggie finally ventured to extract a few explanations from Fernando. With each of her questions, she received only evasive answers. Finally, in exasperation, she blurted, "Fernando, you don't play fair. Please give me the same courtesy with your answers that I give you. Can't you tell me what the problem is? We have only known each other for two weeks, but in all we've done together, you haven't shared one thing about yourself—except where you are from, and that you have experienced family difficulties—"

"My, my, Miss Rockwell, aren't you one for putting pressure on a fellow."

"I . . . uh, I just feel you owe me an explanation . . . as a friend, I mean. I don't want to intrude, I just want to—"

" . . . improve our friendship, your way?"

Even as Fernando spoke, Maggie pressed the brake and came to a stop in front of Fernando's apartment. Turning off her lights and engine, she removed her left foot from the clutch. Except for the small light expelling from the nearby window, all was dark. There was no one around, and everything—even the nearby horses—were quiet. From somewhere close by, Fernando could hear a cricket serenading.

Mentally replaying his sarcastic words, Fernando was suddenly sorry. Gathering Maggie into his arms, he allowed his lips to press lightly against hers, kissing her tenderly. Maggie, hesitant at first, trying desperately to comprehend what was happening, finally allowed her emotions to prevail, and she responded passionately. Cupping Fernando's face in her hands, she drew back, gazing directly into his adoring, shadowed eyes.

"I . . . I've never been treated like that by a friend before," she gasped, catching her breath.

" . . . Just wanted to improve our relationship—my way," Fernando whispered with obvious satisfaction.

Without waiting for a reply, Fernando pulled his face away from her hands, turned the latch on the door, and climbed out. Walking around to Maggie's side, he bent down, once again allowing his lips to briefly touch hers. It was more a brush than a kiss, but as he straightened up and smiled, Maggie felt her heart skip a beat.

Without speaking, Fernando turned and walked into his apartment, feeling a peace and joy that surpassed anything he had previously known. Maggie was not an accident in his life. To the contrary, Fernando knew that destiny was unfolding, even as he closed the door and collapsed on the small divan. He only half-heard the sound of an automobile engine starting up outside. Then fading, as though he had dreamed it, the auto left the stable area and blended into the darkness of the night.

Chapter Seven

Buenos Aires, Argentina

Buenos Aires, affectionately called the Paris of South America, lies nearly 10,000 miles southeast of Los Angeles, California. Its broad, treelined boulevards with sidewalk restaurants provide a beautiful backdrop to its heroic-sized statues and spectacular fountains. Added to this is the grand style architecture in its public buildings. In the evening, elegantly dressed citizens frequent the opera, ballet and symphonies. In addition, the art museums and the expensive stores rivaling New York's Fifth Avenue combine to make it one of the world's most cultured cities.

Argentina boasted per capita more miles of railroad than England, more automobiles than the United States, more telephones than France, more hospital beds than Germany, and more pizzas than Italy. In addition, its consumption of red meat and wine was the highest in the world.

Behind this economic progress was the immense wealth of the fertile *pampas*—hundreds of thousands of square miles of rich, black, loam soil at least thirty feet deep—so rich that commercial fertilizer was never used.

By 1936, the *pampas* of Argentina had evolved into one of the great bread baskets of the world. The production of grains and cattle was so far in excess of local consumption that the surplus for export had begun to feed many nations in need.

The Buenos Aires residence of Don Hugo San Martin Braun

and his British-born wife, Dame Helen, was like the city itself, palatial and excessive. Located in the northern suburbs, this estate overlooked the wide expanse of the Rio Plata. The river was forty miles wide at that point, and on the opposite bank lay neighboring Uruguay. The ocean, a full hundred miles to the east, still affected the level of the river bordering the city of Buenos Aires.

The San Martin estate grounds, located on a high point of the bluff facing the river, sloped down for several blocks toward the shore line. They included formal gardens behind the mansion and tennis courts of red clay made from crushed brick dust. To the side of these courts lay an Olympic-sized swimming pool with diving boards and platforms lined by statuary commissioned by renowned sculptors.

In addition to these amenities, the housing included a ten-car garage with living quarters for several chauffeurs and a full-time mechanic, several guest cottages, and eight strategically positioned security guard posts.

The front side of the immense estate, where the long, sloping lawns extended to the river, was landscaped with pathways and gardens consisting of a variety of flower and shrub arrangements. An aviary and a small zoo adorned the area to the rear of the estate—constructed and populated for the pleasure of the growing family, both young and old. Large, full-foliaged trees planted in strategic places around the perimeter provided total privacy. In fact, from the streets surrounding the estate, nothing but dense vegetation could be observed.

To examine the estate from the river was to observe an expansive green park of detailed perfection, crowned by a multicolumned mansion with a large terrace where the family could watch yacht races or enjoy their meals in private opulence. It was, indeed, every bit a private park. For sheer size and elegance, the San Martin estate would rival the finest of Europe, or even the famous William Randolph Hearst estates in California.

Inside the mansion, and to the immediate right of a three-story-high entry and stairway, was a two-story study. The west wall of the study was adorned with an immense fireplace, framed in imported Italian marble with identical heroic-sized statues of carved marble supporting both ends of the mantle. The fireplace was large enough for a full-grown person to stand inside without stooping.

Elsewhere, the bookcases, filling three sides of the room from floor to ceiling, contained thousands of first edition leather-bound copies of the English and Spanish worlds' best collector books. It was touted as the most complete private library in the entire country, if not in all of Latin America. A full-time professional librarian supervised the collection and lived in one of the servants' quarters. Thus, he could be accessed, as needed, by Don Hugo or any other family member.

The furniture throughout the room was massive and master-crafted—almost irreplaceable antiques imported from ancient European castles. Don Hugo and Dame Helen imported two personal desks of matching mahogany from the West Indies and had these placed side by side facing the large window that overlooked the sloping estate and river.

The master and mistress of the estate were relaxing in this spacious study, discussing Hugo's latest trip. He had just returned from a sweeping tour of various family interests in the southern part of Argentina known as the *Patagonia*.

"*Querida*, Helen," he exclaimed excitedly. "You should see Bariloche and the lakes this year. The wild flowers are spectacular. The lakes are crystal clear and deep blue, right to the edge of the forests that descend from the snowcovered peaks above. Truly, I have never seen the Andes more spectacular.

"Besides, *mi bella*," he smiled, squeezing her hand, "I have missed you greatly. I would have given anything to have had you at my side."

"As would I, *mi amor*," Helen added wistfully. "If only the doctors could find out what's wrong with me and get me well again. But tell me how your work is going."

Dame Helen listened intently as he spoke of the various operations he was handling. She was vitally interested in all that occurred within their domain and kept herself informed of the general conditions of each facet of their stewardship. And that was how she viewed the family wealth—a stewardship, provided by the Lord of Heaven so that the peoples of the world could benefit. As one would expect, her greatest interest was in the welfare of the many hundreds of people who worked for them, along with the workers' families.

"Hugo, how are our people getting along? Do we have the schools and the hospitals for them that we promised?"

Without speaking, Don Hugo stood, walked over to his desk and took a report from the top of a stack of papers. He brought it back to where they were seated by the fireplace. It was too warm outside for a fire to be necessary, but the coziness of the study made it one of their favorite places to talk. No one entered the room, except with the permission of Don Hugo or his wife, since the study was off-limits to the staff anytime either of them were home.

"Here is the school and hospital report. Ricardo prepared it, as you know, and wanted you to see it. He is doing a good job looking after the social welfare of our people. The doctors have finished all the vaccinations, and the dentists have checked all the employees' teeth—even those of the spouses and children. Is there anything else, my dear?"

Knowing the report was well prepared, Dame Helen set the papers aside without so much as looking at them. She would do that later. Now, however, she had many questions that were clamoring to be answered.

"*Mi amor,*" she said, changing the subject, "how about the lodge at Bariloche? What about the lighting plant? Did they get the new diesel plant installed?"

Don Hugo was very proud of his wife. She had remained beautiful and feminine into her golden years, yet was always very interested in everything about the sheep and cattle ranches, the sugar operations, the businesses—and especially the people. And, without fanfare, she always added her touch to the many homes that were being built for them. It was typical that she would remember things like the condition of the fruit, and the lighting plant.

"Yes, the diesel plant is installed and working, but makes more noise than we thought it would. Because of this, we are moving it farther away from the main house. In fact, we used the power this year for electric clippers in the shearing sheds, instead of the antiquated belt-driven mechanical clippers."

Don Hugo felt that it was the duty of the family members to travel frequently, not only to be familiar with the people and operations, but also because of an old Argentine saying, "The eye of the owner fattens the cattle." He genuinely enjoyed traveling around and dropping in on their various operations and knew that having his wife visit the places kept all the caretakers and supervisors on their toes, trying to please her. She was always generous in her praise, and such endearing words made the employees work even harder.

Dame Helen's favorite place to visit was the lodge at Bariloche. It was a huge Black Forest German-type hunting lodge of varnished logs and enormous rock fireplaces. This lodge was the center of their sheep operations in the south, and the center for their other business interests in that region.

In addition to this lodge, they owned and maintained a city home in Cordoba, some fifteen hundred miles to the north. Again, this home was the focal point of their varied business interests there.

Another thousand miles farther north, where they had the sugar plantations and several sugar mills, they also had a lovely home for the family to visit. They had homes at resorts in Brazil, Uruguay, Chile, and Europe, including England. Some members of the family and their children were always traveling and using these various properties, so both Don Hugo and Dame Helen felt justified in retaining and maintaining them.

Don Hugo knew that his wife's interest in Bariloche, or any other place for that matter, was brief, and that she would quickly lapse back into her personal and private worries. Dame Helen had become very introverted with her illness and had not been her usual self these last three years. From Don Hugo's perspective, he knew the core of her problem. Because of this, he decided it was best to address the matter at this time, in the context of his trip.

"I know how you are suffering, my dear. On my trip south, I thought of Fernando more than ever before. Although my heart filled with sorrow as he came to mind, I especially remembered the last trip we made together—just the three of us."

Don Hugo always spoke to his wife in English, although she had long ago mastered the Spanish language. In response to Don Hugo's mention of Fernando in her native tongue, soft tears rolled down Dame Helen's cheeks.

"I am sorry that I am such miserable company," she apologized. "I thought I was listening to the report of your trip, but I guess when my mind wanders, it always shows, doesn't it? I, too, was remembering that last trip, but you need me to be happy and exciting and responsive, and all I can do is to feel so sad . . . and so empty. I am happy you are home safe and sound, and I do love you, Hugo. I get so tired of just sitting here at home, but I just don't feel like traveling. If only the doctors could help me get over the pain . . . ."

Dame Helen had been suffering from a deep-seated internal pain for some time now, but the specialists could offer neither a diagnosis nor a solution for it. At times it was worse than others, but then it would ease up, allowing her to barely tolerate her condition. Don Hugo realized that, in spite of her apparent interest in his trip, she probably had not paid much attention to what he was saying until he mentioned Fernando.

"Helen, do you remember when we went fishing with Fernando, and he caught the twenty-pound trout? And remember when he flew out to the sheep stations with me, where we did some good, hard, horseback riding, and then spent a week camping under the stars? He flew back alone later, to do that veterinary medicine study on our sheep. And then when we came through Bahia Blanca, he played polo with some of the men. They really enjoyed that and still talk about it . . . and about him. Of course, they speak of Fernando as we knew him, not the person who no longer can be called a man. His failures, I'm afraid, have far exceeded the greatness we used to see in him."

"What do you tell your people about Fernando, Hugo?" Dame Helen asked pointedly. Without waiting for a reply, she immediately fell into a deep melancholy mood, then spoke longingly, "I have been looking at the pictures we took of that trip and have almost worn them thin. I keep wondering where Fernando is now—how he's doing. How long has it been since his last letter arrived?"

Don Hugo, suddenly finding himself seething in anger with the turn of the conversation, knew exactly how long it had been. "Five months and two weeks," he said shortly. "The last one came from California, on the west coast of the United States, and for all I care, it will be the last. Fernando is no longer my son, Helen, for his immoral and antisocial behavior has eliminated the love I once had for him."

"I don't believe that for a minute, Hugo" Dame Helen protested. "You have always worshipped Fernando, and his mistakes cannot erase the bond that's between the two of you."

"Enough! I have asked you, Helen, not to use his name in my presence. As far as I'm concerned, he is dead, and that's final."

"It was you who used his name first, Hugo—"

"It doesn't matter who used his name first. The point is, we have lost our firstborn son and have but one son, Ricardo, to carry on our family name."

Dame Helen looked stunned as she listened to the harshness of her husband's words. She didn't challenge him, but continued to speak, stressing the theme Hugo knew well, and from which he suffered deeply. Whenever she spoke longingly of Fernando, she knew it was like turning a knife inside her husband, hurting him once again clear to the core. She did not mean to hurt him, but that was always the result.

Sensing that Don Hugo was deep into his own feelings of anger and denial, Dame Helen continued pressing. "Hugo, Fernando must be suffering, too. Isn't there something we can do that we haven't thought of . . . to find him, I mean?"

Don Hugo felt that, in reality, she was saying, *Couldn't you have done things differently?* That thought produced even greater anger within his heart, as Don Hugo had felt all along that she believed Fernando's distancing was all his fault. But, she was a woman, and Fernando's mother. On both counts, this left her unable to deal with the situation rationally. Fernando had made the same bed at three separate universities, and, as far as Don Hugo was concerned, he must lie in it. He was no longer part of the family, the disgrace was his last unforgivable mistake, and Hugo would die before speaking to him again.

With these thoughts spinning recklessly in his mind, Don Hugo suddenly arose, bolted across the study and out the door. Seconds later, Dame Helen spotted him winding his way slowly down the manicured path toward the river. Her heart was ready to burst, both with anger toward her lifelong companion and with sorrow for the loss of her eldest son . . . the son she would never again set eyes upon.

Three hours later, long after the sun had set, Don Hugo sat limply at the water's edge. Gazing absently at the ships passing in front of him, he finally knew what he must do. "Helen will never be well until I have traveled to the United States and cut all ties with Fernando," he reasoned with himself. "I must take the legal documents, have him sign off all future rights as president and board chairman of the San Martin Corporation, then ask him once and for all—and in person—to end his relationship with his mother. She deserves peace of mind so her health will return, and this will allow that to happen. I must give her the impression that I am going stateside to make peace with Fernando; by the time I return, she will be well. It is deceit born of honor, with her life at stake, and so I shall proceed. After all, the ambassador advised me while down in Bahia Blanca, that they had a fairly substantial tip that Fernando had finally been located."

Sometime later, Don Hugo sat again in his leather chair—his head bowed, and his face between his hands. He had told Dame Helen of his plans and of the ambassador's locating Fernando. Of course, she was ecstatic. She had now retired for the night, leaving him alone with a lie upon his lips. He hated the deception; his marriage had been one of total trust, but he had said the words for her well-being, he convinced himself.

As he thought of his impending trip to the United States, he began to reminisce about the pleasant memories of his son's youth. He remembered what an outstanding and talented first-born he and Helen had reared. Fernando was athletically talented, or gifted, in a way known only to those one-in-a-million athletes. Everything was easy for him—perhaps too easy. He was stronger and bigger than his peers and seemed blessed with hand-to-eye coordination and lightning-fast reflexes that made him superior in games and contests. He had an instinct for winning, and training was never a burden—just a great deal of fun.

Fernando had inherited all these qualities from his forefathers from generations past, who were either part of King Arthur's Round Table on his mother's side, or were casting the Moors out of Spain on his father's side. But polo had been Fernando's first love, and ever since he was just a lad, Fernando and his father had spent hours and hours together on horseback, practicing different polo shots on the best horses in the world—horses which were bred on the family's own ranches.

Don Hugo remembered with bitterness what an outstanding student his son had been. He could get the highest grades in the class anytime he tried to, and this keenness of intellect had likely spawned the problems he had experienced in college.

Fernando's weakness, Don Hugo felt, was that his mind was so fast that the teachers had to challenge him with extra work; otherwise, he became bored with the seemingly slow pace of the class. Long before the class was ready, Fernando would shoot ahead into the advanced concepts of mathematics or science. As parents, Don Hugo and Dame Helen had provided private tutors to utilize Fernando's talents. Even then, he had time left over to take flying lessons from an excellent German instructor who had come to Argentina following World War I. The instructor had flown with the real Red Baron—Baron Manfred Von Richthofen. He was a man among men—a man Don Hugo would never forget.

With a flair for engines, Fernando had asked for and received permission to take the official Rolls Royce mechanic's course required of the top mechanics at the Rolls Royce dealership. This, of course, was routine, since the family owned the dealership. They had long ago discovered that it was better to own the dealership than to be paying retail prices for automobiles and limousines the corporation would purchase anyway.

Don Hugo was well aware that Fernando's problems started after he left Eton and while he was attending Cambridge. He and Dame Helen had sent him to Cambridge, instead of Oxford, primarily because Cambridge was more of a technical school. Fernando was more interested in studying aeronautical engineering rather than history, sociology, or the languages. But after his drinking problem erupted and he had been expelled, they sent him to Paris to attend La Sorbonne. They had thought that in this environment he would polish his French and gain intercultural maturity. Fernando did get top grades the first year, but before the end of the second winter, he had once again been expelled—a direct result of drunken and irrational behavior at a fraternity party. Don Hugo could only assume that immoral conduct with coeds was a part of the problem. This fact was never confirmed, but alcohol and immorality were the twin sisters of

70

failure, and Fernando had assuredly partaken of both.

From that disaster, Don Hugo and Dame Helen had decided to send Fernando to an Ivy League school on the east coast of the United States—Harvard University. After a few months without incident, Fernando's former weakness with alcohol revealed itself, and this time a major disaster occurred, causing profound embarrassment to both the university and the family. Word had come back that, while intoxicated, Fernando had driven an automobile into a river, causing a young lady's untimely death. For that behavior, there could be no forgiveness—not from the honored San Martin and Braun family infrastructure.

The headlines blaring the tragedy were burned into Don Hugo's mind: "Wealthy Latin Jailed," "San Martin Presidential Heir Involved in Drunken Drowning," "Gambling and Alcohol Tragedy, Society Girl Drowned in Car Accident." In Argentina, the papers were a bit more discreet, but shocking nevertheless. Fernando was to have become the head of the family—the Gaucho Prince—but now he had fallen too far to ever recover. True, he had later been vindicated by the law, but this did not erase the fact that his drinking had taken a human life. Blood was certainly upon his hands, and such contamination could never be washed clean.

This final fiasco, considered Don Hugo, was the straw that broke the proverbial gaucho's back. He had sent Fernando away to establish his intellectual ability, intelligence, and competence in order to lead the family dynasty. But his son had failed to show his dependability and character in marrying well and settling down, ready to manage the many family interests with skill and profitability.

This future family leader, Don Hugo continued—now deep in thought—needed to do what was best for the whole family, not just for himself. Such schooling was not unlike the preparation of members of royalty who were in line of succession for the British crown. In his mind, Don Hugo continued going back over Fernando's life—reexamining his own relationship with his son. "Everything in the world to live for," he said aloud and with continued anger, "yet he disgraces his family, his country, and his God. Such mismanagement of talent cannot . . . no, must not go unpunished."

So Don Hugo had done something more drastic than just a little wrist slapping. He had sent a cable, the message of which still rang in his mind: *"You have disgraced us. All accounts closed, all letters of credit canceled. Come home immediately. Signed, Don Hugo San Martin Braun."* He had not even signed it, *Your Father.*

Don Hugo now knew that Fernando had rightly assumed that his use of his formal name, without familial softening, meant that he was disinheriting his son, and Fernando was being dropped from the line of possible succession to his father's position. It had been a family discipline—a means of censuring unacceptable behavior and conduct.

Disappearing with only part of his extensive wardrobe, Fernando had left no trace of his whereabouts. Letters, with no return address, had since arrived twice a year from different cities in the United States. These letters were always directed to his mother, although he had always inferred that he was writing to both by addressing it "My Dear Parents."

Don Hugo had hated those letters because they had always given Dame Helen false hope. Such had indeed been a death knell for Fernando. Don Hugo could never allow hypocrisy within his family circle. *Never!*

Don Hugo's plan to travel to the states and there sever all ties with his former son had actually sprung from a seed planted only two days before. He had received a message from the British Ambassador in Buenos Aires, saying that Fernando had been located somewhere in Los Angeles, California. The wire message from the states asked what the British Embassy should do if the "mystery polo player," as they dubbed him, proved to be Fernando.

With this inquiry firmly entrenched in his mind, Don Hugo stood up and walked to the terrace overlooking the river. The night was balmy and beautiful—the kind of weather that had given the city its name—*Buenos Aires*, or *Good Breezes*. This name, given by the first Spanish sailors who brought their ship into these waters, took hold and remained to this day. He would spend an hour or so there and allow the pain of his emotions to quietly vanish into the night. Dame Helen, he knew, must be protected from his outbursts. She did not understand what Fernando had put him through, and, although he must resolve things once and for all, he must do it independent of her.

Such were Don Hugo's thoughts as he gazed unseeingly out into the sparkling, moonlit water before him. Presently the aroma of frying fish hit his nostrils, and Don Hugo, a connoisseur of fine food, immediately considered its source. Momentarily, at least, his thoughts were diverted. The fish was unquestionably a Southern cod.

The following morning, after breakfast with Dame Helen, Don Hugo returned to the book-lined study to make a private phone call. He did not want to appear too interested in the message from the British Embassy; but, after all, he had just returned from a long trip, so Dame Helen excused him without suspicion.

Once in the study, Don Hugo dialed the ambassador—a man he knew reasonably well—and after going through the telephone operator, the office secretary, then finally the private secretary, he eventually heard the ambassador's booming bass voice on the line.

"Don Hugo, what a pleasure. I have been expecting your call. You did get my message that we needed to see you, did you not?"

"Yes, Mr. Ambassador, but of course. I just returned from my trip to the Patagonia late last night, and I could not call you until now. My office left the message for me at Tres Arroyos, but I skipped my visit there for now because I wanted to get back to see how Helen was doing. Thank you for the interest."

"Glad you returned home safely," the ambassador replied

loudly. "You know, we have important news—from London. As I mentioned, it is regarding your eldest son. It is a bit lengthy to discuss on the telephone. Would it be convenient for you to drop by, or should I bring it to your office?"

Don Hugo decided it might be quicker if he went to the Embassy rather than wait for an open time in the ambassador's busy schedule.

"I'm at home now. It will take me about thirty minutes to be downtown. If you don't mind, I will drop by your office. Is that convenient for you?"

The ambassador agreed that it was, and Don Hugo hung up the telephone, working his mind into even deeper anger than the night before.

Thirty-five minutes later, Don Hugo was escorted to the top floor of the British Embassy in downtown Buenos Aires. There he was ushered into Ambassador Clarke's oak-paneled office. The ambassador stood and walked around his massive oak desk to greet his friend.

"Don Hugo . . . so good to see you again." He greeted Don Hugo with a continental-style embrace, touching cheeks and smacking a soft kiss into the air. "Please, do sit down and make yourself comfortable. Will you have a spot of tea?"

Protocol would have called for small talk and tea, or mate, but Don Hugo was impatient and anxious to get to the heart of his visit.

"Thank you, Mr. Ambassador, but not now. I am more interested in what your people have found out. What news do you have of my son, Fernando?"

Coming right to the point, Ambassador Clarke said, "We feel that we have good news. The identification seems most positive. Fernando is in southern California and is studying aeronautical engineering at a very prestigious private university there. He is soon to graduate—with honors, I must say. He is registered under your wife's maiden name—Underwood. That would not have been hard to do since his passport, according to our records, was made out Fernando Hugo San Martin Underwood. You might remember, in Argentina, actually, in most Spanish speaking countries, the father's name precedes the mother's maiden name on official documents."

Don Hugo nodded silently. He understood the idiotic custom all too well.

Continuing, the ambassador said, "Our informants tell us that your son is working his way through school on a polo scholarship. They have him listed as the team captain when they play other schools or clubs, and he also teaches classes in polo. This job covers his tuition at this very expensive school.

"From what we have learned, Fernando earns spending money and living expenses by managing the university stables and the hands there. Everyone speaks very highly of him, as you would no doubt expect. Our report says that his conduct is exemplary and totally above reproach."

To say that Don Hugo was stunned speechless would be an understatement. He had expected just the opposite because he knew how far down Fernando had plummeted. There must be a mistake, a ruse in the report . . .

"Here is the record, Don Hugo. The only people involved in this private matter are our staff in London and the Earl of Wittingham, our new consul in California. You may remember him since he played polo about the same time you did. Lord Jockham is his name. Later on, he was with the cavalry, then the Hurlingham Polo Club."

With increased anxiety and sensing that Don Hugo was not going to respond, Ambassador Clarke continued. "There is one other person there in California, a British actor, Sir Douglas. He is now famous in Hollywood pictures, but at home he is one of our best Shakespearean actors. This Sir Douglas also played polo with members of the royal family and was a fine Olympic class fencer in his younger days. He uses his skills in many of his films.

"As a matter of fact," the Ambassador smiled proudly, "it seems that Sir Douglas and the Earl of Wittingham saw your Fernando play polo, spotting his unusual talent. They say he is now playing at a ten handicap level. Chip off the old block, wouldn't you say?"

Don Hugo, in spite of his emotions, smiled at the compliment as he asked, "Anyone else involved in your . . . investigation?"

"Well, yes," the ambassador admitted. "Hope you don't mind. We touched base with some of Dame Helen's family for positive identification, but we told them that this is a very private matter and is to be held in the closest of confidence. Our staff can be trusted. We feel that Sir Douglas and the Earl are also completely discreet.

"The Earl has told our people in Los Angeles to keep this under control—treat it as if it were a matter of national security. We did not know exactly what you wanted us to do. That is why I suggested you drop by. What would you have us do next?"

Having made a quick summary of most of the facts, Ambassador Clarke leaned back in his swivel chair, waiting for his words to sink in.

Don Hugo contemplated how best to handle the situation, especially in light of his decision the previous night. It was obvious that the ambassador was sincere and open. The ambassador was aware of Fernando's past problems and did not want to complicate the situation unnecessarily with further intrusion. The San Martin and Underwood families, and their fortunes, were vital to global interests.

After a few seconds, Don Hugo spoke. "Ambassador, I would like to travel at once to the states and locate my son. My request, as you would expect, is that he not learn of my coming. The issues—his often repeated problems—are much too complex to solve through the mail or wire system. I will surprise him, then take it from there. I will turn everything here over to my brother, Roberto. He will probably guess that my trip has to do with Fernando, so I will tell him just that. Thank you for your efforts,

Ambassador. My family is most grateful."

"It is a most delicate trip, Don Hugo. As you requested, our people will not contact Fernando, nor disclose that his secret identity has been found out."

When Don Hugo exited the front entrance of the marbled embassy building, the chauffeured Rolls limousine pulled up, having been signaled by the doorman.

Settling inside the comfortable interior, Don Hugo leaned back, closed his eyes, and considered the phoniness of his conversation with Ambassador Clarke. He detested situational ethics, and thus the deceit regarding his trip to California. Still, what was he to do? Fernando had undermined his character—and the character of the San Martin family—in a profound and permanent way. Don Hugo knew he had no choice but to proceed as he had planned. The trip would be long and arduous, but would lay to rest the notion of a false son and allow him and Dame Helen to move forward in their lives without Fernando's future involvement. There simply was no other way.

Chapter Eight

The Same Day
Los Angeles, California

For both Fernando and Maggie, the next eighteen hours were anything but settling. Their emotions, somehow left unchecked, had betrayed each of them in a very different, although similar way. Maggie, who had successfully avoided romantic involvement for the three years since leaving her high school sweetheart back in Arizona, was for the first time beginning to question the depth of emotion and commitment she had previously depended upon through letters. Even more significant, she had not told Fernando that she was an active Latter-day Saint. She wondered if it was because she was developing such strong feelings that she did not dare to risk complications if he were to reject her "American religion" without giving her the opportunity to explain it to him. She had always planned to marry someone who would share her religious beliefs, which were of utmost importance to her. Then she had met Fernando.

Fernando as well was overcome with a bewildering range of emotions. He had avoided all relationships since his fiancée's death, only to discover that he was falling hopelessly in love with someone else. Was he worthy of such a relationship? he wondered. His one-time preoccupation with alcohol and partying had been so costly that he had spent the last three years struggling with his own self-worth.

Both Maggie and Fernando were deep in thought, attempting to come to grips with the emotions they were now feeling, when they inadvertently entered the lecture hall at the same time. The three aeronautics classes were meeting together, and Fernando and Maggie had previously arranged to sit together.

"Mornin', ma'am," Fernando drawled, again making an attempt at western slang.

"Mornin' to you, Mr. Underwood," Maggie replied, while making every effort not to be embarrassed in Fernando's presence. The magical power of the previous night was still vivid in her mind, and she couldn't deny the emotions she had experienced.

"Are we still on for the horse ride?" Fernando asked, feeling a deep need to spend some time with Maggie so he could discuss his past. It was time, that was certain.

"Right after class . . . if that'll fit your schedule. I've even packed a lunch so we won't starve."

"You must've heard my stomach growl," Fernando laughed. "If it's all right, I'll ride Pepper. That way I'll be able to determine if his ankle has completely healed."

"Duncan will appreciate that, since I'm quite a bit lighter. But I'll carry the lunch bag, and that will even things up a bit," Maggie smiled.

"Great," Fernando replied, immediately glancing around to see if anyone else had heard his exuberance. He adopted a serious, scholarly tone. "Now, Maggie, let us move into the lecture hall and see if we can concentrate on the important subject of aeronautics . . ."

Sensing that his sudden mood change was more put on than real, Maggie grinned and allowed him to open the door in front of them. Entering the room, they took their seats just as the professor began his lecture. The subject was aircraft fuels. Simultaneously opening their note pads, they each began taking notes, their minds suddenly caught up in the subject.

The professor, a stocky, subdued man with a reputation for speaking too quickly, began covering the latest discoveries regarding fuel additives that could reduce detonation at maximum power settings on climb-out after take off, or firewall throttle when air racing. Although neither said a word to the other, both Fernando and Maggie shared an interest in everything that would affect the performance and long term reliability of an engine—especially in a race. Both knew of Maggie's dream of finding a plane and sponsor so she could compete in the Bendix cross-country race.

Much later, as the two left the classroom, Maggie turned to Fernando. "Do you realize, Fernando, what a higher octane rating would mean in a long distance race at full power? Not just a few laps around a closed course, but all day long at full power—ten to twelve hours with every inch of manifold pressure the entire way. What a beating that engine would take—unless, of course, the fuel could be improved to stop any knocking."

Caught up in Maggie's exuberance, Fernando added, "And wasn't that a hilarious story about the race pilot adding tetraethyl lead to his fuel, telling the curious mechanic that it was a secret 'go-juice' from a woman named Ethyl?"

Maggie laughed with Fernando, relishing the growing excitement she felt just being with him.

Don Hugo San Martin Braun was flying north from Buenos Aires in his company's executive plane. He sat immediately behind the corporate pilots who were flying the plane at a level of 7,000 feet, maneuvering between loosely separated fair-weather cumulus clouds.

The plane was a small, state-of-the-art twin engine biplane. It was a wooden-ribbed, wooden-spar wing structure with a welded steel tube fuselage—the entire structure covered with cloth. The two wings were tied together with steel wires crisscrossing like bridge reinforcing. The twin engines were upside down, in-line engines and were considered very efficient for the day. Lastly, the plane had conventional landing gear with a tail wheel, and it responded beautifully to the command of those at its controls.

Don Hugo had hoped to be flown in his newly acquired German-made Junker monoplane. He had leased the aircraft, its well-trained pilot and copilot from the German government, knowing that its advanced performance and speed would be ideal for the extensive travel schedule he maintained. But the plane had not arrived for his scheduled departure, and so he had regretfully gone on without it.

Even with this, Don Hugo had not been able to depart for the states as soon as he desired. The business problems were related to union dissatisfaction over salaries, working conditions, and benefits. There seemed to be growing labor unrest, agitated by Marxist communists and European socialists infiltrating the laborers of the meat-packing plants on the coast, the farm implement factory at Cordoba in the middle of the country, and the sugar plantations and mills in the north. In short, it seemed more like a virus than anything else to Don Hugo.

At the same time that employee relations were disintegrating, the San Martin family relations were also unraveling. Because profits were down, dividends had been cut. Part of the family was challenging Don Hugo's ability to coordinate all the various interests, accusing him of being preoccupied with Dame Helen's health and Fernando's disgrace. These distractions had led Don Hugo to neglect the business, many said, and were calling for his resignation.

The biggest problem for these dissident family members was that there was simply no one to take his place. Don Hugo's second son, Ricardo, was barely in his early 20s and still learning how to interact on an adult-to-adult basis with other hierarchy in the family system. Don Hugo's younger brother, Roberto, was competent enough to take over during Hugo's staged field trips; however, few in the family wanted Roberto to be the permanent chief executive officer for the consortium of investments and interests involved. As for Roberto, himself, he did not understand why Don Hugo had to leave Argentina at this time, in the middle of such major complications. To make matters worse, Don Hugo had not even tried to explain his errand. He had simply announced his departure and left.

Now, as Don Hugo was contemplating these issues, the pilot passed a written note back to him. This communication technique was necessary, since there was no soundproofing between the passengers and the engines outside except thin, doped canvas.

Don Hugo read,

We have crossed over Uruguay and are one hour from landing at Porto Alegre. Last weather report from Brazil is holding up. We expect to land on time. Any instructions?"

He studied the note, looked at the clear blue sky above, then down at the green, coastal fields below. He nodded his head and motioned with the flat of his hand towards the nose of the plane, telling the pilot to continue on course. Then he scribbled two short words on the bottom of the same paper. *Fuel supply?*

The pilot checked his gauges again, made a calculation on paper which he had already computed mentally, and wrote *Two hours fuel at least. Good tail wind.*

Don Hugo smiled, leaned his head back on the headrest, closed his eyes, and returned to studying his itinerary.

He had decided to let their flagship freighter leave the Buenos Aires port on schedule. Traveling by plane, he would later catch up with it, in Brazil. Because the freighter had to stop in Montevideo, Uruguay, and again in Porto Alegre, Brazil, this allowed him an additional week in Buenos Aires. He was glad he had been able to spend the extra week at Dame Helen's side, at the same time structuring short-term procedures for the various businesses.

Don Hugo's last visit with Roberto had been pleasant, and his brother had promised to make no major decisions without contacting Don Hugo on the ship's radio. Any message would be by Morse Code. In addition, the brothers had memorized several code words of their own—covering such things as financial transactions, union matters, and family names.

Don Hugo considered the complexities of the family empire; his mind immediately reverted to where it always seemed to go—thinking of his errant and extremely disappointing son. And, just as countless times before, he experienced a darkness and a loneliness that made way for further pain. This suffering gave birth to bitterness and anger, and before long, Don Hugo was once again thrown into a tailspin of self-pity—a tailspin that lasted the remainder of the flight.

In southern California, the shadows of the trees were growing longer. The ocean breezes lightly wafted the perfumes of spring flowers through the late Friday afternoon air. Fernando and Maggie were the only riders using the long, winding trail into Malibu Canyon. As they rode along on Maggie's matched palominos, Duncan and Pepper, they purposely avoided talking about the events of the previous night, and the change that had taken place in their relationship. Instead, they spoke of horses, flying, polo, exams, and their fast-approaching graduation.

At last, arriving at a secluded terrace overlooking the majestic Pacific Ocean, they dismounted and staked their mounts to a nearby tree. Since the horses were heavily lathered, Fernando insisted on rubbing them down, while Maggie went to the edge of the lookout and began setting out the blanket and food for their picnic.

The sun's rays, bouncing off the distant water of the ocean, made a kaleidoscope of dancing colors. Two swallows, darting in and out of the tree above them, chased each other without regard to Maggie and Fernando's presence. At the same time, a squirrel worked its way along a limb to their left, making a rapid movement with its long bushy tail.

"Penny for your thoughts . . ."

Startled, Maggie glanced to her right as Fernando seated himself at her side.

"Oh, you surprised me," Maggie laughed awkwardly. "I'm afraid my mind was far out on the ocean, splashing with the incoming tides . . . ."

Fernando nodded. "The ocean never seems to be the same, yet almost magically, it never changes. I find that the sea beckons and bathes my mind in a marvelous, singular way. I can't get enough of it."

Maggie simply smiled in agreement, allowing her silence to acknowledge what he had just stated. *Love has a power of its own,* she considered, noting the profoundness of his statement, which etched itself firmly in her mind.

Without speaking, Fernando pushed himself forward on the blanket, wrapping his arm around Maggie's waist. The gesture took her breath away as she not only welcomed it, but leaned her head back on Fernando's chest. Briefly, the two gazed silently out at the ocean, basking in the sense of belonging and love that stirred in their hearts.

At last, unable to resist the feelings she was experiencing, Maggie turned around and put her arms around Fernando. Lifting her face toward his, she slowly rubbed her nose against his face before she smacked a playful kiss on his cheek. Fernando, torn between his Latin passion and his need to sort through his feelings, drew Maggie to him, burying his face in her long, blonde hair.

After a suspended silence, Maggie and Fernando simultaneously heard the squirrel, now perched on a rock close by, scolding them with its chatter. They laughed and slowly pulled away from each other to begin their meal. The horses were also eating, munching the tall grass behind them as though it were their last meal.

Twenty minutes later, after they had finished eating, Fernando lay back on the blanket, placed his hands behind his head, and sighed. "You do pack a delicious picnic, Maggie. I haven't eaten that much since the night of the steak barbecue."

"That's funny," Maggie replied, "I remember that night as the night of the tango."

"Ah, ha! There you have it, Maggie, the difference between a man and a woman. Men think of their stomachs, while women think of romance."

"It wasn't just a woman thinking of romance last evening, Fernando."

Caught off-guard by Maggie's statement, Fernando felt a myriad of emotions that he wasn't prepared for. Turning on his side, he leaned up on one elbow. "Maggie, about us. I hope that I haven't—"

" . . . Violated my space?" she questioned, completing what she thought was his thought.

"Well, yes . . . and, no, Maggie. I am thinking about my space as well. For three long years I've protected myself by remaining detached, hoping that by keeping a distance from others, I would gain a peace of mind that would allow me to forget."

" . . . And you can't forget, can you, Fernando?" It was a statement rather than a question, and the soft, gentle firmness of her voice completely disarmed Fernando.

"Where did this remarkable woman come from?" he asked himself. In spite of his resolve to remain in control, his eyes moistened, and he was flooded with emotion.

"No, I can't," he replied, choking back the tears. "The . . . the accident was actually caused by a broken front axle, although I'm convinced that if I hadn't been drinking, I could have responded differently."

"You said her name was Rachel?" Maggie prompted.

"Yes . . . Rachel Cummings, actually, from Sarasota, Florida. She was so . . . so alive, and so much like you that at times I wonder if—"

"If you are reliving your past?"

"Yes, perhaps . . . . But, there's more, Maggie, much more. My emotions for each of you are really quite different, although both filled with a power I can't explain. Still, there is the guilt. I simply can't get past the guilt I feel for her dying . . . ."

"My grandmother Caroline was killed by being thrown from

86

a wagon drawn by a team of horses that were seldom used. My grandfather Soren talked about that for years, blaming himself for having sent her south to Flagstaff with these horses rather than the team she was used to. That memory haunted him for over ten years, until just before his death. Then something happened—an event that one day I may share—that seemed to settle his mind and give him peace."

"I wish that could happen to me, also. My soul died when Rachel died. Her death has been a dark cloud covering my mind, causing me to see things in black and white with all the colors drained out. You could never know, Maggie, how many conversations I have had with myself—conversations of guilt, shame and regret. I have wished futilely that I had the power to roll the clock back and to somehow pay for what I did—"

"Perhaps that has been your problem, Fernando."

Fernando looked up at Maggie, perplexed. What on earth was she talking about? he asked himself. But he remained silent, allowing her to continue.

"You are a Christian, aren't you? I mean, you do believe in Christ?"

"But, of course. Our family has been Catholic for centuries, and—"

"You should know that it is *He* who must atone, Fernando . . . not you. Just think of it. The Savior paid for our sins—beginning in the Garden of Gethsemene and concluding on the cross. And . . . all this so we can experience peace."

Maggie spoke with such conviction and enthusiasm that Fernando was once again astonished. *Where on earth did this young lady come from? he questioned. And how did she obtain such spiritual depth?*

"Maggie," Fernando continued, "you speak of Christ with such familiarity. In Argentina, it is likewise the women and children who pray, and who speak of Biblical things. . . ."

"People in all nearly all cultures have been guilty of relying excessively upon their own strength," Maggie said. "My great-grandfather, Seymore Rockwell, settled on what has evolved into our ranch, almost seventy years ago. Anyway, he led a group of colonizers across the southern plains, through the Mexico Territory, and on to Arizona. On one occasion, when this group of travelers found themselves surrounded by hostile Indians, someone suggested they kneel in prayer and petition for relief. That was when a fellow traveler, Edward Bunker, was supposed to have said, 'Pray? Hell, I'm up-to-date on my prayers. Circle the wagons and get ready to fight.'"

Both laughed, then Fernando spoke somberly, "At least he had said his prayers, Maggie. In Argentina, men are too *macho,* or proud, to pray. It is a cultural tradition that I'm afraid I have shared."

Maggie described how she had grown up in a home filled with prayer, and told Fernando about her neighbors at home, Dan and Katie Morris, who had moved up from Phoenix.

As the two continued to talk with increasing urgency, Fernando—for the first time in almost three years—began to feel strangely hopeful. It came as no surprise to Maggie that finally, after they had exhausted themselves in conversation, Fernando knelt and asked her to join him in prayer. Taking her hand in his, he gazed heavenward and began to speak. His words were halting—unsure. Even so, they were sincere and fill with emotion. It was the first vocal prayer Fernando had offered since he had been a young lad in Argentina, and when he concluded, he took Maggie into his arms and wept unashamedly.

Maggie, caught up in the emotion of the moment, found her eyes moistening, too. Fernando had shown greater humility than she had thought possible. In addition, his heart seemed to no longer be stony. It was malleable, and she knew that in time he would experience the peace he had just prayed for. For Maggie, this thought not only gave her hope for him, but for *them.* Never had she felt so close . . . so drawn to a man.

Holding each other with a fierceness that included, yet extended far beyond romance, the two talked until the sun gathered in its rays and slowly descended beyond the ocean to the west. Their conversation, one of learning and exploring, evolved into one of love—the Savior's love. *If only Fernando were a member of the Church*, Maggie sighed with some frustration. But he wasn't. And yet, that fact seemed to offer no solution to what was happening within Maggie's heart.

When at last they saddled their horses and began their descent into the canyon, each had been affected in a way that would forever alter the nature of their relationship. For Maggie, the change was subtle, since she had always considered the Christian and Latter-day Saint ethic to be the center of her life. To this point, she had felt constrained to not share her membership in the Mormon Church with Fernando. There were simply too many other issues to be dealt with, and the Church could come later.

For Fernando the afternoon on the mountain was a prelude to an evolution of emotion and spiritual understanding which had already begun.

A few hours later, and less than a mile off the coast of Brazil, Don Hugo was standing on the bridge of his biggest ocean-going freighter, the *Star of the Patagonia*, enjoying the unmistakable smell of the early morning air. They were just entering the spectacular harbor of Rio de Janeiro, one of the most dramatic harbor entrances in the world, with Sugar Loaf Mountain rising abruptly from the sparkling azure sea. Behind it and inside the harbor was the famous Botafogo Yacht Club, which was full of world-class yachts.

As the huge freighter cut the water below him, Don Hugo remembered the days when a teenaged Fernando had captained their ocean-going racing yacht nonstop from Buenos Aires to Rio to win the coveted South American Cup. Fernando had been the youngest captain ever to enter the event, let alone win it.

Just thinking about his son, who had held so much hope and promise, brought tears to Don Hugo's eyes. First, tears of fatherly pride, then tears of anger and total despair. His grief could not be measured, and the inescapable, painful knot in the pit of his stomach was consuming his emotions even more than he cared to admit. Not only had he lost his eldest son, but he had lost face in the eyes of his family and employees as well.

Looking up at the majestic Corcovado Mountain, crowned with the world's largest statue of Christ, he forced his thoughts back to the present. Silently he offered a prayer in his heart that he would have the strength to sever all ties with his son. In many ways, he reasoned, it would have been much easier on him and Dame Helen for Fernando to have died in the automobile crash—instead of living and casting such a dark shadow on the San Martin Braun family tree.

Don Hugo calculated that after discharging cargo and taking on new freight, they would be about twelve days from New York City, their destination. He was booked into the Waldorf Astoria to take care of financial affairs related to export financing for their products to Europe, England, and the United States.

The seas had been calm off the Brazilian coast, but the news from California had not been so peaceful. A few hours out of the Rio harbor, the radio operator brought him a sealed envelope. The sealing was only symbolic, since the radio man had carefully copied each letter of each word as the signals came in over his earphones.

"This message just arrived from your New York offices," relayed the messenger.

Hurriedly Don Hugo opened the envelope. Upon examining its contents, he realized that it came from California, relayed through the New York office. In essence, it explained that Fernando would graduate soon, and he appeared romantically involved with another student, the daughter of an Arizona rancher. Don Hugo was advised to hasten his arrival, if he had any hopes of affecting the outcome of Fernando's likely marriage.

After he read the telegram, Don Hugo gazed absently into the distance. He wondered at the effort Jock and Douglas had expended to work out the careful wording of the cable. They knew it was not their prerogative to pry into this delicate family matter; but they also knew that Don Hugo had no other source besides themselves, and, having initiated the whole thing, they felt a sense of responsibility to help this most unusually influential family in any way possible.

Unbeknownst to Don Hugo, Jock and Douglas had become aware that the relationship between Maggie and Fernando had grown like a brush fire, escalating far beyond what either of them had been led to expect from Fernando's conduct during his last three years of self-imposed isolation. And that worried them because they knew the importance of a proper San Martin mate-selection—a fact that had been heralded in the press for as long as either could remember.

Neither Jock nor Douglas knew Maggie, but both knew that such a romance could have far-reaching consequences—both in Argentina, and especially in England. They had no choice but to contact the famous Don Hugo and inform him of such a potentially explosive and devastating eventuality. They realized that the San Martin family would feel that the heir apparent to the financial throne could not marry a cowgirl from somewhere in remote northern Arizona.

Jock and Douglas had said nothing up to now to the British home office. Nor had they felt free to contact the San Martin family directly. However, after receiving Don Hugo's travel schedule from one of their investigators, they realized that he might want to know about the escalating romance. Thus, they obtained permission to send the radio message to him. Originally, they thought that Don Hugo would arrive in the states early enough to take care of matters himself. But now that it was apparent he was arriving much later, they felt it their obligation to give him foreknowledge of what might be developing.

Don Hugo responded quickly, sending a radiogram to New York, requesting it be forwarded to California. In it, he thanked them for their information and indicated that he would be flying to the west coast immediately upon his impending arrival in New York City. Requesting that they arrange adequate accommodations for his stay there, he signed his name and sent it.

What Don Hugo did not mention, however, was his lack of interest in Fernando's deepening romance. The girl was of no concern to him, as his errand would result in measures that would make further contact unnecessary. She could be a peasant from Pagatonia for all he cared. He would not even meet her; so of course, it was as though she didn't exist.

While in Rio, waiting for the ship to discharge and load cargo, Don Hugo visited with the local offices of his international bankers from New York and London, and he was able to handle the business arrangements he had planned to take care of on Wall Street while in New York City.

Finally, after what seemed like forever, his ship cleared the harbor with a sundown sailing. Don Hugo stood on the extension of the bridge, in the balmy ocean breeze, watching the pink-colored evening clouds drifting above the city. Copacabana Beach lights twinkled vividly, casting shadows on the intricate patterned tile sidewalks along the beach. Don Hugo's only regret was that the excitement was a facade, as his heart remained heavy, yet empty, while he envisioned the seemingly impossible task of disowning his eldest son.

In spite of his oppressed spirit, Don Hugo had just settled down to his evening dinner with the Captain and First Officer, when the radio-operator brought another bombshell message. It was from his brother, Roberto, back in Buenos Aires.

With a first glance at the contents of the sealed envelope, Don Hugo excused himself without touching his meal, then quickly retired to his private quarters. The news was not good at all. Don Hugo studied the text, furrowing his brow deeper and deeper as he read:

*REGRET TO INFORM YOU OF RIOT AT TUCUMAN
SUGAR PLANTATIONS AND MILL STOP UNIONIZED
WORKERS WENT ON STRIKE STOP PLANT MANAGER
CLOSED COMPANY STORE TO STRIKERS BY REFUSING
CREDIT STOP RIOT ENSUED STOP PROBLEMS
INCREASING AT PORT PACKING PLANT STOP WILL
KEEP YOU ADVISED STOP*

ROBERTO S M B

Don Hugo stared out the suite porthole, looking at the sea
and marveling that it could be so smooth while there was so
much turbulence back home. Being a steward to literally thousands of workers' lives, with their differing needs and perspec-
tives, was certainly not easy. He knew that Roberto's natural
inclination was to please all factions; but in conflicts of this pro-
portion, a strong, authoritative stand had to be taken. Although
he had no way of knowing what had transpired since his brother
sent him the cablegram, Don Hugo knew that he must rely upon
Roberto's judgment to squelch the riots and disquiet at the plan-
tation and mill.

These thoughts escalated, and, before long, Don Hugo was
considering the similar family turbulence in California. Although
Fernando's behavior was not riotous, it was rebellion against the
San Martin name. Therefore, it became even more imperative
that he break off his relationship with Fernando. Contact with
his son had to be severed because of Fernando's weaknesses, so
that Don Hugo and Helen might continue, undeterred, to steward their massive financial responsibilities.

This thought triggered another, and immediately Don Hugo
was replaying a broken phonograph record about his eldest son.
He thought back to Fernando's teen years, when Fernando had
worked at the dirtiest jobs alongside the slaughterhouse butchers.
He had also worked with the sugar plantations' cane cutters, the

factory mechanics and had ridden with the gauchos of both the cattle and sheep ranches. He had been called "the Prince of the Gauchos" with great endearment even by those restless union agitators who looked down on the rest of the aristocracy.

That advantage had been lost when Fernando started drinking and gambling, and then was dishonored in the press because of his conduct in Europe and the United States. Now, after disgracing the San Martin name, Fernando was preparing to cover up his past by marrying some waif from an unknown wasteland called Arizona. However, that was irrelevant. Don Hugo would see his son but one last time. Then he would return home.

Chapter Nine

The following morning, in southern California, Fernando busied himself with his tasks at the stables. Although he went through the motions of a rigorous schedule with those he supervised, still his mind was daydreaming. He rehearsed, again and again, the unusual feelings of the previous night. When he had awakened during the night, his emotions had seemed so different that Fernando immediately climbed out of bed and wrote them down in minute detail. As the day progressed, Fernando found himself becoming more and more anxious to share his newness of peace with Maggie. He had never experienced such a transformation of emotions as this, and he didn't know how much of it was real and permanent, or how much was just the product of an enlarged imagination brought on by the previous day's dialogue.

Maggie had invited Fernando to go with her to a western rodeo that night, to celebrate Fernando's twenty-eighth birthday. He had announced that it was his birthday as they arrived back at the stables, secretly knowing that they would celebrate by spending the evening together.

For Fernando's birthday celebration, Maggie had gone to a store and had purchased cowboy Levi pants, a plaid shirt, and a pair of western boots for him to wear for the occasion.

Although Fernando was appreciative as Maggie presented the gifts to him when she came to pick him up, the gifts embarrassed him because he had no way to reciprocate. Nevertheless, he accepted the new wardrobe and wore them to the rodeo. His conversation with her would have to wait until later, perhaps the end of the evening. For now, he would put it aside and make every effort enjoy his birthday festivities.

As the evening began to unfold, Fernando was surprised at how exciting and enthralling the American rodeo was. Sitting in the stands, he not only enjoyed each event but also the memories the rodeo evoked of his long-ago rides with the gauchos while they worked cattle on the famous Argentine Pampa.

There was not much about the handling of calves, cattle, and horses that Fernando did not know. He had never tried western style bullriding, and that event impressed him, especially with the clowns there to distract the wild brahma bulls from trying to gore a thrown rider. Argentina, he remembered, had almost exclusively bred British cattle such as hereford, angus, and short-horn. Fernando had heard of the large American-bred brahmans, but had never seen them up close—especially in an arena where the huge bulls made every effort to destroy their antagonists.

The couple good-naturedly exchanged points of view through all the events, remarking on how interesting it was that cultures do the same tasks so differently.

Finally, the last event of the rodeo came with the wild bronco riding, both bareback and with saddles. Maggie had announced to Fernando that this was to be the most dramatic event of the evening, with many of the cowboys getting dumped, some result-ing in broken bones. No one liked to see anyone get hurt, but the cowboys were eager to test their skills against the horses as well as against the other cowboys.

When the event was nearing completion, Maggie turned to Fernando and asked, "Do you break broncos in Argentina the same way we do, or do you have a different way of doing that, too?"

Smiling while shaking his head, Fernando replied, "The gau-chos used to tame wild horses your way, simply because it is faster. Even so, my family discontinued that technique on our ranches at least fifty years ago."

Again Maggie was both surprised and intrigued. "How in the world do you break a horse for riding and show him who's boss? I can't see any way to do it, other than by simply jumping into the saddle and having it out with him. He throws you, and you try again—until you win and he gives in."

"Well, most of our horses are thoroughbreds and very valuable," Fernando responded. "We feel that we can't afford to run the risk of injuring an expensive animal by a fall. But more important is the concept that we do not want to break our animals' spirit. For polo, for the race track, or even just for ranch work or breeding, we value highly the courage, the boldness, and the spirit of our horses. We don't want to diminish any of the natural personality that we have tried to breed into them."

Seeing that Maggie was interested in what he was saying, Fernando continued. "We want our ponies or horses to become obedient and well-trained . . . *manso*, we call it—not through fear of the rider, but rather through trust and confidence in him. We train with love and tenderness, precisely to nurture the independent spirit of the animal. Doing it that way seems to make the horses far easier to train, and they love the game of polo or the challenge of the race—working harder to win for us."

Maggie had never heard a man talk so knowledgeably of horses. Fernando's reasoning made sense, and his way did seem more civilized than spurring or whipping a horse into submission. In fact, she and her father had worked with her palominos that way almost from the day they were born. They were never wild and never resisted the saddle or the rider.

Suddenly, Maggie realized that Fernando had just referred to his family's ranches in the plural, and he spoke as though his family had a lot of property and many horses. When would he open up with the whole story of his life? She felt so close to him, yet she somehow sensed that there was so much more.

"Maggie! Wait up a sec, will you?" Fernando and Maggie were on their way to the parking lot after the rodeo and stopped at the call. Hurrying towards them was a lanky, suntanned cowboy, who could have appeared on a Levi's advertisement poster. He looked the part of a very successful young professional cowboy, which, in fact, he was. His hair was blond and tousled, and the crow's-feet wrinkles in the corners of his eyes seemed to accentuate his dark, sun-baked tan. He was tall and thin in a tough, wiry way; and with an infectious grin, he threw his arms around Maggie and gave her a big kiss. His Stetson was tipped casually back on his head, and he spoke with a low, mellow voice with a distinct western drawl.

"Honey," he began, while Maggie blushed a bright crimson, "I've had a hankerin' to see ya for what seems like forever. Where ya been hidin' out?" He ignored Fernando standing beside her, as though he didn't even exist.

Maggie stammered, "Uh . . . Fernando, this is an old friend of mine, Curly Jackson. We used to do rodeos together, and he is one of the best on the circuit. He was the winner of the bullriding and the bronc-busting events, remember? Curly, this is Fernando Underwood. We're classmates at the university."

Curly was a bit quicker than Fernando in courteously extending his hand. "Well, Mr. Underwood, you're in the company of a great lady. I've been in love with her all my life, and as soon as I get some money ahead I'm goin' to propose to her." Turning to Maggie, he continued. "Just have to give ya fair warnin', Maggie. All's fair in love and war, ya know."

"Curly's always been a teaser," Maggie said, blushing even more deeply.

Fernando was overwhelmed with such jealousy as he had never known. He was also angry that Maggie would refer to him simply as "her classmate." He wanted to turn around and leave but couldn't think of how to gracefully withdraw, so he stood quietly, allowing the scene to play itself out.

Curly was asking Maggie about her brother, Will. "I haven't

seen him around here. Don't you two do the rodeos anymore?"

Relieved that the conversation was suddenly less personal, Maggie answered, "William broke his hip and leg in a bronco riding accident, so both of us dropped out of the circuit. I decided to go back to school for my degree. I've been doing a little stuntriding for the movies, and William is back on the ranch, recuperating. He married his nurse, so I don't think we'll ever get back to rodeoing. What about you? How's it been going with ya'll?"

Although Maggie was unaware that she had slipped into a cowboy-type drawl, Fernando noticed it and attributed it to a habit of long and easy friendship with Curly. Feeling more and more uncomfortable, Fernando grimaced inwardly, but remained silent. Curly, noticing the brand-new clothes Fernando was wearing, leaned down to whisper in her ear, "Where'd ya get the drugstore cowboy, honey? Ain't ya runnin' with us real boys any more?"

Maggie desperately hoped Fernando didn't understand the insult, but decided she better put a stop to Curly's teasing. Although she had dated Curley for awhile and knew he had a lot of good qualities, Maggie knew he wasn't the type she was looking for. She decided to set the record straight for Fernando's sake.

"Fernando can hold his own with any of you guys on any day of the year," she said forcefully.

Surprised at her vehemence, Curly backed quickly away, saying, "Hey . . . okay . . . just wanted to make sure ya weren't lettin' us down. Ya know I'm just in love with ya, that's all." Curly turned to Fernando. "Been good ta meet ya, pardner." Spinning quickly around, he disappeared into the crowd of people.

Completely flabbergasted and embarrassed, Maggie apologized to Fernando for Curly's rudeness. Fernando just shrugged his shoulders and smiled awkwardly. Taking Maggie's hand in his, he followed the crowd, hoping the exchange with Curly Jackson would not put a damper on their evening and on their relationship. Although he desperately wanted to talk with Maggie, it would have to wait until the timing was right.

Chapter Ten

Off the channels in New York harbor, Fernando's father, Don Hugo, stood quietly on the bridge of the *Star of the Patagonia*. He had been studying the navigation charts, which showed the ship to be only a short distance from the coast of New Jersey. It would soon dock at the company pier. The trip from South America had been smooth all the way, but the radio messages had been anything but smooth. The company news worried Don Hugo enormously, which no doubt aggravated his feelings, causing him to be more upset about the unhappy errand upon which he now found himself.

Don Hugo shifted his thoughts to his beloved wife, Dame Helen. She was very ill and going downhill rapidly. Was her illness psychosomatic, he wondered, related to the tragedy of being alienated from her eldest son, or was it some other serious malady that was perhaps terminal?

As he considered this never-changing question, Don Hugo knew more than ever that he must eradicate Fernando from his family system. It was Fernando's irresponsible behavior that was destroying Dame Helen. Don Hugo would take care of his business affairs in New York City, then charter a plane directly to California. He resolved that his errand must be swift and sure. He knew that he would not experience peace within his own heart as long as Fernando continued to abuse his family name. The end for his cowardly, womanizing son must come quickly. There was no other way.

Three thousand miles away, Maggie and Fernando drove into the polo stables with the top of the convertible down. They had spent the evening with Roscoe and had begun to develop a strategy how they could possibly enter the Bendix Cup race, with Maggie piloting the plane. It all seemed remote and impossible, but both Maggie and Roscoe—for their own reasons—were convinced they could pull it off. Fernando, on the other hand, viewed the adventure as an absurd fairy tale. Still, he kept his feelings to himself, sensing how important it was for Maggie to believe, if such was her dream.

The urgency of the evening's conversation seemed to now vanish in the darkness of the night. And so, even though Fernando wasn't holding Maggie's hand, he felt an uncommon stirring deep within his soul. Some kind of primeval instinct was encouraging him to override his natural cautions. Once again he felt himself falling deeply into the risky territory of love.

In the past few days, he had come to realize that more than anything else in this world, he wanted a permanent relationship with Maggie. He could not tolerate the thought that within a week—after graduation—he might lose this beautiful, gifted woman. Although she had been offered a steady job by the movie studio, Fernando feared that she might vanish into the air, pursuing the air race; or, she might even go back to Arizona, to her family, who would likely try to keep her from a foreigner like himself.

Due to an unexpected request from the movie studio, Roscoe had asked Fernando to help film the Bendix Cup air race—whether or not Maggie was involved. Fernando was intrigued by the offer, despite his own longing to return to Argentina and confront his parents with the ghosts of his past.

Fernando knew he was in love with Maggie, and that losing her would be catastrophic. He knew that he must propose to her at once or risk losing her altogether. Curly, the arrogant cowboy, would certainly grab her if Fernando didn't. As compelling as his feelings were, however, Fernando could not put aside his spiritual experience of the previous week. *That has to be dealt with first,* he cautioned himself, and at last the time to discuss it had arrived.

At the conclusion of the evening, he and Maggie sat silently in the little convertible, savoring the long-awaited solitude that presented itself. Without speaking, Fernando reached over, took Maggie's hand, and they intertwined fingers. The soft glow of the lights under the arches of the stable complex dimly lit the area around them. It was late and by all appearances, the stable hands were in bed. Inside the stables, a horse whinnied and was answered by another.

"Maggie," Fernando paused, turning so that he could look into her eyes as he spoke. "This has been the greatest week of my life. Thank you for . . . for allowing me into your life."

"Thank you, Fernando . . . especially for being so patient tonight, with Curly."

"Let's forget about him and about the race. I mean, let's deal with us, and with what's happening."

"What is happening, Fernando? Please tell me."

"Actually, Maggie, I've been waiting all evening to tell you."

Maggie waited patiently for Fernando to find the words to express his feelings.

He continued, "It's quite simple, really, although I don't totally understand it. For three years I have been consumed with guilt. But since we have talked . . . and especially since I have begun to pray, I have had a great sense of peace."

"Oh, Fernando, I'm so happy, I don't know what to say."

"Then, let me hold you, Maggie, while I savor the newness of life that I feel. What is happening to us?"

"Since you asked, my darling," Maggie smiled, "I think it's called growing—growing in love, or falling in love, however you want to say it."

Darling? Maggie's use of the endearing term sent chills throughout Fernando's body, as he realized what she was saying.

Silently pondering Maggie's words, Fernando at last spoke.

"Will you be my darling, Maggie?"

"But, of course, you old romantic. I'll also be your greatest fan . . . ."

"Thank you, Maggie for showing me the way for my soul to know peace. It is a gift that I have never expected, but one which I hope will continue to soothe the pains of my past."

Nestled snugly in Fernando's arms and in his heart, Maggie felt tears well up in her eyes, then cascade down onto her cheeks. Never had she felt such ecstasy, such joy. It was a moment she had longed and hoped for, a moment that must never end.

"You know," Fernando whispered, "I love you, Maggie Rockwell. I love you more than anyone, or anything, in my entire life."

"I love you, too, darling."

With Maggie's head resting gently on his shoulder, Fernando lightly stroked her hair. Heaven, he thought happily, could never be more gratifying than this.

Maggie, sensing that this was what she had long anticipated, suddenly became frightened with the sudden unknowns in her future. Where did this now lead her? Would she be able to pursue her dreams? Would she be racing in the Bendix Cup? So many questions, each almost exploding in her mind.

In spite of these unanswerable questions, the one thing Maggie did know was her own heart. Never in her life had she felt such admiration and had such love for a man. Fernando had become a soul mate and a true protector, the likes of which she had only dared to dream. Now, suddenly and without warning, she had felt the nesting instinct stirring within her breast. She truly wanted to make a home for and with Fernando—complete with cottage and children—and most of all with the fullness of the gospel. She admitted, as she snuggled safely in his arms, that she was hopelessly, and eternally, falling in love.

Lifting her head and gazing into Fernando's eyes, she finally spoke. "Sweetheart, I give you my heart . . . forever."

Squeezing Maggie even more tightly, Fernando whispered tenderly in her ear, "On this most beautiful evening, I ask . . . will you marry me, Maggie?"

The question, spoken softly, sent chills of electricity throughout Maggie's entire frame. Immersing herself in the magic, she placed her hand on Fernando's neck and kissed him. Drawing away, she broke into a smile and said, "Oh, yes, Fernando. I will marry you."

For hours, the two talked about their future, and then about their past. As Fernando told Maggie about the complex San Martin Braun family, Maggie was spellbound. She was completely fascinated that one person could have had so many unusual experiences—both positive and negative—in such a relatively young life.

When Fernando had answered all of Maggie's questions, he asked Maggie about her own family history. Still attempting to digest all he had shared with her, Maggie took a deep breath and began. At last, she knew, this was the time to tell him about her beliefs and about the Church.

Maggie began by explaining how she came from European immigrants, who were among the first settlers of the northern Arizona cattle country. She talked about her earlier progenitors as though they were still alive. Fernando sensed that she had a love for past generations and their accomplishments and the heritage they had given her.

Maggie spoke of her "spiritual inclinations," as she put it. Fernando had never heard anyone speak so familiarly about their relationship with deity and did not respond. He noticed that Maggie's voice seemed to transcend her natural pitch, containing a reverence and a profound sureness.

"Darling," Maggie continued, suddenly knowing what she would say, "there is something you must know . . . something I have been wanting with all my heart to tell you, but which until now I haven't felt comfortable doing."

"Yes, Maggie," Fernando said encouragingly.

"Have you ever heard of the Latter-day Saint faith? The Mormons?"

"But, of course. I know that they are an American religion, and that Brigham Young led their early members across the plains to the desert of the Great Salt Lake. What about them?"

"The real name of the Church— my church—is The Church of Jesus Christ of Latter-day Saints."

Fernando could not speak. Words would simply not come, and he suddenly felt as though he could cut the thickness of the air with a knife. Sensing a need to allow this crucial time for her words to settle in, Maggie simply waited for him to speak.

At last, realizing he must reply, Fernando whispered, "I see . . . ."

His words hung suspended in the air. Drawing a deep breath, Maggie spoke. "Fernando, darling, I have the deepest respect for all Christian faiths, especially those of the Catholic persuasion. To have remained true down through the Dark Ages must have taken great courage—especially with so much persecution raging.

"And yet," she continued, "there is so much more. You see, darling, God's priesthood . . . His power . . . lies within the Mormon faith, and it contains the power to bond us together forever."

As Maggie's words crescendoed in his mind, Fernando sensed a need to hold back his emotions of betrayal. Maggie belonged to a relatively new cult, and he didn't know how this would affect their future together. For now, he would simply listen. After all, it was her spiritual insights that had led to his experience of the other night, and so—

"Fernando, I want to tell you why my Great-grandfather Seymore forsook all that he had in Europe and crossed the plains with his family." With these words, Maggie began to unfold the events of the Restoration and of the revered prophet, Joseph Smith. She spoke and Fernando listened for almost two full hours.

Without speaking, Fernando did the only thing he could

think of. He gathered Maggie into his arms, held her fiercely, and began to cry.

"Please don't speak, darling," Maggie whispered. "Let's enjoy the quiet of the moment. It will be etched within our hearts forever . . . ."

It was some time before Fernando was able to collect himself enough to speak. Drying his eyes, he asked, "Maggie, may I ask a favor?"

"Of course. Your request is my command," she tried to speak lightly but she did not know how he has taken all that she had told him.

"Tell me about your family," he said quietly. "I know about your ancestors and about your religion. Now I would like to know about you.

"Actually," Maggie began, "I am a simple girl with simple needs. This dress that I'm wearing was made by my mother while I canned pears two Septembers ago. Although I love wildlife— especially horses—my greatest love, present company excluded, is my family."

She paused and Fernando spoke. "My parents are the greatest people I know, and my greatest fear is that I will never again enjoy the warmth of their fire, and their embrace . . . ."

Maggie responded impetuously. "Oh, but you will, Fernando, I know."

"You what?" Fernando was surprised at her tone of complete sureness.

"Well," she admitted, "I was praying about you last night, and about your parents. I was completely taken back with how good I felt as I spoke their names."

Fernando spoke slowly. "You are a wonder, Maggie . . . a pure and natural wonder. Still, that doesn't mean—"

"Hush! My father always said that emotions of fear must be replaced with emotions of faith. It's the only way to be truly happy."

After a short silence, Fernando reminded Maggie that she had been telling him about her family. So she described her family's home and ranch, her parents, her older brother, and younger brothers and sisters. She told him of the scenic desert country that surrounded their ranch, including the nearby Grand Canyon, and other sights that were different from anything he had seen in Argentina.

As Maggie spoke, Fernando found himself strangely experiencing peaceful feelings about her religion. Surprisingly, he found himself wanting to visit her family and her homeland—to see for himself where she was born and reared. As he expressed this request, Maggie assured him that nothing would mean more to her, and that they would perhaps consider going there for the wedding.

This sobering thought caught them both off-guard, bringing them swiftly back to reality. Would they really marry? Would Maggie's Mormon faith bring a wedge between them? Each considered these questions, yet neither spoke of them. Instead, they began to speak of the marriage, itself. When would they plan for a wedding? Where would it be? Who would be invited? How would Fernando's family react—especially to the fact that she was not of royalty?

As if sensing that he must bring closure to their discussion of Maggie's Latter-day Saint faith, Fernando squeezed her shoulder, then spoke. "I don't know where this takes us, darling. I mean . . . I'm Catholic and you're Mormon. Somewhere there must be a meeting of the minds . . ."

Maggie spoke firmly. "That won't be difficult. I promise. We both believe in Christ, and for today, that is what's important. What's also important is that we love each other, and that we have the foundation for a happy and lasting marriage. Those were my thoughts last night as I was praying."

Fernando sensed that it would be best conclude their conversation at that point, rather than to say something that might mar the spirit of their conversation.

"I believe that," he said at last, while cupping Maggie's face in his hands. "You're the most beautiful, most unselfish person I have known, and I also think what you have told me tonight will work itself out. Just be patient with me, okay?"

"And you be patient with me, darling. We have so much to share with each other."

As the tension went away, both Fernando and Maggie realized the lateness of the hour and decided further conversation could wait for another day. It was well past midnight, and the unexpected religious differences had left them both totally exhausted.

Fernando opened the door to the car and stepped out. After pulling Maggie after him, he surprised Maggie by dropping to one knee and making a wide sweeping gesture with his hand. "All that I am," he pronounced solemnly, "and all that I ever hope to be, I gladly give to you, Maggie Rockwell."

Laughing, Maggie threw her arms around Fernando, knocking him over backward into the grass. Quickly kneeling, Maggie took Fernando's hands in hers and replied, "Oh, darling, I have never been so happy. Can this be happening? Can I really be falling in love with the most handsome, charming—"

"And broke!" Fernando interrupted. "But we'll make it, Maggie, I assure you. And I'll make you the happiest flying cowgirl—and Mormon—in all the world."

"Oh, I know you will, Fernando," Maggie sighed, relieved beyond words that he hadn't rejected her religion. "And I'll make you the happiest gaucho polo player that ever climbed into a saddle."

"Maggie," Fernando added, suddenly changing his tone of voice, "I do have one more request . . . ."

"But, of course, darling."

"It is very important that we make no announcement until after we have spoken with both sets of parents. I must ask your father for your hand. And of course, I must somehow restore myself in the eyes of my parents, and . . . and ask their permission, as well . . . without their knowing of your religion."

"I understand," Maggie nodded. "These are our secrets,

right?"

"Right," Fernando responded, rising to his feet and pulling Maggie to hers. Tenderly, the two embraced, kissed briefly, then parted.

As Maggie stepped back into her car, Fernando closed the door, leaned down, and again allowed their lips to touch. "Goodnight, my American sweetheart," he whispered, surprising himself that he had used the word "sweetheart" for perhaps the very first time.

"Goodnight, darling . . . ."

Maggie's words lingered in the air, as she started the engine to the car. While both were totally oblivious to the world about them, each was keenly aware that, in spite of Maggie's announcement about her religion, the events of the evening had unfolded in a miraculous way, thrusting their relationship forward at an accelerated speed.

Chapter Eleven

Douglas Boynton, the renowned British actor, had Fernando Underwood very much on his mind. He was seated at his reserved table in the remote corner of the famed Beverly Hills Country Club restaurant. This was his favorite place to meet friends without being bothered. He had picked up the morning newspaper, and it now lay open on the table in front of him. He appeared to be scanning it, but the truth was he was not even reading it. Rather, it was a ruse to keep passersby from pausing at his table.

Douglas knew a major showdown was imminent in Fernando's life, and he worried about whether it would be good or bad for all concerned. Originally, Douglas had felt it might be a great idea to bring to light the fact that one of the world's best polo players was hiding incognito at the local technological university. Since he and Jock had traced Fernando's background, his thinking had taken a 180-degree turn in his mind. Douglas had come to genuinely admire Fernando, especially after privately visiting with several of his professors.

Jock entered the semi-dark interior of the restaurant. Knowing he was late for their appointment, he waived the maitre d' aside and strode directly to where Douglas was sitting.

"Good afternoon, old boy." Jock's jovial greeting startled Douglas.

Smiling in recognition, Douglas tilted his head and said, "G'day to ye, me lad. Just sit yerself down—I've been holdin' it fer ye. Got our usual drinks a comin'."

"What's in the paper this morning, Douglas? The headlines, the business news, the social stuff, or the movie news? What's up?"

"Matter of fact, Jock, I couldn't tell you a thing of what's in this paper. You know me—my thoughts have been drifting all over southern California ."

"Well, if you're not reading, old boy, where are your thoughts? You looked deep into something, I dare say."

As usual, Douglas and Jock enjoyed lapsing in and out of the different accents from different parts of the British Isles, mimicking the well-known idioms and expressions from their homeland.

Douglas hesitated before speaking. "I was just thinking about our boy, Fernando, and what the arrival of his father, Don Hugo, will do to him. I mean, he is so shipshape, then everything will be suddenly stripped away, with his true identity being disclosed."

"I see, " Jock replied, sipping from the tall glass of water. "Bit of a risk, wouldn't you say, old chap?"

"To be sure, Jock," Douglas sighed pensively, "I surely hope our boy won't be hurt by all this. In my opinion, I think the old man, Don Hugo, is coming to America at just the right time. Graduation is next week, Fernando is on the peak of his game, so to speak, and his girlfriend—this Maggie Rockwell—seems to have given him a lift."

As Douglas spoke, Jock could sense an increasing excitement in his voice. Instead of interrupting him, he simply nodded and smiled agreeably.

"You know," Douglas continued, "I have really taken a liking to him, especially since our cruise out to Catalina Island last week. Oh, maybe I didn't tell you that I had invited him once before, but he had to take a raincheck. It was good that we did, too, because the weather was simply fabulous this time."

"Wish I could have accompanied you, Douglas. I'm afraid my

schedule is leading me around by the proverbial nose, if you know what I mean."

"Most certainly. But, let me continue. While we sailed, our boy Fernando watched the crew work that new boat, making a frightful number of technical mistakes. Finally, and to our collective surprise, the true sailor in our lad from Argentina could stand it no longer."

"Sailor? I'm afraid I don't follow you, Douglas—"

"Our Fernando is a man of the sea, Jock . . . I swear he is. He asked me if he might give a bit of assistance, and what an understatement that was. We needed a lot more help than a bit. Since I was aware that he knew much more than myself, I asked him to take over for awhile. In a jiffy, he had a different set of sails up and the crew working together better than I ever could have. We immediately picked up some speed, and to my surprise, the vessel moved more rapidly than I ever imagined it could. It was simply fantastic!

"Within minutes," he continued with increasing energy, "another boat came by and challenged us to a race around a distant buoy, then back to a buoy that was off starboard side. Fernando asked me if I was up to some fun, so I gave my permission.

"The ships lined up," he continued. "The signal was given, and the race began. We were running just a little ahead to the designated buoy, but when we negotiated our turn, the other boat switched sails to a giant spinnaker for the run downwind. Seeing what was happening, Fernando asked me if we had a spinnaker sail and pole down below in the sail compartment.

"I had no idea if we did or not, so quick as a flash he had me take the wheel while he went under the deck to look. He immediately found what he was looking for, retrieved it topside, then taught the crew how to negotiate a fast take down of the Genoa jib and raise the balloon spinnaker. Soon we had the biggest full sail I had personally ever seen. And, by jove, we quickly gained on the other boat, then won the race hands down. It was absolutely marvelous."

Jock smiled widely, enjoying the enthusiastic and animated narrative that his friend, Douglas, had just related. "Do you remember," he asked, "that in the original dossier on Fernando from England and Argentina, it said that a decade ago he had captained his family's racing sailboat from Buenos Aires to Rio?

"But, of course! And the southern Atlantic Ocean is not for amateurs. I've also heard that the *gaucho* sailors of Argentina are supposed to be totally fearless when racing against their arch rivals, the equally competent *cariocas* of Brazil. These two countries have a long-standing tradition of fierce, but friendly competition. If Fernando could sail that race as captain while still in his teens, in that kind of sea and wind conditions, I would suspect that he can sail almost anything."

Jock continued to be impressed with young Fernando and what he was learning about the rest of the famous San Martin family. Now it was his turn to share with his friend some additional information that had just turned up.

"Douglas, I received word from the London office that our plans for the graduation have been approved by the family—at least those in England. It is strange, however, they did not confirm Don Hugo's accord. Perhaps we have not heard back from him because he's at sea. But that, in any case, is a family problem. We are committed on our end, and if things go well, the London people will be credited with great diplomacy and for having healed a deep family wound. On the other hand, if things go poorly, we are setting ourselves up to take all the blame. Are you ready for the curtain to go up on our little play?"

Douglas suddenly became very pensive. "I'm ready—at least as ready as I can get. Still, I don't know what to do about the girlfriend problem. She may be no obstacle at all, or her presence could damage Fernando and offend his father completely."

He continued. "You know, don't you, that Fernando and Miss Rockwell are spending more and more time together every day? In fact, I believe they are secretly engaged although there is not as yet any ring. But I have a reason now to develop a closer and more natural contact with both of them. Have I told you of the studio's new plans for me that involve both Fernando and his girl?"

"No," Lord Jockham looked intrigued. "Some new movie, I dare say."

Douglas nodded, "Yes, a new adventure of gigantic proportions beginning next week. This new film is about a cross-country air-race. A good lot of planes in it with, surprisingly, both male and female pilots participating. You'll be impressed, Jock old boy, that I am to be a race pilot."

"Most interesting, Douglas, I dare say . . . ."

"The character I am to play is a different kind of hero than I've ever played before. Instead of a historic setting, with pirates or knights in armor, this is an ultra-modern scenario. And, of all things, I must develop a Yankee accent. There will be a love plot between myself and a lady pilot—along with the excitement of engine failures, air crashes, planes lost in storms, the whole works. They've really pulled out all the stops for this one.

"But, listen to this, Jock. The fellow who is providing all the planes, pilots, and stunt flying is a race winner by the name of Roscoe Turner. He's the model for the role I am to take. He has a flying school, together with an aircraft sales office, hangars and maintenance shops, plus a charter service that provides stunt flying for the film industry.

"The other day," Douglas continued, "when I went to meet this man, Roscoe, he was not there. But, who do I run into, right there in his office, but Fernando and Miss Rockwell."

Douglas interrupted his narrative to pick at his food. Jock prompted him impatiently, "Go on with it, man. What happened then? Of course, Fernando knew you from your sailing jaunt, but what about the girl? All I have on her is what I hear from others."

Douglas chewed calmly and swallowed. "We already knew the girl was graduating with Fernando, with a full-fledged aeronautical engineering degree. Naturally, this is unusual as there are very few women in the field of aeronautics. This Maggie, as she is called, is a very pleasant girl, and quite beautiful. She is sharp as a tack as well—a quick study, I dare say. And along with everything else, she is working as a stunt pilot, rumored to be one of the best, although I understand her hours in the cockpit are rather limited.

Douglas paused and produced the pièce de résistance. "But, Jock, get this. She is a stunt woman for my own studio. That's right. She stands in for the leading ladies who don't like to take unnecessary risks. The studio says she pulled off a fabulous stunt in a movie that has just been released. The studio boss asked that I view it as soon as possible as I will be working with her and the other women pilots. Seems they want me to understand this new kind of woman," he concluded with a lift of the eyebrows.

The two conspirators continued to talk about the details of both the air race movie and their involvement in the mysterious plan they were devising, which had to do with Fernando.

"Douglas," Jock continued, "it seems to me that if Don Hugo arrives in our fair city before Fernando's graduation, it would be best to just take him directly to the polo stables and let the two of them be alone. Why, in the king's good name, does London want to do it the other way—having them meet after Fernando's graduation?"

"I haven't the faintest idea, Jock, but however we set things up, it had better meet with Don Hugo's approval. The ramifications of a mishap could be disastrous for relations with Argentina, and for the San Martin family."

"Without a doubt, old boy. Still, what do we do if Don Hugo insists on meeting with Fernando before graduation?"

"We'll just have to think of something," Douglas mused.

"Just take him out on your new boat and have it conveniently run amuck," Lord Jockham suggested. "Or, better still, hire Fernando to fly you to Nevada, or Mexico, returning just in time for his graduation. There will be a way to keep him from his father, I'm sure."

After the bill was paid, the two men exited the restaurant, each deep in thought. Their conversation had revealed much, and their resolve to do all within their power to help the esteemed San Martin family was of top priority. Don Hugo's arrival in California must be orchestrated to perfection.

Chapter Twelve

Roscoe Turner paced his office nervously, as his pet adult lioness nonchalantly groomed itself. The office was usually cluttered with papers, various airplane engine parts, and instruments on the floor and desk. Today, however, was special, and Roscoe had taken great care to straighten things up. In addition, several folding chairs had been brought in for the expected visitors.

Maggie and Fernando stood beside his old roll-top desk, rather than relaxing in the comfortable leather sofa as they normally did when visiting. Maggie winked at Roscoe. "Boy, have you ever spiffed things up. Tell us again—just what did the studio do to get you so all fired up?"

Roscoe stroked his moustache, twisting the ends into perfect points, then replied. "Well, as I mentioned to Fernando on the phone, Mr. Goldsmith, the charter executive at the studio in charge of stunts, called to offer our firm an astronomical amount of money for their new movie. He said that they wanted to shoot a major epic picture surrounding the Bendix Cup cross-country air race. It appears as if the entire country is talking about it. He emphasized the fact that women will be challenging men in the most dangerous of sports, which is stirring up public interest in air racing. You see," he smiled, "it's a real battle of the sexes."

Roscoe paused, then continued. "But that's not all. As you both know, the country is divided as to whether women should, or should not, be allowed to participate. They all remember back a few years when women started competing in short races around pylons, and there were some tragic crashes. You remember, Maggie . . . wasn't Ruth Stevenson a close friend of yours?"

Maggie nodded soberly . "Yes, I was there. I saw the wing of her plane peel off on the third lap, just as she rounded the back pylon. She was far out in front, flying a nearly perfect race, but her plane had been put together without the full stress analysis used today. She put too many G's on the plane, and it broke the main spar in the wing." Maggie sighed. "In fact, that accident was one of the things that made me want to become an aeronautical engineer. I simply had to know how to avoid such a tragedy in the future."

Maggie glanced down at the floor, emotion etched deeply on her brow. "The race officials asked me to phone Ruth's parents to tell them she didn't make it. She had been killed instantly. That was their only consolation—that she didn't suffer. She had always been afraid of fire burns and of being disfigured, they said, but she had never been afraid of dying. She and I were the same age, you know. She was a good friend."

"I'm sorry, Maggie," Fernando said gently.

"That's all right, Fernando . . . . I think I'm slowly getting over it.

There was a moment of awkward silence. Each of the three knew that flying was a demanding mistress. There were real dangers as they worked at the leading edge of a new science, extracting lessons from every accident so the same thing would not happen again. Breaking the silence, Maggie changed the subject. "What else did Mr. Goldsmith say, Roscoe?"

Roscoe seemed relieved to get back to the present. "Well, he said that they want to tell a story about cross-country long-distance air racing, highlighting the kind of people the winners are. They especially want to emphasize the women who fly and what motivates them to compete in such a dangerous sport.

"At the same time," he continued, "they want to include the male pilots, the engineers who are designing the planes, and all those who work together to make up what they're calling the racing family. Since I've flown more races than anyone else who is competing, he said they would like to hire me to be their technical advisor.

"I have also been asked to do the stunt scenes where crashes are involved. They expect to destroy a few planes in the filming, so they want me to build or purchase some expendable planes. I'm expected to work with the writers and the director." Roscoe grinned. "I'm pretty excited."

Maggie and Fernando glanced at each other, wondering if they were sharing the same thought of how this would all play into their future plans.

"Listen to this," Roscoe added, "and don't faint when I say it. They told me they wanted to build the story around a woman stunt pilot—and asked about you, Maggie. Goldsmith knows that you and I have worked together; he knew the horse-to-flying-ladder stunt was fresh on everyone's mind. Because of this, he asked that I invite you here today. I think they may have a contract for you to consider. I know they have offered you a full-time stunt performing contract, but this solidifies it."

Roscoe was enjoying Maggie's reaction, as was Fernando, for she had her hands cupped over her mouth and was staring at them wide-eyed.

"Goldsmith," Roscoe continued, "told me that they would bring the head of the studio, plus the director and the screen writers, out here today to see our operation—and, of course, to meet you. Their objective is to have a lot of local color in the film—nothing phony. All real planes with real pilots doing the real flying. And they'll try to have cameras at certain places along the route during the race so they can film the refueling and turnarounds."

"So, then," Fernando asked, "they've made a final decision to film the actual Bendix Cup, itself? It'll cost a fortune, but I think it'll fly with the movie-going public, pardon the pun."

"I'm sure it will," Roscoe laughed. "That's Hollywood, for sure, and if I don't miss my bet, they'll make back every dollar they spend, and then some. At any rate, their storyline, as the screenplay is evolving, is to have me be the winning pilot, with you, Maggie, as the leading female pilot. My big selling job, as I see it, is to convince all the other pilots to agree to play themselves. The other pilots won't have much in the way of speaking parts. I'm sure the studio will use regular actors wherever they can, to keep it professional."

Maggie was still in shock. "I can't believe this is happening. Doing stunts, yes. But this? It's more than I could ever have hoped for."

Without speaking, Fernando placed his hand on Maggie's shoulder and drew her to his side.

"Now, Maggie," Roscoe added, obviously enjoying himself immensely, "they want you to also be a technical advisor regarding the feelings of women in aviation. Goldsmith said that they want to bring women further into the limelight, so to speak."

Roscoe then shifted his attention to Fernando and continued. "Fernando, as you both know, as a foreigner isn't qualified to enter the race. However, knowing that you probably want to be involved—and I spoke to at least one studio executive about this—I'd like you to pilot a camera plane and maybe do some stunts as well. What do you think?"

While Fernando was flattered by the compliment Roscoe had given him, he was especially excited with the prospects of joining Maggie in such a once-in-a-lifetime happening. Nevertheless, he knew his primary concern at the moment was sorting out his family obligations, his future relationship with Maggie, and her religious beliefs.

"Thank you for the offer, Roscoe," Fernando said. "Maggie knows how much I would like to join such a remarkable cross-country adventure, and I support her with all my heart. At the moment, however, I have some fairly weighty matters to sort through, so if you will permit me, I must defer my decision for the time being.

"As for you, my beautiful new movie star," he continued, turning to Maggie, "I couldn't be more excited for you."

Glancing at his wristwatch, Roscoe said, "They're due any minute now. I asked you to be here a half-hour early so I could fill you in. I don't need to tell either of you that my getting this contract means everything to my having the ability to keep this business afloat. In fact, without this movie opportunity, I don't know how I'll be able to get my own plane ready for the cross-country race. It isn't that I don't have the assets; it's just that a lot of people owe me, and with the depression, they haven't been able to pay up. The bank has already said that they won't increase my line of credit. They counted on my winning the same race last year—to amortize a lump of what I owed at that time. I came in second place, as you know, so that canceled my ability to reduce my deficit."

"Why don't you put your trophies on your desk to show them off?" Fernando asked. "Where have you hidden them? I saw them here the last time I visited you."

Roscoe mumbled something about recently moving the trophies out with the junk, but, taking Fernando's advice, he left to retrieve them. Moments later he returned, carrying several large trophies he had been awarded in past years for major races. Within seconds, Maggie and Fernando had helped arrange them strategically around the room. Included with the trophies was a photo of Roscoe and President Franklin Delano Roosevelt taken three years earlier, only weeks after Roosevelt had taken the oath of office as the country's twenty-seventh chief executive officer.

"I thought I was overdoing things," Roscoe confessed. Taking the photo from Roscoe, Fernando hung it on a nail behind his desk.

Maggie, herself impressed with Roscoe's humility, spoke up. "Roscoe, when they get here why don't you lead them on a tour of your operation? Let Jake explain the difference between radial engines and in-line engines, and why you prefer the radial. Then perhaps you can take them to the airframe department where your men are recovering your last year's racer with new linen.

They can see for themselves how strong the welded steel tube inner structure is. I noticed the wing spars have been beefed up, and the gas tanks are bigger. I presume you're doing this so that you can cross the country with only one gas stop, instead of the two you made last year.

"In fact, why don't you show them your route map?" she continued, the pitch of her voice rising with added excitement. "You can explain the different tracks you have planned over the ground depending upon the weather conditions forecast during the race. What do you think?"

Roscoe nodded appreciatively. Maggie had suggested a brilliant plan of action. At that moment a convoy of luxury cars drew up beside the hangar.

After an exhausting set of negotiations and disclosures, the movie executives finally left. Roscoe had been offered a significant job as airplane coordinator, and Maggie had been hired, not only as a stunt pilot, but as one of the actors in the movie itself. She would be given speaking lines, and would actually come in second in the race—if she could get a sponsor, of course.

The cross-country air race would take place on the Labor Day weekend in less than three months. The producer and director had put together movies before in that length of time, and they were confident that they could likewise meet the challenge with this one. The difficult part of the job would be setting up a suspense-filled backdrop for the film, then cutting and piecing together the best parts of the actual race for the final version. They knew the editors would throw away at least ten feet of film for every foot they retained. They also knew that they would have to drive the writers, actors, and film crews unmercifully. But a monumental movie classic was in the making, and an exciting race was getting ready to be staged in the skies—across the entire width of the continent.

During the meeting with the movie executives, Maggie and

Fernando were surprised to learn that an unknown Russian was going to fly in the race. He was living in America and had become a U.S. citizen, and so qualified both as the designer and the pilot to be in the race. He was a fighter pilot for the Soviet Union during the great World War and was also an engineer.

"It is rumored," said Roscoe, "that he has an all-metal military fighter plane that is so secret that no outsider has seen it. From what we just learned, this Russian-American is deeply worried that another war is approaching, and that the United States has no advanced plane with which to fight the antagonistic Germans.

"On the other hand," he continued, "the Germans have the very fast Messerschmitt fighter with an in-line V-type engine. England also has a similar streamlined fighter, but they can't manufacture them fast enough. The unnamed Russian-American thinks he can save the world with his country's plane. The trouble is, no one has seen it. This is only a rumor, and if it is ready to fly, I doubt the U.S. military will allow him to race it, simply because of the publicity. For the time being, it is a top military secret."

Roscoe paused to allow Fernando and Maggie to assimilate the details he had just shared.

Fernando spoke up. "My professors have expressed their feelings that the Russians do, in fact, have a secret flying machine. Even so, I seriously doubt that the military will allow the craft to fly in an open, world-renowned race."

Roscoe sighed, "I might add that the Russian believes that the round radial engine is the best combat and racing engine made to date. This thinking, of course, is in direct opposition to those who favor the in-line V-shape engines."

There was silence and Maggie thought it was a good time to lighten things up. "There's a funny story about Miss Amelia Earhart," she said. "It's said that she took Lockheed's president aside, and whispered, 'We'll buy your craft for the race, sir, on one condition—that you install a ladies' potty. A twin is big enough to have a powder room for women pilots.' And the president said she could have it."

The three laughed, then Roscoe added satirically, "You see now why the officials took so long in admitting women to cross-country racing. It has nothing to do with flying ability—only with personal convenience."

"You're always telling us how special we are, and how you'll do anything for us," Maggie teased, "so I am pleased that at least one airplane manufacturer is sensitive to our needs."

Late for another commitment, Roscoe excused himself, inviting Maggie and Fernando to remain as long as they desired and talk over the unusual events of the day.

After Roscoe left and having poured two fresh glasses of water, Maggie began. "Fernando, when we spent our first minutes together, I asked 'A penny for your thoughts.' So much has happened today that I would give a bushel of dollars to know what you are thinking . . . just where, or how, you see yourself fitting into all of this?"

"My goodness," Fernando replied, smiling broadly. "You do get right to the point, don't you, Miss Rockwell?"

"Only because I plan on spending the rest of my life with you, darling, and I'm curious to know how the next several months will play into those plans."

"Well," Fernando hesitated, grappling with his emotions, "such an opportunity is certainly a once-in-a-lifetime proposition—especially for you. Roscoe's job offer as a technical flight advisor and the director's invitation to teach Douglas Boynton how to fly are exciting possibilities. But my first priority must be contacting my family and healing the rift that exists between my father and myself as well as assuming my responsibilities with the family business, of course. It's not a clear-cut decision . . . especially since my first choice would be to share with you what appears to be the fulfillment of your dream. I just don't know, Maggie . . . I just don't know."

"I understand, Fernando, and I don't want you to feel pressure from me to—"

"Don't say it, Maggie, for I cannot escape the pressure. Your founding father, Benjamin Franklin, once said that 'Time is the stuff life is made of,' and at least I seem to have the time to decide what I must do.

He stood and took Maggie's hand in his. "Right now, I'm famished, as I'm sure you are. What say we go to Santa Monica Boulevard and enjoy a sandwich at Ralph's Drug and Eatery?"

As Maggie followed Fernando out into the quiet of the evening, she felt an excitement and an anticipation that she could not put into words. She had faith in her future, and in their future, and she could hardly believe the direction the afternoon meeting had taken.

Chapter Thirteen

Don Hugo planned to be at the Wall Street offices of his international bankers at precisely 9:00 a.m. Then he hoped to leave immediately for the West Coast. However, that was before receiving Roberto's telegram.

In a surprise decision, the New York bankers insisted that Don Hugo personally sign the loan documents for their new industrial complex in Brazil. This delay would cost him almost a full day.

Don Hugo's telegram to the Earl of Wittingham in Hollywood had been perfectly clear. Stating his scheduled arrival at the Los Angeles Airport on June 22nd, at 2:00 p.m., Don Hugo requested that a limo meet him at the airport. He directed that the Earl invite Fernando to his hotel later that afternoon to meet someone, although Fernando was not to know that it was Don Hugo he was to meet. Fernando's girlfriend, said Don Hugo, was of no consequence to him; he saw no need to meet her. *At last,* he sighed as he wired the cablegram, *the stage is set to take care of Fernando once and for all.*

The cablegram arrived in Los Angeles within minutes and was delivered to the British consulate two hours later.

Reclining in the large desk chair in his office, Jock picked up the phone, dialed the actor, Douglas Boynton, and read it to him.

"This delay in his arrival, and his new requests, eliminates our problem of distracting Don Hugo. But the comment about Fernando's girlfriend is most puzzling."

Douglas mused, "All we can do is allow Fernando's father to direct our actions, Jock. We certainly can't risk offending him."

"That's right, old chap. Thankfully, we haven't tipped our hand to Fernando, so we won't have to retrace our footsteps."

"To be sure," answered the consul with visible relief in his voice. "The university officials will just have to meet Don Hugo following the graduation exercises.

"Douglas," Jock continued, suddenly remembering something else, "I am still counting on you to host a celebrity party at your place, to honor Don Hugo and Fernando. Guests of great importance must be in attendance—celebrities Don Hugo cannot ignore. You may use my driver to escort them, of course. We must certainly put our finest foot forward, mustn't we, old boy?"

"Without question," the famed actor agreed.

The two friends continued to discuss details, then before concluding their conversation, Douglas remembered one more thing that he wanted to say to Lord Jockham.

"Say there, Jock, I almost forgot. I met with studio executives today, at Roscoe Turner's hangar. We discussed the air-race movie of the annual Bendix Cup, and believe it or not, our man Fernando and his lady were in attendance. They were surprisingly helpful to the director and writers who were developing background material for the script. I observed Fernando and the girl carefully," he continued gleefully, "and I could swear that they are engaged. They were just too comfortable with each other. Still, the girl wears no ring, so at this point this is just conjecture."

The two British strategists concluded their conversation, each anxious but pleased with the way the "Argentine Affair," as they had begun to call it, was coming together.

It was late at night, and all lights were out except for those under the arches of the corridors next to the horse stalls. In the shadows, Maggie and Fernando sat closely together in the convertible parked in front of the polo stables. Maggie cuddled in Fernando's arms, enjoying a sense of safety and well-being. They quietly discussed the activities of the day and the changing plans that faced them.

"Maggie, it is all working out perfectly for us. I have Roscoe's job offer on this air-race movie deal, plus an offer that my university advisor found with an aircraft manufacturer in the East. There is also my obligatory return to Buenos Aires to take my place with the San Martin conglomerate, although that appears a highly unlikely option right now. But who knows what unexpected events might unfold?

"At any rate," Fernando concluded, "it looks to me like we have enough job security to marry soon."

Maggie sensed that it was not in Fernando's nature to wait long for her to make up her mind about a wedding date. She had been reluctant to choose a date, although that was not her nature either. Only days ago she had hoped for something to cause Fernando to open up, trust her, reveal his past, and propose to her. The unexpected appearance of her old bronc-busting boyfriend from the past had obviously triggered Fernando into action. He had proposed that same night.

Now it was Maggie, not Fernando, who needed time. She wanted time to introduce Fernando to her parents in Arizona and to plan the wedding she had always dreamed for. It would not be a temple wedding, of course. That would have to wait. Following continued prayer, Maggie had been feeling more and more constrained to allow her religion to simply remain in the background. She knew that when Fernando was ready to discuss it, she would have plenty of time to share the glorious truths she knew had been revealed. It was difficult to not be marrying initially in the temple, but they would be temple worthy as her bishop had explained, and for now this provided the comfort Maggie needed.

In addition—and first and foremost—Maggie wanted time to

film the movie and participate in the Labor Day cross-country race. That was, of course, if she could find a sponsor. While with each passing day the possibility was diminishing rapidly, she told herself that she must not lose hope.

Maggie was aware that Fernando was still waiting. She spoke carefully. "Fernando, darling, let's settle on mid-September, after the race, for the wedding. Please, not now. It's too fast for me to rush into marriage this soon, even though I love you fiercely and would do anything not to lose you.

"I am the first of my generation to marry, Fernando, on both sides of my family, and I've told you how my family will need time to adjust to your culture and customs. I've always dreamed of marrying with my family present, and I know they will want a big celebration at home on the ranch."

Maggie looked pensive for a moment."There's something else, Fernando. My family has . . . had some problems. I haven't talked about it, but it looks like my father might lose our ranch. He's behind on the mortgage, and the bank is threatening to foreclose. I've sent some money home, but it hasn't been enough to save the ranch. Oh, it's not like the western movie plots where the bad guy gets hold of the mortgage and forces the girl to marry him or he will foreclose on the family place. This is just a situation where the bank has done the best they can. From what my parents have told me, the bank is in trouble, as well."

"I'm so sorry, Maggie, I really don't—"

"Please, darling, don't say it. Our family has been blessed with an unusual imbuing of faith, and we're sure a solution will present itself."

"Imbuing? I'm afraid the meaning of that word escapes me, Maggie . . . . Could you please run that past me again?"

"It means a fullness, or a completeness, Fernando. We're of pioneer stock, the kind of folks who truly believe that this faith will provide a solution for us. My parents don't have their hand out—that isn't their way. What they do have is plenty of spiritual backbone, if you will. It's difficult now, and of deep concern for all of us, but we trust, Fernando, and if it's important that our family retain the ranch—for whatever reason—then retain it we will."

A new and deeper admiration filled Fernando's heart. "Well, if you aren't the most unusual person—or family—I've ever encountered. And, a Mormon family, no less. What you're saying makes perfect sense in a way, yet it is such a foreign way of looking at life that I have a hard time digesting your words, let alone the full meaning behind them."

"I'm sorry, darling, but it is who I am . . . who we are."

"And hopefully, Maggie Rockwell, it's who I will become. Perhaps not a Mormon, but at least a more devout Christian."

Maggie smiled tenderly at him. "They're one and the same, my darling, believe me."

Without replying to her comment, Fernando continued with his previous thought. "I have thought more of spiritual imbuing, as you call it, since I met you, than I have in my entire life. It's quite stirring, really . . ."

"Oh, Fernando," Maggie exclaimed, throwing her arms around Fernando and kissing him earnestly. "I don't know what's happening, but I've never been this happy. I know things will work out—both for my family, and for us—and I want to thank you for adding your faith to my own."

"Maggie," Fernando replied, suddenly exhausted with the many complexities of their conversation rushing through his mind, "let's not talk anymore right now. Let's just enjoy the magic of the night, and of the serenading crickets. Things have a way of happening on their own timetable, and I have a hunch that our marriage and the solution to your family's ranch will come together in the way that will be for the good of all of us.

"Now, my beautiful, flying equestrian," he added, "what do you say we announce our engagement next week after our graduation party? We can then get married—just as you suggest—the third week of September, after the race. After all, I wouldn't want to start out at odds with your parents, now, would I?"

"Oh, sweetheart, you are the most understanding man in the world. How could I—"

"Now, now, Miss Rockwell, I know you Americans say that 'love is blind,' but I wouldn't want you to take it to the extreme. I'm just a polo jockey from South America, who happens to have fallen deeply in love with the most beautiful—and intelligent—woman this side of Fredonia, Arizona."

"As long as there isn't another lady of your liking east of Fredonia," Maggie said pertly.

"East and south, actually," Fernando replied with a teasing note to his voice. "Her name is Dame Helen Underwood de San Martin. You'll love her as you do your own mother. And even though I doubt she's milked a cow or fed any chickens, she has ridden plenty of high-spirited horses. She has truly been my anchor . . . that is, until now. Thank you, Maggie, for helping me breathe the fresh air of love. Because of you," he concluded, "I will never be the same."

"Oh, Fernando," Maggie whispered urgently, still nestled safely in Fernando's arms. "I love you with every fiber of my being. The Lord has been so kind in bringing us into each other's lives. . . ."

As Maggie's words trailed off, the romantic spell of the night fell in upon them, allowing each to marvel at the emotions they were experiencing, while providing the way for both to know that their lives, and their future, were inexplicably and eternally woven together.

Chapter Fourteen

The executive twin engine plane descended gradually into the great Los Angeles basin. Inside the plane, accompanying the pilots and stewardess, was a very weary and beleaguered Don Hugo San Martin Braun. During his arduous journey across the broad expanse of America's heartland, Don Hugo had been mentally reviewing the life of his disappointing eldest son, Fernando. He remembered when Fernando was born and the unspeakable joy he and Dame Helen had as the child had learned to walk and to talk.

Don Hugo reflected sadly that during his son's youth, strong personality traits appeared that had eventually become his undoing. When Fernando became a teenager, these traits became defined by leadership, as Fernando became an outstanding athlete and student leader. His athletic prowess, on whatever level he participated, proved him to be almost without peer. Likewise, his mind was so insightful and quick that his teachers soon pushed him to the forefront of his class, grooming him, even at that early age, to ultimately assume the head of the San Martin business conglomerate.

Don Hugo remembered angrily that Fernando was always pushing against his boundaries, trying to prove his wings like a young bird that just wasn't content to remain in the safety of his mother's nest. Rather, even though his feathers were not adequately developed, he constantly tried, prematurely, to spread his wings.

Don Hugo was lost in disappointing reverie as the tops of the houses grew larger and larger beneath his view. He recalled Fernando's youth, as he began dating, and how in desperation Don Hugo and Dame Helen had moved him from place to place, in an attempt to keep him clean and unspotted from their country's growing lack of moral values. But, even with all of these precautions, Fernando had left home, blatantly throwing his values and future opportunities to the wind while tragically and permanently disgracing the sacred San Martin name.

It was because of Don Hugo and Dame Helen's efforts to get Fernando away from a blossoming romance that they found a solution that caused him to forget about girls. His parents had suggested he take flying lessons. Their suggestion took root, and within months Fernando had become an accomplished pilot. Then, in Fernando's late teens, the polo bug bit hard, and he quickly became a leader in the highly popular polo circles. The training to prepare for international matches was so intense and time consuming that adoring young ladies were left far behind on his list of priorities.

Dame Helen had been successful in rearing Fernando free from the entanglements of alcohol and other vices, and she had convinced Don Hugo that their eldest son should be trusted to go to England, there to advance his technical education as well as his leadership skills.

As Don Hugo's plane approached from the sky and rolled along the runway of the newly expanded Los Angeles Airport, he reflected on how he and Dame Helen had first become aware of Fernando's departure from his early teachings and values. News had arrived at their home in the form of an alarming report from the university he was attending. The regents, along with Fernando's professors, had reported that their son's social life was irreparably interfering with his studies. Then came word of his growing addiction to gambling, and his dismissal from the university. Don Hugo and Dame Helen were heartsick in the belief that they had failed as Fernando's parents.

Yet, even with all of this, Don Hugo had been willing to forgive and to allow his son to return and take his position at the head of the family empire.

As the plane rocked to a stop at the edge of the tarmac, Don Hugo was still deep in thought. Aware that several moments would pass before he would be cleared to disembark, Don Hugo allowed his memory to continue through the wreckage of his eldest son's life. The final blow, which had resulted in Don Hugo's current plan to disinherit his son, had been the murderous death of the girl, Rachel Cummings. *Murderous?* Just the thought of that word repulsed Don Hugo. It was not fair! It was not right that Fernando's behavior sabotage all that Don Hugo had worked for in his life . . . the reputation of his family's name, which had come to stand for integrity and honor. But now he would pound the final nail into the coffin of Fernando's abandoned inheritance.

Outside, the limousine he had requested was waiting for him, which would facilitate his plans without undue involvements with the British consulate. He had asked that the limousine come without Lord Jockham and his associates. Don Hugo was totally exhausted, as he had expected he would be. His meeting with them could wait.

Don Hugo planned to go directly to his hotel. There he would gain knowledge of Fernando's whereabouts from Lord Jockham's memo. After that, he would take time to prepare to meet his son. At the thought of his son, Don Hugo felt a tightening in his chest. Fernando would have no knowledge of the meeting; he would simply be waiting in a privately reserved conference room at the hotel in anticipation of a meeting with the British actor, Douglas Boynton. But the actor would not arrive. Instead, Don Hugo would enter the room and matter-of-factly announce Fernando's disinheritance. He would then extract the necessary disinheriting documents from his pocket, demand Fernando's immediate signature, and march swiftly and permanently out of Fernando's life.

For Don Hugo, the next few hours passed excruciatingly slowly. At last, however, after a soothing bath and brief rest, he dressed quickly and walked briskly to the room that was being held for his rendezvous with his son. The room was in the west wing of the hotel, not far from the elevator which he was entering. A smiling young woman was seated in the corner of the elevator, manipulating the controls as though her task were the most important in the world.

"Good evening, Mr. San Martin," she acknowledged politely. "Welcome to Los Angeles. I understand you have had a long flight from New York . . . ?"

The young lady's gracious manner, and her knowledge of Don Hugo's identity, surprised and impressed him.

"Longer than I care to remember—from Argentina, actually," he replied. Indeed, it had been a long two-week journey.

"I've never been south of Los Angeles," the elevator operator replied. "But, perhaps one day. Your meeting room, sir, is on level two, Room 240. It is down the hall to our left, and from what I have been told, your son has arrived and is awaiting your arrival."

"Thank you, young lady," Don Hugo nodded stiffly at the mention of his son. "Do come visit us one day." He bowed and stared toward the door. He knew that Fernando was not awaiting his arrival, but rather was anticipating a meeting with Douglas Boynton. Just as well, Don Hugo reasoned. He wanted his errand to be swift and private; the plan he had asked Lord Jockham to arrange was the best he could come up with.

As the elevator doors opened, Don Hugo experienced a growing knot in his stomach that prevented him from breathing normally. Could he do this? Could he follow through with the plans that had taken weeks for him to formulate in his mind? For Don Hugo, it was the most painful moment of his life, and he found himself consumed with the spirit of anger and disdain.

Finally, after leaving the elevator and walking down what seemed like an eternally long hallway, Don Hugo arrived at the designated meeting place. He checked the number on the door, took a deep and pain-filled breath, then turned the handle and entered the unlocked room.

His back to the door, Fernando was looking out the window to the busy street below. At the sound of the closing door, Fernando turned and found himself unexpectedly and impossibly staring into the weary eyes of his father.

"Father, I—" he began.

"Please . . . say nothing." Don Hugo interrupted, pushing his hands out in front of him, not wanting to give his son the opportunity to speak. "My words will be brief, as I—"

"Oh, my father . . . " the anguished cry tore itself lose from Fernando's throat as the repentant son covered his face with his hands. "How I have longed—" But he could not speak for the great sobs that broke away from him like giant waves upon the sandy shore. He wanted to rush to his father, kneel at his feet, but he did not dare. The shame he had brought upon his father!

Don Hugo searched in vain for the angry, cutting words he had rehearsed for this moment, but found, to his amazement, that they no longer clutched at his heart as they had for, it seemed, so many years. Instead of anger, there was an outpouring of gratitude at the sight of his beloved son, pain for the pain he had suffered, and love for this his firstborn. Don Hugo took his son in his arms and his tears mingled with those of his son.

Fernando allowed himself to be swallowed up in his father's loving arms. Strangely, he felt like a young boy, fearing the wrath—then feeling the love—of the man who meant more to him than any other in the world. But he was no longer a child; rather, he was a twenty-eight-year-old prodigal son, being welcomed back into his father's heart.

"Fernando, my son," Don Hugo whispered, again in his preferred English. "How I have missed you . . . and how I have wronged you by turning my back on you when you needed me most. Please . . . forgive me, my son. Allow me to once again claim you as my own and to be the father you so deserve."

Don Hugo's unexpectedly humble words took Fernando completely by surprise and touched him deeply.

"It is I who must ask forgiveness, Father," he spoke painfully. "I have betrayed you and Mother, I have betrayed myself, and most of all, I have betrayed God. With all my heart I ask your forgiveness and ask that you give me one more chance. . . ."

"Oh, my son." Don Hugo tried to smile through his tears, then took a handkerchief from his pocket and wiped away, first the tears from his son's face and then his own. "Your mother—although she has been ill—goes to mass and prays for you daily. How vigilant she and your brother, Ricardo, have been in their faith in you. I'm afraid it is I who did not believe and allowed my my mind to be filled with horrid, contaminated thoughts—"

"No, Father," Fernando interrupted him. "It is I who placed these thoughts there, for my poor judgment with alcohol has caused me greater pain and sorrow than I can ever express. But you must know, my father," Fernando continued, now drawing back and placing his hands squarely upon the shoulders of his father, "even with all of the partying in which I became engaged, the standard of virtue you instilled within my heart has remained intact. I have never allowed myself to walk down the long, dark corridor of moral decay, but instead, I have honored each woman I have known, as though she were my sister . . . ."

Fernando paused, allowing his words to penetrate his father's heart. Don Hugo felt a wince of pain, as he had wrongly judged his son's moral character for many years.

Fernando continued regretfully, "The stream of alcohol within my system did dull my senses, causing me to watch the life of someone I loved slip quickly, and uncontrollably, away—"

As Fernando spoke these words, tears again flowed down his cheeks at the thought of she who had been his fiancée, Rachel Cummings.

"I have never known the truth," Don Hugo admitted. "I judged you in my heart knowing nothing of your story. Will you speak of it to me, my son?" Don Hugo feared that his request was selfish, and yet he wanted desperately to know what had happened.

Taking a deep breath, Fernando began to describe the events that led up to the automobile accident, how the axle had shattered and he had been unable to keep control the car. He spoke of the funeral and of how strangely kind and nonjudgmental Rachel's parents had been.

When Fernando concluded his account, both father and son stood silently, as if in quiet reverence for the passing of the young and innocent Rachel Cummings. Then, after tears were dried and noses were blown, Fernando took his father's hands in his own. Fernando again spoke.

"Father," he began cautiously, yet with increasing composure, "there is more. I have recently met a young lady—Maggie Rockwell—who has reintroduced into my life the power of prayer. At Maggie's insistence, I have asked God's forgiveness for my horrid, inexcusable behavior, and for placing one of his beautiful daughters in such peril. I have also asked for peace, and for—as Maggie so wisely taught me—a new brightness of hope."

Don Hugo, for one of the few times in his life, was speechless. His son's words revealed such a profoundly different and mature outlook, that Don Hugo could not find the words to respond.

Sensing his father's surprise, Fernando smiled even more broadly. "I know what I'm trying to say may sound odd to you, Father, but believe me when I say that I have felt the wonderful cleansing of forgiveness. I feel that Rachel and her family have forgiven me, and that the God of Heaven has forgiven me. The most difficult part has been to forgive myself. Prayer has been of great help to me."

"Prayer? Fernando, I . . . I don't know what to say. Your words seem so foreign to my way of—"

A voice interrupted him gently. "Perhaps I could help you, sir . . . ."

Don Hugo and Fernando turned simultaneously toward the person who had just spoken; and there, standing in the open doorway, was Maggie. Both men stood respectfully, and Fernando walked quickly to her side.

What a beautiful young woman, Don Hugo thought as Fernando made his way across the room. While she was attractive, to be sure, there was more . . . much more than that. It was almost as though her skin were illuminated with a light that brightened the entire room.

"Father," Fernando said, "meet my fiancée, Maggie Rockwell. She is from nearby Arizona and is—"

"Please, Fernando," Don Hugo held up is hand as if to protect himself. "I am aging rapidly—especially after the last hour. Please take things a little bit more slowly. I'm afraid my mind needs more time to assimilate—"

"Excuse me, Mr. Underwood," Maggie spoke up. "I hope you will forgive my interrupting your conversation with Fernando. I thought he was meeting with Mr. Boynton."

Fernando coughed, "Maggie, Underwood is my mother's maiden name. Father's full name is Don Hugo San Martin Braun."

Maggie looked at Fernando in surprise. "You mean, your name is not Underwood?"

"No matter, my dear," Don Hugo replied, breaking into a lively grin. He found himself thoroughly enjoying the spontaneous nature of the young woman before him. "It is our way. Do allow me the pleasure of congratulating you, Miss Rockwell."

With that, Don Hugo embraced Maggie warmly and lightly kissed her on both cheeks in the Latin custom. "If I may be so bold, my beautiful daughter-to-be, I would much prefer calling you by your first name . . . ."

"My first name," Maggie smiled, "is actually Margaret. No one but my mother calls me that . . . so please, just call me Maggie."

"Then Maggie it is," Don Hugo exclaimed. "Fernando and I have just been . . . how do you say? . . . yes, reintroducing our souls to each other. It has been too many lonely and misunderstood years. "

Fernando nodded silently, suddenly acutely aware of the profound vacuum the absence of his father had created in his life.

The three then spent the next hour visiting, updating each other on their activities, and introducing Maggie and Don Hugo to each other's vastly divergent lives. For Fernando, this portion of the conversation brought great relief and elation, as the two seemed to bond almost immediately. In fact, Don Hugo became so effusive and complimentary of Maggie that from Fernando's perspective, it seemed they had known each other for years.

Finally, after enjoying a catered late-afternoon meal, Fernando and Maggie escorted Don Hugo back to his room for a much-needed rest. As they left him, Fernando wrote down specific time and location instructions for the following morning's graduation ceremonies and festivities. Maggie's parents, Wilford and Doris Rockwell, were due to arrive from Arizona on the 10:00 p.m. train, and Maggie had invited Fernando to meet them at that time.

Chapter Fifteen

The warmth of the sun directly over the university stadium revealed the time to be near noon. The sky was sprinkled with high floating cirrus clouds, and all around the polo stadium, birds sang and bees and butterflies flew in and among the vast arrays of the surrounding flower displays.

Don Hugo's head was spinning as he seated himself in the President's Box, a cordoned-off area in the bleachers that had been reserved for Dr. Rheinhart, the university president, and his distinguished guests. What Don Hugo hadn't known until earlier that morning was that he was one of those for whom the area had been reserved.

As Don Hugo took his seat, he smiled and politely nodded to the individuals who had just dined with him at a special breakfast hosted by Dr. Rheinhart and his wife, Amelia, at the president's home. Included in these guests were Don Hugo's hosts, Lord Jockham, and the famed British actor, Douglas Boynton. He had enjoyed meeting them and appreciated the opportunity to thank them for their obviously sincere interest in Fernando and his family.

Also attending the president's breakfast, and much to Don Hugo's surprise, were Maggie's parents, Wilford and Doris Rockwell. They had safely arrived by train from Arizona late the previous night and were staying with Maggie at her apartment. Don Hugo was glad to meet them, especially as they would become family in the very near future.

Wilford was a roughhewn American gaucho, if there ever was one. He was well over six feet tall, with a square jaw that framed one of the most smiling faces Don Hugo had ever met. There was simply no end to his engaging smile. Doris, on the other hand, was refinement in its purest form—a regal blonde lady who was almost a twin to Maggie, only a generation older. It was obvious that Maggie came from good stock, although never in his wildest imagination had Don Hugo considered that Fernando would marry someone from a remote western area such as Arizona, let alone the United States and another culture. Yet, hadn't he himself married someone of a culture different than his own? Such a question, answered by his own admission, put his mind at ease, and Don Hugo was strangely proud of the selection his son had made in a companion. In fact, in truthfully evaluating his feelings, Don Hugo was surprised with how totally accepting he was of this Maggie Rockwell. She was a "cowgirl" after all, and would understand the vast San Martin holdings. It was good, and it was enough.

Now, as Don Hugo sat in the audience and waited for the graduation ceremonies to begin, his only regret was that Dame Helen had not been along to enjoy these totally unexpected, yet special new friendships. He would be sure to send her a telegram in the day and explain the unexpected turn of events. She would be surprised, to be sure, but would rejoice in the softening of his heart and in the reunion he was having with their eldest son. She would also, in all likelihood, experience a renewal of energy and health. These thoughts brought with them unexpected humility and joy for the powerful Don Hugo.

As the graduation ceremonies finally began, Don Hugo found himself gazing out beyond the stadium, taking in the blossoming trees and the finely manicured flower gardens. In every way, the balmy June weather of southern California reminded him of Buenos Aires, and he drew in a deep breath, savoring the moment.

Getting used to the western American customs, Don Hugo

was likewise impressed with how the visitors matched the surroundings, dressed in their finest. Most of the ladies were wearing wide-brimmed hats, while the men wore their best summer straw panamas. The dignitaries, wearing their colorful robes of the universities from which they had received their doctorate degrees, had a reserved area on a raised platform in front of the graduates. Looking for the first time at the printed program, Don Hugo found Fernando and Maggie's names. To his astonishment, he found that Fernando was receiving a special award—the Presidential Citation. The print below Fernando's name read:

Mr. Fernando Hugo Underwood is given special recognition for scholarship and for exceptional contributions to the advancement of aeronautical science. This award, given annually, is for achievement in the Science of Aluminum Extrusion for Aircraft Application.

Don Hugo was speechless. He had no idea that Fernando was receiving an individual honor today, let alone one of such intellectual magnitude. Fernando had only said that he had to sit on the front row of those graduating.

Music heralded the beginning of the ceremonies. Dr. Rheinhart, the university president, then announced the program exactly as it was printed, making special mention of the guests, including Mr. Don Hugo San Martin Braun, who had traveled so far to attend the ceremonies. Don Hugo was both flattered and embarrassed in being singled out, but he nodded graciously and smiled proudly in Fernando's direction.

The program then proceeded, as one-by-one the speakers, then administrators, made their contribution. At last, Dr. Rheinhart again took the stand and invited Fernando to come forward and receive the special award. Fernando did so with great dignity, looking very thoroughly the part of a new professional engineer in aeronautical science.

Dr. Rheinhart had never known Fernando's full name, but he

pronounced every syllable with significant emphasis as though he had been coached. Carrying his full name, Fernando seemed to stand taller, his face glowing with justified pride.

As Fernando returned to his seat, Don Hugo joined in the thunderous applause, his eyes shining with tears of joy at the accomplishments of his eldest son. He was equally proud of both Fernando and Maggie as they, along with the other graduates, stepped forward to receive their diplomas. Maggie's parents were sitting behind Don Hugo and to the right, and he made eye contact with them when Maggie was walking across the stand, sensing the deep joy and pride they had in their daughter. He also noticed, as he observed them, that theirs was an obviously loving relationship. Such a thought evoked optimism for Fernando's future, as Don Hugo believed strongly that children coming from happy, loving homes made the most successful spouses and parents.

These impressions were running through Don Hugo's mind when Dr. Rheinhart stepped forward, took the microphone in his hand, and proudly announced, "Margaret Rockwell is one of our most famous and esteemed graduates. She is an accomplished pilot and has performed some of the greatest flying and horseback stunts the movies have ever filmed. Her latest film is now being shown around the country."

Then, turning back toward Maggie, Dr. Rheinhart added, "We are all proud to claim you as our own, Miss Rockwell. We wish you well in your future endeavors."

Maggie, standing down on the platform, was overwhelmed. She had never before met the president of the university, yet he spoke of her as if she were an intimate friend. As far as she knew no one on campus had paid even the slightest attention to her movie connections. She had tried to keep them unknown, but somehow word had reached as far as the university president.

Maggie did not want to delay the line, so she thanked the president graciously and moved on. As she came down the steps, an usher took her by the arm and whispered, "Dr. Rheinhart would like you to take a seat next to Mr. San Martin Braun."

Surprised, Maggie walked quickly to her new seat. Sorting through what had just taken place, and how excited she was to have Fernando's father and her parents sitting together in the stands, she squeezed Fernando's arm and whispered, "Well, big boy, you carried the day. I'm so proud of you I can't stand it."

"You know, Miss Rockwell," Fernando replied, smiling tenderly, "this may very well be the happiest day of my entire life."

"And mine," Maggie agreed, then added humorously,"If only my feet weren't killing me in these new heels."

Standing there beside Maggie, Fernando felt as though his heart was about to explode. Never in his wildest expectations had he imagined himself experiencing the joy that was his now. As he gazed up into the stands, he saw his father looking in his direction so he waved at him. Don Hugo, who was savoring the moment as he watched Fernando and Maggie, waved back enthusiastically in reply.

As the ceremonies concluded and the thrown caps and tassels had been retrieved, Fernando and Maggie made their way to the prearranged corner of the field where their guests were awaiting them.

Don Hugo was the first to notice them coming, and stepping quickly forward, he wrapped his arms around his son. Squeezing tightly, he whispered into Fernando's ear in Spanish, *"Felicitaciones, mi hijo. Nos ha hecho muy orgullosos de ti.* You have made us very proud of you. *Tu mama manda besos.* Your mother sends kisses. *Un beso de ella y uno de mi.* A kiss from her and one from me."

Then, his voice breaking, he whispered, *"Perdoname, perdoname, perdoname.* Forgive me, forgive me, forgive me."

Answering his father with his own embrace, Fernando saw that he was only beginning to comprehend the miracle of his father's presence at his graduation and his welcome of Fernando back into the family fold, and with him, his fiancée.

Clearing his throat, Fernando replied. *"No, papa. Tenia que recuperar tu amor y llegar a ser digno de tu confianza por mi propia cuenta.* No, Father, I had to recover your love and become worthy of your trust by my own effort. *No se si lo he hecho todavia, pero dedicare el resto de mi vida para lograrlo.* I don't know if I have accomplished it yet, but I will dedicate the rest of my life to doing it."

Don Hugo caressed his son's cheek with his hands. Their exchange in Spanish had been meant only for the two of them; but Maggie, standing to the side, somehow understood their meaning, if not their exact words. The prodigal had returned, the overly proud father had been humbled, and the newness of their love had become exquisitely delicious for them both.

While father and son embraced, Maggie was welcomed into the circle. This time was one they would each treasure for the remainder of their lives, and one that would set the stage for the evening's activities. They then turned to visit with Maggie's parents, tears of joy unashamedly glistening on their faces.

That evening, after Don Hugo had returned to his hotel room for a rest, he bathed and dressed for an evening with Fernando, Maggie, and her parents. Don Hugo had arranged to host a dinner in Fernando and Maggie's behalf, and as he had been making the arrangements, received a cablegram from Dame Helen—two cablegrams, actually. One, a very brief statement, was addressed to himself. In it, Dame Helen simply expressed her love, and her anxiousness to once again have him back in Buenos Aires. The second one was written to Fernando.

Stuffing the cablegrams into his shirt pocket, Don Hugo hurried through the corridor and into the parlor. As he walked into the room, he was met with applause. Gathered around the punch bowl were his four guests—Fernando, Maggie, Doris and Wilford Rockwell.

Seeing that their host, Don Hugo, had arrived, all eyes focused on him. Extending a glass of freshly made orange juice, Maggie's father, Wilford, promptly proposed a toast—

"To our graduates, Maggie and Fernando."

"May your future," Maggie's mother exclaimed, "be met with joy, and with the same fullness of love that Wilford and I have enjoyed for the past twenty-seven years."

"Yes, yes!" Don Hugo added, not to be outdone, "And in behalf of our family, especially my wife, Helen, we wish you the most prosperous life imaginable."

Glasses were raised, all present made their cheers, and Fernando and Maggie touched their glasses together, then completed the toast.

When everyone was seated and eating, Don Hugo stood, lightly tapped a spoon on the side of his glass, and announced:

"I have a very special gift for you, Fernando. You'll never guess what it is, and so I shall simply give it to you—a cablegram from your mother. I give it with my love, *mi hijo.*"

Fernando took the piece of yellow paper, unfolded it, and silently read the cable.

MY DEAREST FERNANDO STOP MISS YOU TERRIBLY STOP AM FEELING BETTER STOP FATHER ROBERTO AND I ARE VERY HAPPY YOU HAVE GRADUATED STOP FORGIVE US ALL AND COME HOME AS SOON AS POSSIBLE STOP UNDERSTAND YOU HAVE A GIRLFRIEND AND POSSIBLE OBLIGATIONS THERE STOP PLEASE FEEL FREE TO DO WHAT IS BEST AND WE WILL UNDERSTAND STOP KNOW HOW MUCH I LOVE YOU STOP LOVE MOTHER

As Fernando read the words of the cablegram, his eyes became blurred, and he found himself swallowing hard. He could almost feel his mother's softly spoken words. Her words seemed to almost jump off the paper with her unique Argentine accent. She had not requested that he come to her side, so he reasoned that she must not be dying. And how in the world did his mother know about Maggie? His father had obviously informed her of Maggie in his telegram to her. If only she had accompanied his father to the states. If only he could go to Buenos Aires at this time, and enjoy the newness of his acceptance back into his father's graces. But those thoughts were only dreams for the time being, for Maggie and the race now seemed to engulf his entire waking moments.

Maggie . . . dear beautiful Maggie. She had, in fact, become the very center of his life. Still, his family was not known for easily accepting someone into the family, especially without money, titles, and prestige. An unknown rancher's daughter from a remote region in the western United States—and, of a strange and little-known religious cult—might be a bit hard to swallow for some members of the family.

Fernando cleared his throat, before reading aloud the words his mother had written. When he concluded, he simply folded the cablegram and stuffed it into his shirt pocket. He would show it to Maggie again later, as evidence that his mother accepted her, sight unseen.

Maggie embraced Fernando and planted a full kiss on his lips. He responded genuinely, then invited everyone to resume eating.

Throughout dinner, Don Hugo and Maggie's father carried on a lively discussion about cattle and horses, and the ranching business in general. To the surprise of both, they found that each appeared as well informed as the other. However, when her father indiscreetly asked, "How many head do you run?" Maggie wanted to kick him under the table. She had no idea how Don Hugo would respond, but she was sure that the San Martin Braun ranch was many times larger than their Arizona spread.

Sensing Maggie's discomfort and knowing how important it would be for both Maggie and Fernando that he not create a disparity with the Rockwells, Don Hugo said simply, "Oh, I don't actually know, Wilford. We've lost quite a few head with disease recently, and I'd be surprised if we had more than a small herd by the time I return home.

"Which reminds me," he continued quickly, hoping he had diffused the issue, "do you American ranchers brand your cattle like our gauchos brand ours? Each head, I mean, and on one of the rear flanks?"

"Well," Wilford drawled, leaning back, "that's how we treat our Rocking "R" brand. Branding calves each year is always a backbreaking experience."

"Who's been doing the inoculations, Father?" Maggie asked, breaking into the conversation. "I mean, since I left home."

"Oh, we've taken turns, honey. But none of us do it as well as you used to."

As the conversation continued, Fernando sat quietly, taking in Maggie's intoxicating vocal expressions. Hers was the voice of an angel and would be a song to his heart throughout his lifetime.

When the dinner was finally completed, Fernando walked Maggie out onto the veranda. It had been a most busy day, filled with emotion and excitement, and now Fernando simply wanted to relax and reminisce with Maggie.

"Things are a lot different in Argentina than they are here," he began. "We have land that has been handed down to us from old Spanish land grants. These grants were initially bestowed by the king—over four hundred years ago, actually. We have some ranches of half-a-million acres. They seem to go on forever . . . ."

"How many cattle would run on a ranch that size?"

"The two ranches this size that I'm aware of carry 200,000 head of cattle. I also recall three less productive tracts of two million acre ranches that can carry only 100,000 head."

Maggie had no idea anyone in the world held property so large that they could talk numbers like that. Not even the cattle barons of the last century ran outfits of that magnitude.

"Please understand, Maggie," Fernando explained, "that the perspective is totally different down there. A thousand acres here in the states might be worth more than one hundred thousand acres down there. It's not even on the same scale."

After learning more about the St. Martin Braun ranches, Maggie kissed Fernando lightly.

"Darling," she whispered, nestling into his arms, "what about your family's experience? Have they been in the business for several generations?"

"Oh, yes, and then some. In fact, there is one well-known family story of how my great-great-grandfather once gave to General San Martin—a distant cousin who was our equivalent to your General George Washington—one million head of cattle to help feed his army. This was the army that conquered the Spaniards and allowed our people to achieve our independence. In addition, General San Martin asked for and received 100,000 head of horses for his cavalry—and that was from only one of the family's ranches. When Father was a young man, his father and uncles split that ranch into several smaller properties, so that each could control its own profit center."

Fernando sensed that his statement had shed an entirely new light on the vastness of the San Martin Braun empire; yet, he also knew that he owed it to Maggie to give her an accurate perspective of his family's commitment to South American society.

"Ours is an almost inconceivable stewardship," Fernando continued, "and my father has always used that word, for he hasn't laid claim to being any more privileged than anyone else. Our family had been granted a legacy that has assisted in forging the very character of Argentina, and although this legacy has allowed for near-global perspective and influence, in some ways it has been a greater burden than a blessing. Still, literally thousands of lives have been impacted by the wise and giving nature of my forefathers. This fact has always been difficult, yet profoundly sobering for me to consider."

"What you're telling me, Fernando," Maggie whispered, as she stared out into the darkness of the night, "is that your future—our future—is predetermined . . . almost written in the stars."

Maggie's statement caught Fernando off guard, as he had been dwelling on that thought ever since his father had arrived in southern California the day before.

"I haven't really thought of being part of the San Martin Braun future," Fernando admitted. "My estrangement from my family eliminated that. But now . . . I just don't know. What I do know is that I have been restored in my father's eyes, and that will undoubtedly impact our lives to one degree or another."

"Whatever happens, Fernando," Maggie said softly, "I want you to know that I'm with you. I've never been so happy, and with my parents' blessing, I want to simply be 'the wind beneath your wings.'"

A smile breaking across his face, Fernando replied, "But for now I need to be your wind, as we enjoy the upcoming air race and movie production."

"It really will be a summer to remember, dearest . . . the summer of our engagement."

Maggie's father interrupted their conversation. "Hey, kids!" he drawled as he walked out onto the veranda. Behind him were Doris and Don Hugo. The entire party congregated unexpectedly where Maggie and Fernando were standing.

Startled, the two engaged graduates looked up and drew quickly apart. Although the privacy of their moment together had been interrupted, they both sensed that something was happening that was not simply routine. What they didn't know was that Doris was about to drop a bombshell that would set in motion a chain of events which would change, and accelerate, all that they were talking about.

"You shouldn't have left us alone," Doris smiled, "for these two men have spent the last twenty minutes conniving like you wouldn't believe."

Don Hugo raised his hands in front of his chest. "Let me make the request in behalf of your parents—all four of us."

Maggie and Fernando looked at Don Hugo, then Maggie's parents, in bewilderment.

Clearing his throat, Don Hugo continued. "Please permit an

old man to make a statement."

Fernando detected an unusual twinkle in his father's eyes and fidgeted nervously. Don Hugo, meanwhile, sensed that he had cast a suspenseful spell over the two young lovers, and he revelled in the magic of the moment.

"I have been doing a great deal of thinking," he added, almost mischievously, "and Wilford and Doris graciously approve of my proposal—"

"Proposal?" Fernando asked, hoping to unravel the puzzle that had suddenly presented itself.

"Why, yes . . . " Don Hugo smiled, his mind reeling in anticipation of his well-conceived plan. "You see, children," he continued, winking at Wilford as he lightly squeezed Doris's hand, "I am a teetering old romantic. I don't have many requests left inside me; but, I do have one. It is all too obvious that the world has never known two young people who are more deeply in love than are the two of you . . . ."

Maggie's arms and neck rose up in goosebumps as Don Hugo spoke. Truly, theirs was a remarkable love story, one that would rival any other. What was he leading up to? she wondered

"And so . . ." Don Hugo continued, drawing a deep breath of restorative air into his lungs, "I would propose, simply, that the two of you marry in three weeks, on the twenty-fourth of the month. Doris tells me the month of June in northern Arizona is spectacular in its desert beauty, and she has just the man of the cloth who could marry you."

Don Hugo's words hit both Fernando and Maggie squarely in the stomach, leaving both speechless. *Three weeks?* they each asked themselves. Neither could comprehend the request, but likewise neither could deny the emphatic manner in which it had been made.

"Now," Wilford drawled, stepping up and putting his arms around the shoulders of the stunned Fernando and Maggie. "Such a scheme makes me more anxious than a fly-bit colt. But, like Doris said in the other room, this date would allow Don

Hugo to attend and to join with us in the festivities."

"But Father," Fernando questioned, "how could you attend?"

"You forget, Fernando, that I'm the captain of our ship in South America, and I can pretty well do what I want. It's one of the few luxuries of carrying so weighty a stewardship. I'll fly back to New York and use this time to stabilize the activities I've got going on there, and then fly back to—where is it, Wilford?"

"Fredonia, in Arizona," Wilford answered proudly.

"Yes, Fredonia. Wilford tells me there's a little-used road there that he can cordon off for the purpose of landing our plane. He even tells me he'll lead us all on a guided flying tour of the great Grand Canyon. I've heard of this wonder, but have never actually seen it."

As Don Hugo spoke, Fernando found that the idea appealed greatly to him—especially since it would allow him and Maggie to travel together, as the summer and the filming of the movie unfolded.

Maggie, on the other hand, suddenly reeled in panic. *Three weeks?* Just the thought of marrying so quickly, not to mention the myriad of tasks that must be performed in preparation, seemed impossible for her to accept. And what about their religious differences? She hadn't even told her parents of his response to their being Latter-day Saints.

"I-I'm not sure what to say, " she blurted, burying her face in her hands. "Mother, I . . . ."

"Now, Maggie," Doris interrupted, stepping forward and drawing her only daughter into her arms. "I know this is sudden. But, I've seen miracles performed on the ranch before, and with the support of our friends, I know we'll be ready. After all, it would be most selfish of us not to include Fernando's father in such an event."

Her calming words reassured Maggie, and she suddenly found a peaceful calm settling over her. *Of course it will work*, she told herself silently. *How could it not work?*

"What about your mother, Fernando?" she asked, her brow

furrowed deeply in concern. "How can we do this without her?"

"Mother will be with us in spirit," Fernando replied calmly. "And when she meets you," he added, winking at Don Hugo, "she'll understand why I couldn't wait for summer to bring you into our family."

Our family, Maggie said to herself. Just hearing the words caused a new wave of emotion to sweep over her, encompassing her entire frame with an unexpected chill.

"Then, it's settled?" Don Hugo asked, rubbing his hands together in excitement.

"Well, darling," Fernando smiled. "What do you say? I'm game, as you say it, but it is really your wedding. A lady only gets married once, you know, and that day should be hers to . . ."

As Fernando's unfinished sentence floated out into the air, Maggie felt a second wave of excitement sweep over her; this time it was accompanied with a sense of peace, of knowing that the proposal was right. The Holy Spirit had permeated her own soul, and that meant only one thing—proceed.

Taking a deep breath, and swinging around while she took Fernando's hands in hers, she said, "Fernando, my handsome gaucho, I will thee wed . . . on the veranda of our ranch house, overlooking the red cliffs of Kanab. And I'll do it on June 23rd, in the company of your father, who just happens to be one of the most persuasive gentlemen I have met."

"Now you know why he gets so much accomplished," Fernando replied, squeezing her hands even more tightly. "But then again, he can see that a summer flying unmarried all over the country with you is a high risk proposition for his son—and he doesn't want me to take the chance of losing you."

They all laughed, and as Maggie buried her face in Fernando's chest, a sudden emotion swelled within her breast, and she began to softly cry. Never in her wildest imaginations had she anticipated the emotions she was now experiencing. Love was encompassing and compelling, she realized, and Fernando was the greatest miracle of her life.

Chapter Sixteen

The next three weeks for Fernando, Maggie, Don Hugo, and the Rockwell family were harried, to say the least. While Fernando and Maggie began preproduction work on the movie, Don Hugo flew back to New York and made major strides in solving the global difficulties his seemingly incompressible empire had been experiencing. His brother, Roberto, had orchestrated things beautifully from Buenos Aires, and through the long-distance help of Lord Jockham, the British government had likewise become involved. Doris and Wilford had returned to Arizona and with the aid of William, Maggie's younger brother, their ranch hands and friends, they had pulled off the impossible. They were prepared, both with food and decor, and never had the Rocking "R" Ranch looked so well-groomed and decorated.

There was no way that an outsider would have believed that the ranch itself was under siege—and in foreclosure. And for right now, neither Wilford nor Doris wanted to make that fact an issue. This was Maggie's day to be remembered, and they had pulled out all stops to make her proud and to be the perfect hosts to Fernando and his father. What they hadn't anticipated, as they drove their friend Dennis Barney's new Packard to the makeshift airstrip, was the surprise that was now only minutes away.

Fernando and Maggie had arrived in Maggie's rental car two days earlier. And now, as they stood next to the car by the side of the improvised landing strip, they were surprised when the anticipated plane appeared from the east. For, instead of the plane

Don Hugo had flown to Los Angeles three weeks before, descending was a strange-looking plane, the likes of which Fernando had never before seen.

The three-motor transport plane landed safely and taxied to a stop in the designated leveled field to their left. As it pulled broadside the waiting party, Fernando was even more puzzled with the German markings on the rear tail fin. The unrecogniz-able pilots waved their greetings, and the engines quickly shut down. As the propellers came to a stop, the side door opened, and an aluminum four-step ladder was lowered to the ground. Don Hugo soon appeared, smiling and waving like a little boy.

Fernando and the others waved back; and then, to Fernando's surprise, into the doorway appeared his younger brother, Ricardo. Fernando ran forward, quickly embraced his father before throwing his arms around Ricardo, each backslapping while they choked to hold in their tears. Before Fernando could grasp what was happening, out of the plane and down the steps descended his beautiful mother, Dame Helen San Martin. She smiled cheerfully at first, but upon making eye contact with Fernando, she exploded into a flood of tears.

Joyfully and emotionally the two embraced, kissing each other again and again.

"Mother," Fernando exclaimed, catching his breath, "I can't believe you're here! Where have you and Ricardo come from?"

"You know your father, Fernando," Dame Helen laughed, while still drying her tears. "He is always one for drama, and this had to be his surprise."

"Father, I—"

"Please forgive an old man for being selfish, Fernando. I had not seen our new JU 52 Junker—which I recently leased from the German government—so I sent your mother a cablegram requesting that she and Ricardo bring it up to the states. Its fuse-lage is topped with a corrugated metal roof, making it look somewhat like a flying barn. Its three radial engines are state-of-the-art and very dependable, even though it only travels 150 miles per hour. In addition, it has comfort that the world can't appreciate in this advanced year of 1936." ·

"Mother . . . Ricardo . . . let me introduce you to the most beautiful blonde in the world, and a family that has taught me more about being a gaucho in the past two days than I ever learned in the Pampas."

With that exaggerated setup, Fernando walked hand-in-hand with his mother, Dame Helen, and the four of them soon joined Maggie and her family in what each, in their own way, felt was truly a miraculous reunion. They also introduced themselves to the two German pilots—brothers, actually—Manfred and Seigfried Rudolph. These men, exhausted from several days of nearly nonstop travel, asked that they be excused from the day's activities and soon disappeared back inside the plane to take a long-overdue rest.

The following morning at precisely ten o'clock, Fernando sat nervously staring out the open window in Will's bedroom. A slight breeze caused the curtains to sway invitingly. Without thinking, Fernando walked over and knelt with his arms folded on the sill of the window. Looking out into the vacant north yard, he noticed a swarm of bees working their way through a patch of blooming rose bushes. At that instant, two humming-birds swooped into view. Immediately they began drinking from the pan of water that had been placed there for them, and Fernando marveled at how they could fly in a still position, their wings a mere blur of activity.

"Hello, big brother. Mind if I come in?"

It was Fernando's brother, Ricardo, and even as he spoke in a thickly accented English, he entered the room, closed the door, then positioned himself in the corner rocker.

"Hi, Ricardo," Fernando answered, while turning and sitting with his back against the wall beneath the window. "How're things shaping up out there?"

"People are coming in from all directions," Ricardo answered, smiling. "Tell me, Fernando, how does it feel?"

"You mean getting married?"

"Yes . . . to such a beautiful lady gaucho."

Both laughed, then Fernando replied. "Actually, she is even more beautiful on the inside than she is on the outside—if that's possible. She has taught me more about life and about love than I can ever articulate."

"What I love is her spirit," Ricardo added enthusiastically. "She is like a finely trained thoroughbred racehorse. It is as though she lights up the room whenever she enters."

"Thank you, Ricardo. I'll pass along your compliment."

"Fernando," Ricardo replied, a tone of nostalgia creeping into his voice. "Have you missed me as much as I've missed you?"

"Probably more, little brother. There has hardly been a day that I haven't thought of you, your boundless energy, your million-dollar smile, your wavy dark locks, and of course your . . . love."

Ricardo smiled appreciatively, then lowered his eyes to the floor while Fernando continued.

"I want to thank you, Ricardo . . . ."

"Thank me? For coming all the way from Buenos Aires just to meet your bride? *Por nada.* It is nothing."

"Well, for that, too. But mostly for forgiving me for the many mistakes I've made since leaving home. I really let you down . . . entangling myself in the middle of some harmful habits."

"I don't want to disillusion you, Fernando, but I've made my share of mistakes, too. As Mother has often said, we all do. But, deep down inside, I knew you would pull out of it. You're only the greatest man I know . . . and I get to always be your little brother."

Ricardo's words found their way quickly into Fernando's heart, and his eyes moistened. "I want to promise you, my brother, that I'm back. I'll never touch alcohol again as long as I live."

Ricardo paused as he searched for just the right words. Then

162

he continued, "I'm sure she has forgiven you, Fernando. In fact, from what Maggie told me last night, I suspect she is in paradise enjoying her new life, while taking full responsibility for her early departure here."

"You spoke with Maggie?"

"But, of course. You were in town with Mother, buying produce for today's festivities. Maggie is one remarkable woman."

"And, as you have found out firsthand, she's a very deep thinker. In fact, if I can shed a bit of my Argentine male pride, I will admit that she has caused me to explore my motives—and my emotions—more deeply than ever before. She just plunges into deep water as though she were born to it."

"Well, I'm not dating anyone in particular right now, but after meeting Maggie, the woman I choose will have to be pretty special for me to fall in love with her."

"Maggie's father came up with what Americans call a one-liner. He said that it is better to aim at the sun and miss, than to aim at a pile of manure and hit it."

"He said that?"

"He's always saying things like that. It's corny, I know, but it still rings with truth, and I highly recommend the notion."

"Well, big brother," Ricardo sighed, "it sounds like the natives are restless out there, so perhaps we'd better go."

As both brothers stood to leave, they looked lovingly into each other's eyes, then embraced. It was a fierce embrace, with back-slapping and pure Latin tears. They had missed each other, and each in his own way hoped that their future would be kind, and that they would be able to enjoy their renewed friendship.

"It's time, gentlemen." The intruder was Maggie's brother, Will. "It seems my room here was made for brothers—me included."

"You're a fine man," Fernando responded, slapping Will on the back. "Ricardo and I were just having a little premarriage chat, if you know what I mean."

"I really don't know what you mean, although when I bite the dust, Maggie had better be around here to send me safely into that crazy world out there."

With that, the three men left the room, and went out into the gathering crowd.

Maggie was upstairs in her own room, putting on the same wedding gown her mother had worn twenty-seven years earlier. It was form-fitted, with a white lace overlay that her grand-mother had hand-sewn over a five-year period before her mother's marriage. It was a priceless treasure, and Maggie smiled as she looked into the mirror, knowing that her grandmother's gift of sacrifice was now hers.

"You look absolutely stunning," her mother whispered. "Now, if I can just pin this in back here . . ."

As her mother made final adjustments on the dress, Maggie stared at herself in the mirror. Her radiant blonde hair cascaded over her shoulders, accentuating her tanned, olive complexion. She had brushed her lips with the newest Hollywood natural color of lipstick and had even rubbed a little rouge onto her naturally rosy cheeks.

"Katie Morris surely worked hard to make you a new veil," Doris said, almost in a whisper. "She wanted to thank you for all you have done for her four daughters. She really sees you as their role model, you know."

"I know she does," Maggie sighed, "yet I feel so undeserving. I just loved her daughters, especially Elizabeth and Carolyn, just like they were my younger sisters."

"Regardless," Doris concluded, "you have an unusual gift of influencing others, Maggie, and I feel the Lord will have you working with the young women in the Church wherever you may live. It is part of your destiny."

"Mother," Maggie countered, "whoever I am, I owe to you and Dad . . . and of course, the Lord. You have been my very best friend, Mother, and all that I am, I owe to you and your example. You are so close to my heart . . . my heroine, if I can borrow a term from Hollywood."

"Maggie, you really have grown during these past two years in California. But, do you know what?"

"What, Mother?"

"You're still my little girl."

At once, mother and daughter melted into each other's arms, their eyes moist with love, and a bond of trust between them that would reach deep into the eternities. The moment was brief, yet compelling for them both. At last, drawing back, Doris caressed Maggie's hair, placing it perfectly upon her shoulders.

"Mother," Maggie blurted, looking out the window, "Katie and Dan just pulled up in front. In fact, I think everyone's out there, ready to begin."

"Your father said he would let us know when Bishop Barney and his wife, Ann, arrive. He is such a great bishop—a gentle, Christ-like giant, I call him—and I appreciate Fernando not insisting on a Catholic ceremony."

"Religion is a new thing for Fernando, Mother. Somehow, I think the social customs and traditions of the Argentines prevents men from taking things too seriously. One day, though, on the Lord's timetable, I feel Fernando will embrace the gospel and allow us to have a temple marriage."

"Oh, I hope so, Maggie, as does your father. But, at least you'll be able to tell your children that you were true to your feelings, even though you weren't able to initially marry in the holy temple.

"Now, Maggie," she continued, taking her daughter's hands in hers, "perhaps if we could change the subject. I have just a couple of things I'd like to say . . . ."

"Yes, Mother," Maggie looked at her expectantly.

"The festivities will begin shortly; but before they do, I want to say that I think you have found one of the finest young men in the world. Fernando is so polite, so sensitive."

"Thank you, Mother. I think so, too."

"But there's something more, Maggie, and I think I've put a handle to what I've been feeling about him. I think, that in addition to his virtue, Fernando is presenting you with the greatest gift that a man could give to his bride. It is a gift that few men master in a lifetime, let alone while in their twenties. It is the gift of honesty. I truly believe that Fernando does not have the capacity to tell a falsehood."

The profound depth of her statement stunned Maggie because she had not expected her mother to say anything of the sort. But, she was right. Fernando was a truth-teller, and she felt totally safe in the things he told her. Still, until that moment she had had no idea of the importance her mother placed on this trait.

"You should know, Mother. You have often expressed how appreciative you have been that Dad has been a man of his word. But I must say, I'm surprised that you would mention this in particular. . . ."

"Well," Doris continued, motioning for Maggie to sit down on the window ledge, "there are two more things I would like to say . . . ."

"Please do . . . I'm just so nervous . . . ."

"The first, actually, is very personal. It is about you, Maggie . . . about us, as women. We're built quite different than men, you know . . . ."

"Oh, Mother, stop embarrassing me."

"I don't mean physically," Doris laughed, "but emotionally. Men are at times more sensible, more rational, as it were. Women, on the other hand, lead with their emotions. Being emotional creatures, we are able to give a depth of loving attention to our children that is necessary. The Lord created us this way, so we should rejoice in it. But this gift is a two-edge sword, Maggie, and one that must be handled with great care."

"What do you mean, Mother?" Maggie asked.

"What I mean is that if we allow our mood swings to get the best of us, then we compromise the intimate expressions our husbands appreciate. We don't need to check in and out of our marriage . . . emotionally, I mean. We must learn to put our husbands first, even when our emotions suggest otherwise. I have found that by doing this, your father likewise makes a greater effort to fulfill my needs—even when he is consumed with so many obligations on the ranch. Just make Fernando your theme, Maggie, and your marriage will blossom and flourish just as ours has done."

Wilford called from the base of the stairs. "Ya'll ready? The Barneys are here, and folks are anxious to begin."

Smiling, and adding just a touch of powder to her cheeks, Maggie embraced her mother, fought back further emotion, then proceeded to lift her skirt and petticoats a few inches from the floor so she wouldn't trip over them as she descended the stairs.

Reaching the bottom step, Maggie's father handed her the bouquet of beautiful roses. They were a deep red and had been given as a gift by Bishop Barney's wife, Ann. She had cut them early that morning, so they would be fresh, and she had fashioned them with an elegant white ribbon. Pausing, Maggie and her mother both smelled the inviting fragrance. They smiled, Doris left, and Maggie and Wilford waited to make their entrance.

Fernando had joined the nearly hundred guests, and now found his heart leaping almost into his throat, as the live band music began. The entire backyard had been decorated for the occasion, and the blossoming flower garden provided a scent which was purely intoxicating. The daffodils were especially lovely, long rows of them, and served as the backdrop for the ceremony, itself.

"Stand over here by me," Bishop Barney suggested to Fernando, his voice too deep for a whisper. "That way you'll be able to see your bride as she appears through the back door."

Even as the kindly bishop spoke, Fernando gazed in fixed anticipation as Maggie stepped out onto the veranda. She smiled broadly in Fernando's direction, took her father's arm, and slowly and gracefully descended the three stairs onto the back lawn.

"Well," Fernando whispered, forgetting his close proximity to Bishop Barney, "if you aren't the most beautiful creation in the universe, I don't know what is."

"Are you speaking to me?" the lay bishop queried, smiling over at Fernando.

"Pardon me, sir," Fernando coughed, realizing that the man's attempt at humor had indeed been embarrassing.

"Just kidding . . . trying to loosen you up, is all. You were speaking of my wife, Ann, of course . . . ."

"Well, her, too," Fernando whispered, realizing that their private conversation needed to cease since Maggie and her father were approaching them.

Seconds later, Maggie stopped directly in front of the bishop and looked up into Fernando's eyes. The music faded and Bishop Barney began.

"It's a very special pleasure for Ann and me to be here today," he began, "especially to see that Maggie takes the mighty leap into the right man's arms."

Everyone laughed, enjoying the homespun humor of their dear friend and clergyman. Dennis Barney had moved his family up from Gilbert, Arizona only two years earlier, after involving himself with a commercial tourist venture at the famous Grand Canyon. In that time, he had endeared himself to everyone he met. A huge man physically, his smile and his heart was as large as his frame; and his commonsense approach to life made it very compelling to like him and to listen to what he had to say.

It had come as a surprise to no one, really, that only three weeks earlier Bishop Barney had been selected to lead the newly formed Fredonia Ward. His genuine love for people made him the only choice for the one to marry them to each other. Although Maggie had met him just briefly the summer before, her parents had entered a horsebreeding venture with him and had become the Barneys' closest friends.

Bishop Barney continued uninterrupted; then, after providing a good fifteen minutes of marital advice to the bride and groom, he performed the actual ceremony. When he concluded, he invited Fernando and Maggie to kiss, which they readily did—with a lingering tenderness that caused all in attendance to giggle and laugh amongst themselves.

Finally, after what seemed like forever—although it lasted only a few seconds—Fernando released Maggie from his arms and smiled broadly to those in attendance.

"You won't need counseling on how to love each other," the bishop teased, "and so we'll simply proceed to the exchange of rings. Just remember," he added honestly, "that if you keep your love alive, and if you are true to yourselves, you will always enjoy the peace that your hearts now hold."

With that, the rings were exchanged. Each was a sparkling gold band, which the bishop explained represented the eternal circle of their love—with no end. The metaphor was not lost on either of them. They then shared a second, though equally compelling kiss, and an even more encompassing embrace.

In response, the guests clapped excitedly, then arose and immediately formed a line in which to greet the bride and groom. The day was perfect—a brilliant blue sky, kindly smiling faces, extended hands of friendship, and of course, the forming of a new family unit. It truly was a day never to be forgotten.

Chapter Seventeen

That evening, seven miles to the north and in a small rough-hewn log honeymoon cottage on the outskirts of the hamlet of Kanab, Utah, Fernando and Maggie snuggled together on the divan. A cool breeze swept through the open windows, sending a slight shiver through them.

"Penny for your thoughts, darling," Maggie whispered, breaking the magical silence that filled the room.

"That's what you asked on our first date," Fernando reminded her teasingly.

"Oh, so I've married a man with an elephant's memory," Maggie teased, poking her finger into Fernando's ribs.

"Let's just hope my nose doesn't keep growing," Fernando quipped, "although with your ranch-style cooking, I'm afraid that I'm in for a lengthy and active nasal lifetime."

"Well," Maggie countered, "as a friend of mine would say, 'No one knows what the nose knows—speak, beak.'"

Again they laughed, and then Fernando became suddenly very somber.

"Maggie, darling," he began in earnest, "I . . . I never dreamed life could be so filled with energy . . . and with promise."

"You are an old romantic, aren't you, sweetheart?" she responded, her own mind searching for a way to respond.

"Fernando," she added, not waiting for his reply, "can it always be like this? Our emotions, I mean."

"I surely hope so, Maggie, although from what our folks were telling each other, it gets even better."

"'Deeper and richer,' I think your father said," Maggie added, closing her eyes in quiet reverie.

Just then, Maggie burst out laughing, instantly changing the mood.

"Penny for your thoughts, ma'am," Fernando asked, mimicking Maggie's western accent.

"Oh, it's nothing really," Maggie answered, "only a silly poem that my father has repeated over the years."

"Well, then, let's hear it," Fernando pleaded. "It seems you're full of one-liners today. So, if it's that funny, I've got to hear it."

"Very well, I memorized it one night while I was milking the cows, so I'll try to recite it correctly. It goes like this:

> *A bride white of hair*
> *Stooped over her cane,*
> *Her footsteps need guiding.*
>
> *While down the church aisle*
> *With a wan, toothless smile*
> *The groom in his wheelchair came riding.*
>
> *And who is this elderly couple thus wed?*
> *You'll find when you've closely explored it—*
> *That here is that rare, most conservative pair*
> *Who waited 'til they could afford it.*

Fernando laughed out loud, as did Maggie, then suddenly became very serious.

"Your father has a great sense of humor, sweetheart," he began, searching for what to say. "But . . . perhaps this is the time we should deal with it."

"Deal with what?" Maggie countered, not understanding.

"Well, deal with me. You see, Maggie," he continued, clearing his throat, while pausing to sip a glass of Maggie's freshly squeezed orange juice, "last night, when my father and I took our walk into your orchard, he gave me a piece of paper. It was a reinstatement, Maggie, a document that placed me squarely in the middle of my parents' will."

"But . . . what does that mean, darling?" Maggie asked breathlessly.

"It means, Maggie, that you are married to a different man than you imagined. Yesterday we could hardly afford the gas to travel the last hundred miles from St. George. Today, without having any say about it, you and I are worth more money than I can even comprehend. Father conservatively places our net worth in the millions and has opened a $400,000 savings account for us in Los Angeles."

To say that Fernando's disclosure sent a shockwave throughout Maggie's system would be a clear understatement. She was totally dumbfounded by his all-too-casual announcement, and strangely she found herself resenting the disclosure.

"So, does this mean that we change our lifestyle, Fernando?. . . that we are forced to live our lives at your father's beck and call?. . . that he now controls us?"

Maggie's words stung Fernando deeply, cutting away at the very core of his character. To be placed in such an unexpected position was something that had appeared from nowhere, and he could see that if he didn't quickly resolve it, their unexpected affluence could destroy the mutual dependency he and Maggie shared with each other.

The silence that fell upon them became thick and ominous, forcing each to consider the words they had just spoken and to try to search for a reply.

At last, after what must have been ten full minutes of only a nearby cricket chirping, Maggie took a deep breath. "Fernando, I'm sorry if I hurt you. I truly didn't mean what I said. It's just that I blurted out the first thought that came into my mind."

"Please don't be hard on yourself, Maggie," Fernando replied, smiling warmly with Maggie's gentle reply. "I really think we're filled with more character than to change our relationship just because of money."

"If we do what your father has done?" Maggie blurted, interrupting him, while surprising them both with her unexpected boldness.

"What do you mean, Maggie? What has Father done?"

"Well, darling, from what you've told me, your father doesn't feel like he owns anything. Didn't you use the word stewardship? Don't your parents regard their wealth a stewardship, rather than an ownership they can selfishly hoard?"

"You were listening that night, weren't you, Maggie." Fernando's reply was more a statement than a question, and Maggie was inwardly pleased with how she had processed his words.

"Your telling me about your parents' wealth, and the almost incomprehensible holdings they have, didn't change a thing for me, Fernando. It really didn't. Oh, I would be less than honest if I didn't say that I was jealous, at first—although not for myself."

"What does that mean, Maggie? What are you saying?"

"Oh, just that I felt a twinge of jealousy for my parents, knowing how they were sacrificing to even be in California, knowing their ranch was on the chopping block."

"How much do you trust me, Maggie?"

Fernando's question came out of the blue, and Maggie paused in her thoughts to again process his question.

"About as far as I can throw you . . . that is, if I were holding you on the edge of the Grand Canyon."

Again both laughed, smashing the wall of tension into smithereens. Fernando cupped Maggie's face in his hands, following a custom that was now several months old. Then, kissing her affectionately, he replied, "Remind me to never allow you to carry me when we're near the Grand Canyon . . . or any canyon, for that matter. But seriously, darling, I need you to express your trust in what I have to say."

Realizing that Fernando was dead serious, Maggie nodded

agreeably, and said, "I do, Fernando . . . lock, stock, and barrel."

"Whatever that means," Fernando smiled.

"It means *with my life*," Maggie stated emphatically. Then, speaking almost in a whisper, she added, "Please tell me what *you* mean, darling."

"Very well," Fernando replied, stroking her hair with his fingers, as though they were a comb. "I've thought a great deal of how our net worth can affect us, and I would like to propose that we use our money discreetly, and with the intent of quietly sharing it to lift the burdens of debt from others. . . ."

"What a wonderful idea," Maggie sighed, again closing her eyes. "Please, go on."

"Well, Maggie, I don't think I could live with myself if I knew I had the ability to ease your parents' financial burdens at this time and didn't. In respect of their privacy, and so our relationship with them won't change, I would like to propose that we wire in the funds, anonymously pay off the mortgage, then instruct the bank to send your parents the deed."

"And, if they ever ask us if we're the culprits?"

"We'll just admit it and tell them it was Mother and Father's payment for passing the cumbersome stewardship of their son over to you. We'll then swear them to secrecy, give them a giant *abrazo,* and tell them how much we love them."

"Oh, Fernando, I don't really know what to say. I . . . "As Maggie spoke, her voice cracked, and a sudden tear worked its way down her cheek. Their prayers had been answered, but in a totally unexpected way. The thought of her parents not having to move, and of preserving their dignity and self-respect at this time in their lives, was overwhelming.

"There's one more thing, Maggie . . . ."

Fernando's words hung suspended between them. As Maggie looked up at him, he added casually, "We now have the means to sponsor you in the Bendix Cup race."

Chapter Eighteen

The following morning, after enjoying a leisurely breakfast at the town's only cafe, Fernando and Maggie climbed into their rented '33 Chevrolet Roadster and drove north. They wanted to see the spectacular Zion's National Park, and after winding their way the seventeen miles up through the canyon on Highway 89, they reached Mount Carmel Junction. They then turned left onto Highway 9, crossed what was identified as the Virgin River, and proceeded through the mountains to a giant rock formation that had been named the East Temple. Here they had lunch—a picnic Maggie's mother had prepared for them the day before— and they enjoyed a brief walk along the floor of the canyon.

Although they planned on traveling west and then into St. George for the night, Maggie suddenly felt a constricting in her throat, sensing a foreboding like she had never known before.

"I can't explain what I'm feeling, darling," she whispered, barely able to get the words out of her mouth. "But neither can I ignore my fears."

"Perhaps you're just climbing down from the emotional high we've been on these past two days, and that you're—"

"It's not that," Maggie interrupted, surprising herself with how abruptly she spoke. "I've never felt this way before, and I'm thinking that perhaps we should go back to the ranch—"

"Back to Fredonia? But we're well on our way to Los Angeles."

"I know, darling, I know." Maggie could feel her voice soften, as just the thought of returning to Arizona seemed to remove the pit of discomfort that was in her stomach.

"Well, then," Fernando sighed, his disappointment almost as great as his desire to respond to Maggie's impressions. "Let's be on our way."

When Maggie didn't reply, Fernando stopped the car in the middle of the dirt road. Backing up, he worked his way from shoulder to shoulder and finally projected the car back toward where they had just come from. Putting the roadster into first gear, he accelerated, and soon they were moving along at a full 40 miles per hour.

Two hours later, as Fernando and Maggie rounded the bend which headed south out of Kanab, Maggie saw something that caught her eye.

"Fernando," she gasped, "that's Father's truck!"

Glancing to the side of the road, Fernando instantly recognized not only the truck, but Ricardo and Will standing next to it, waving. But they weren't just waving. They were shouting and running out to the road, signaling for them to stop.

Slamming on the brakes, Fernando backed up and swung to the right shoulder of the highway, stopping only a few feet from where Ricardo and Will were now standing.

"What's going on?" Maggie called out, as she rolled down the window.

"It's Father," Ricardo shouted in English. "We've got to get back to the ranch. Father's had a heart attack, and the doctor's not sure he's going to make it."

"Why don't you climb in, Ricardo, and ride with us."

"Is he still at the ranch?" Maggie asked.

"Yes, he's resting in Mom and Dad's bedroom. Dr. Fielding and Fernando's mother are there and we just took off in hopes of somehow running into you. Manfred and Seigfried wanted to take the plane up and see if they could locate your car that way. We thought we'd check out Kanab first, and started out."

Ricardo climbed into the backseat of the roadster, and Will ran back to his truck. Then the two automobiles sped down the seven-mile stretch toward Fredonia. As they passed the state line, Ricardo detailed the tragic events to Fernando and Maggie, omitting only Dame Helen's emotional outburst at the moment of the attack.

"Well, Maggie," Fernando said gratefully, "now we know why you were having those feelings. Don't let me ever discourage you from doing what you think we should."

Fernando's words echoed resoundingly in Maggie's ears. "I'm so sorry, darling. I just hope he'll be all right."

"He's in God's hands," Ricardo said slowly. "I just wish he weren't in such great pain."

"How is Mother taking it?" Fernando asked. "Is she okay?"

"She's being her usual strong self," Ricardo replied. "She won't leave his side, and Mrs. Rockwell is a great help, as well."

"When did it happen? . . . The heart attack, I mean."

"This morning about nine. Mr. Rockwell had just taken some cattle over to Pipe Spring. I don't know if he's back yet, or not, since we left for Kanab a couple of hours ago."

They rode a little longer in silence, and then Fernando turned to Maggie.

"I guess this is a time for faith, Maggie."

"Yes, and trust. We need to pray in our hearts, trusting the Lord's will be done."

Ricardo, leaning forward in the back seat, looked first at Maggie, and then at Fernando. *Faith? Trust?* What had happened to this older brother of his? Even speaking the words seemed so foreign, so out of character from not only Ricardo's frame of reference, but from his perception of who Fernando was. In truth, his mind could not assimilate the exchange that had just taken place.

Fernando spotted the ranch house and pushed lightly on the brake. Coming to a near stop and seeing that Will was right behind him, Fernando turned to the right and wound up the lane to the Rockwell home.

Stopping the vehicles in a cloud of dust, all four climbed out of their automobiles and ran to the house and entered. Will led the way, and one-by-one they bounded up the stairs. Once on the balcony, they slowed to a walk and soon were tiptoeing into the master bedroom.

"Mother," Fernando whispered urgently, kneeling next to the rocking chair where Dame Helen was napping. "Mother, are you awake?"

Dame Helen slowly opened her eyes, coming gradually out of a deep sleep. Realizing that the voice she had heard was Fernando's, she reached out and took his hand.

"Oh, Fernando," she said, making barely audible her words. "Ricardo found you?"

"Yes, Mother." Ricardo answered for him, then knelt next to Fernando before their mother.

"How is he?" Fernando asked, pleadingly.

"He is heavily sedated, as you can see, but the last time we spoke, he was in a great deal of pain."

"Helen . . ." Don Hugo cleared his throat as he pushed the word out of his mouth.

"Father?" It was Fernando who spoke, at the same time walking on his knees to Don Hugo's bedside. Ricardo and Maggie followed him and stood behind him as Fernando took his father's hand.

"Fernando . . . Maggie . . . they found you . . . ."

The huskiness in his voice brought Maggie's emotions to the surface. During the brief days she had known her new father-in-law, she had come to love his gravely voice. Now, as he fought for his very life, he sounded little like the Don Hugo she had grown to love and revere.

Although Fernando knew his father would be exhausted from his ordeal, nothing had prepared him for the almost unimaginable effort needed for Don Hugo to speak.

"You'll be all right, Father," Ricardo whispered from where he was standing. "It is a miracle that Maggie and Fernando are here."

"A miracle is right," Dame Helen said from where she sat in her rocker. "My prayers have been answered, and Hugo will now be just fine."

I have something to say to you, *mis muchachos* . . . ." Don Hugo spoke to his two sons. "Your *madre* is so proud of you both, as am I . . . ."

Don Hugo's voice seemed to be gathering strength, and as he spoke, he clasped Fernando's hand more tightly.

"Thank you, Father," Fernando answered solemnly. Don Hugo's words were plainly spoken, but carried such warmth and love that Fernando was swept with emotion. However, before he, or any of the others in the room could speak further, Don Hugo continued.

"I have lived such a good life . . . drinking from the love of the most beautiful woman in the world—equalled only by your beauty, Maggie . . . ."

Don Hugo's endearment, both to Dame Helen and Maggie, was met with smiles. He was starting to reveal his Latin humor, which meant recovery, for sure.

"Does your chest still pain you, Father?" Ricardo asked.

"Please, son, don't take me away from my thoughts . . . ."

Don Hugo's response surprised everyone present, especially Maggie's mother who had just entered the room with a new set of damp towels. He was surely feeling better, Doris reasoned. Without speaking, and with these thoughts in her mind, she replaced the towels on his forehead and chest, then retreated behind Dame Helen's rocker.

"Thank you, Mother," Maggie whispered, for the first time making eye contact with Doris. "Is Dad home yet?"

"No, but Manfred and Seigfried just returned from town, and they say he is on his way."

The two German brothers had been quickly briefed as to the goings-on at the ranch and had been most helpful in first alerting Doctor Fielding to Don Hugo's attack.

"Tell those men to keep the Junker ready. I'll be ready to fly by tomorrow morning."

Hearing Don Hugo's words brought a sense of relief to those present, and he smiled and winked at Fernando as he continued.

"My chest . . . it is feeling better. . . . Now, where was I? Oh, yes, I was just thinking about the first time your mother and I kissed . . . . It was a passionate Argentine kiss, for sure . . . ." He gave a little laugh, and seeing that he was accomplishing his goal of easing the anxiety in the room, Don Hugo briefly closed his eyes. Drawing a deep breath of restorative air into his lungs, he added, "Fernando, you have been gone from our home for what seems like forever . . . ."

"I know, Father, and after the race, Maggie and I—"

"Let me finish, please. Maggie, your future almost has a life of its own. It is different from what I am used to. But that is okay. You are a woman of destiny, and as you soar through the skies, I will be there to help . . . ."

Her eyes brimming with tears, Maggie could only place her hand over her mouth and listen. Making every effort to understand, Fernando spoke, "We are thankful for the deposit, Father, and our friend Roscoe will indeed keep you in mind when purchasing the right plane for Maggie. You will be with her, in spirit, even from Buenos Aires."

Fernando had spoken with emphasis, and he smiled warmly into Don Hugo's eyes, confirming what his father had just said.

"I mean . . ." Don Hugo continued, this time taking two short breaths before finishing his sentence, "that I will really be with you . . . but only if you ask . . . ."

"Thank you," Maggie answered, not knowing how to respond to his puzzling words. "I have already decided to name the plane *Don Hugo*, after you. I will need the additional power your name will provide . . . ."

"That's marvelous, Maggie," Fernando replied, turning and looking up into her eyes.

"Now, before I go on . . ." Don Hugo again breathed deeply, his eyes focused directly on Dame Helen. "Helen, *mi amor,* please come over and sit by my side. These children aren't old enough to hear what I'm going to say to you."

Obediently, yet puzzled by her husband's request, Dame Helen immediately arose and walked to the other side of the bed. Then, sitting lightly so as not to upset him, she grasped his other hand, bent down, and kissed him gently on the cheek.

"I love you so much, darling." Dame Helen's words were barely audible, but understood by everyone.

"And I, you," Don Hugo answered, smiling bravely. "Now, come closer. . . ."

Dame Helen leaned over again, only this time placing her ear next to Don Hugo's lips. Whispering what the others sensed were words of love, Don Hugo finally stopped speaking and closed his eyes. Dame Helen, suddenly realizing what he had said, buried her face in her hands and wept.

Without waiting for the others to respond, Don Hugo turned back toward Fernando and spoke, "My eldest son, you have given your father so much honor with your accomplishments. I shall cherish our days in America together . . . and the memory of your beautiful marriage . . . . In addition, I have felt a spirit in this home that is . . . how do you say? . . . different. I don't know what that difference is, son, but find it, and build it into your home."

"I know what you mean, Father," Fernando replied, while a sense of foreboding began to swell within his chest, "and I will. Besides, you and Maggie and I will have many more days together this coming year. Why, we may even bring you a grand-son to play with, when we come to visit you."

Maggie, deeply moved by Fernando's words, simply dug her fingers into his shoulders, while remaining silent. Her eyes were welling up again, and it was all she could do to keep swallowing back her emotions. Don Hugo's conversation was direct and nostalgic, to be sure; but his statements made no sense, not when—

"Ahhhh!!! Mi padre!!!" With those agonizing words escaping

loudly from his mouth, Don Hugo arched his shoulders back and threw his arms directly above him into the air. Then, grimacing in obvious pain, he slowly slumped back into the waiting arms of his wife and eldest son. After three short breaths, he paused for several seconds, and finally drew an unusually long breath. At that instant, while those in the room gazed in horror, Don Hugo slowly released the air from his lungs for the last time. He then quietly slipped away, the corners of his mouth lifting subtly into a smile of infinite sweetness.

Dame Helen, overcome with grief, buried her face into his neck and sobbed uncontrollably. Maggie took her hands from Fernando's shoulders and made her way to the other side of the bed and gently caressed Dame Helen's hair, weeping with her.

Fernando continued to kneel at his father's side, clutching the lifeless hand, betrayed by his own tears which now cascaded unashamedly down his cheeks. Ricardo also wept, then replaced Fernando, as the eldest son arose and motioned him forward.

Stunned, Will remained silent, and he placed his arm comfortingly around his mother's shoulders. Doris buried her face in his chest, allowing the emotion to gently sweep over her. The father of her new son-in-law was gone. She must now give comfort to her new friend, Helen, and to Helen's two sons. "If only Wilford were here," she whispered, allowing only Will to hear her plea. "We need him so badly . . . ."

Wilford did return, although not until an hour later. By this time the Rockwells had left the room and sent for the mortician, while Dame Helen, Fernando, and Ricardo continued to remain with Don Hugo's lifeless form. Each in their own way prayed quietly, giving comfort to the others during what proved to be the most difficult hour in their lives.

Finally, when Miles Anderson, the funeral director, arrived with the hearse, they left the room and came down the stairs to meet with him.

"I-I don't know what we should do," Dame Helen stammered, searching for answers.

"Perhaps we should bury him here," Ricardo replied. "After all, that is our custom."

"What is your custom?" Wilford asked. "What do you mean?"

"Well," Fernando interrupted, "in Latin America, we do no embalming. It is our law that a person's remains must be buried within twenty-four hours of death, and so there is no need for preservation."

As Fernando spoke, even his very words seemed so cold, so distant from his emotions. He couldn't bear the thought of his mother having to return to Argentina without his father. It just wasn't right.

"Mr. Anderson," he continued, taking in a deep breath of air as he spoke, "could you prepare Father's remains, as is your custom, and then allow him to accompany Mother and Ricardo back to Buenos Aires?"

"Yes," the mortician answered kindly, "that will be no problem at all. We could have him ready by tomorrow morning—perhaps even bring him back here for a short memorial service. It is your choice. As to preserving his remains, our methods are the very latest, and his body will be fine for the return trip."

"Oh, my darling," Dame Helen whispered, tears once again forming as though she were speaking to her husband. "We'll take you home where you belong."

Moving to where his mother sat, Ricardo placed his hand on her shoulder, then gently rubbed her back. It would be a difficult flight home, to be sure, but he knew that he would be given strength. This was the least he could do so that Fernando could meet his obligations with the movie company and assist Maggie in her race.

"Thank you very much, Mr. Anderson," Fernando added. "I'm sure Bishop Barney would conduct a memorial for us—a brief one, as Father would have directed."

"Yes," Doris replied quickly, "I'm sure he would."

The next several hours were spent in quiet reflection and preparation. Fernando, numb from the tragedy at hand, spent part of the afternoon with just his mother and brother. They took a long walk into the orchard, reminiscing about memories of their youth, and reflecting on Don Hugo's gentle, yet powerful personality. Sensing their need to be alone together, Maggie busied herself with cleaning the house for the next morning's services.

Nighttime finally arrived, and following dinner, Fernando and Ricardo accompanied Will on his round of chores. It had been several years since Fernando had milked a cow, and so, graciously obliging his guest, Will stepped aside when they got to the barn and allowed Fernando the task of milking their cow, Sally. Ricardo, remembering similar times from their youth, routinely grabbed and held onto Sally's tail. It was filled with cockleburs, but that didn't matter. It felt good to be with be with his elder brother, and they shared their thoughts and feelings while the milking took place.

Afterward, the three returned, without speaking, to the house. Under Will's supervision, the milk was strained and placed in the icebox to keep it cold and to allow the cream to rise during the night. After washing the bucket and straining cloth, they removed their shoes and entered the house.

"Have Manfred and Siegfried left yet?" Doris asked, breaking the silence which had loomed in the kitchen.

"They went to the bunkhouse right after dinner," Ricardo replied. "Said they needed a good night's rest before tomorrow's five-day marathon."

"They're such fine young men," Dame Helen replied softly. "I just hope we're not putting too great a pressure on them by flying straight through."

"Actually," Ricardo replied, "when we talked about that, they indicated that this was their preference. I have my pilot's license, and I'll spell them off as copilot, so they can take their turns sleeping."

"Thank goodness for that Junker," Fernando added. "I've never ridden in a plane like that, but with how it's set up, you should get plenty of rest as you wind your way south."

"Did they speak of our routing?"

Dame Helen had made the inquiry, and Fernando knew she was worried about returning a different route than the one they had taken just days earlier.

"I have it right here," Ricardo interjected, pulling a yellow sheet of paper from his shirt pocket. "Let's see . . . okay, let me read it."

"If you would, please," Dame Helen pressed, her anxiety very visible on her face.

"First, we fly directly south to Nogales, Mexico. We'll have to check in with customs there, then get clearance to Guadalajara. After refueling, we'll fly to Acapulco, then on to Guatemala City."

"I can't believe all the stops," Maggie said in amazement.

"It's a lot farther to Buenos Aires than one would think," Fernando replied, smiling.

"Well," Ricardo continued, "from Guatemala, we travel to the Panama Canal, and refuel at the military base. The canal, itself, will be spectacular to see from the air. It's been in use now for several years, so we should see ships actually moving through it.

"Anyway, from there we fly to Guayaquil, Ecuador, then to Lima, Peru. I know that sounds exhausting, but we will take an extra long rest in Lima—say, four or five hours. Then we'll fly directly to Antofagasta, Chile. From there, we'll need to refuel in Santiago, then head due east."

"From what I learned in geography," Fernando interjected, "that should be the most beautiful leg of the journey."

"I think so, brother. We fly across the Andes in the shadow of Aconcagua Mountain. It's the tallest mountain in all of the Americas—only 1,000 feet shorter than Mount Everest. From what Manfred and Seigfried have been told, we will make it all the way to Buenos Aires—that is, if the weather holds out."

Wilford joined in the conversation. "I haven't even seen inside the plane. Does it just have the twenty seats installed, or has it been customized?"

"Father leased it with a full custom interior already installed," Ricardo replied. "There are four beds—two sets of bunk beds, and a sitting area with a sofa and two swivel chairs. There are also four regular seats—two on each side near the front. But, I doubt we'll use them. There is a large storage section to the rear, and we'll place Father's casket there. We won't be breaking any speed limits at 150 miles per hour, but with the personalized comfort, it shouldn't be too tiring."

The rest of the evening was spent in visiting, and then for most of the household, the night was long and sleepless. Although Dame Helen was experiencing the greatest sense of loneliness, she was actually able to get more sleep than the others. Her body, having exhausted itself throughout the long ordeal of the day, seemed to shut down, and for that she was grateful. Fernando, on the other hand, slept less than anyone. Not only was his mind pressed to consider the sudden emptiness in his heart, but he rehearsed again and again the miracle of having resolved their relationship prior to Don Hugo's passing. His mind went from this to Maggie, then to the filming and the race. So many issues presented themselves, that it was at the crack of dawn that he was finally able to relax and slip into slumber.

All who attended the memorial services felt a genuine outpouring of love and encouragement. It was held in the large sitting room to the rear of the Rockwell home, and, because it had rained lightly during the night, a cool breeze brought relief to the otherwise warm and balmy mid-summer morning.

At one point in the services, Bishop Barney paid special tribute to Don Hugo by saying, "The great philosopher, Plato, died in the year 348 B.C. Aristotle was his protegé, just as he had been Socrates' protegé. Anyway, Aristotle was invited to give the eulogy at Plato's memorial service. Not long ago I read this eulogy, as he said 'Plato showed us by his life that to be happy is to be good.'"

Then the bishop concluded, "From what I have learned about Don Hugo San Martin Braun, he has also shown us this key to happiness. His life was one of doing good to others, especially those who had special needs. The Rocking 'R' Ranch will never be the same after having had him spend his final hours treating each of us in that same selfless manner. He is, after all, one who truly learned to live as the Savior taught. His life was indeed a sermon for each of us."

Further words were also expressed, both by Wilford and by Fernando. When the services finally ended, each member of the San Martin family knew they had witnessed something different—something good—that had lifted their spirits and given each of them a sense of peace.

Then, before Fernando realized it, the time came for his family's departure. They had used a crane from the hayloft to lift the corrugated top from the plane and had then placed Don Hugo's casket safely in the rear cargo area. After strapping it into place, the family exchanged hugs and kisses, each side making a commitment to have a reunion in Buenos Aires within the year. Dame Helen especially insisted that such a trip would be their treat, and that Doris come down and spend at least a month with her. She concluded by insisting that she would send the Junker back for them whenever their schedule permitted.

And so, after watching the large three-motor transport plane taxi down the again cordoned-off highway, Fernando and Maggie quickly prepared a second picnic lunch and bade farewell to Maggie's family.

"Be sure to write," Maggie called, as the roadster moved slowly down the lane toward the main road.

"I will, darling," Maggie's mother called back. Their arms were waving long after either of the two could see each other, and their hearts pined for the day when they would once again be together as a family.

"You know," Fernando said, as they turned onto the road and headed north toward Kanab, "the thing I enjoyed most at the services was Bishop Barney's remarks. He is such a warm-spirited man, and I can surely see how his congregation elected him to serve as their leader."

"Well," Maggie countered, "he wasn't exactly elected, Fernando. He was chosen, through the prayers of other Church leaders, and was then sustained by the members."

"However he was called," Fernando smiled, "it had to have been with God's approval. That man is truly a follower of Christ."

"Which part of his sermon did you enjoy most?" Maggie asked with interest.

"I think his quote about Plato," Fernando answered. "That was quite a statement for Aristotle to make."

"And then to think that, even though the bishop didn't really know your father, he compared Don Hugo with Plato."

"Well," Fernando reasoned, "being good is what life's about, isn't it?"

Chapter Nineteen

The next three weeks passed quickly, but with a cloud of loneliness and emptiness that still hung in the air. Dame Helen and Ricardo had long since departed for Argentina with Don Hugo's remains—a task that was indescribably painful for them both—and painful in a different way for Maggie and Fernando, in that they could not accompany them.

Wilford and Doris Rockwell continued working their ranch, while each remembered the unusual day of the wedding, Don Hugo's untimely passing, and the blessing of having Fernando's mother and brother with them during their hour of need.

Words could not adequately express the myriad of emotions Wilford and Doris experienced when, exactly twenty-one days following Don Hugo's memorial service, they received their mortgage note in the mail. It was marked *PAID IN FULL* and was accompanied with the canceled foreclosure papers. That they were stunned would be an understatement. That they were relieved would be accurate. That they correctly guessed their benefactors would be incorrect. In fact, they didn't even have a clue. What they did know, however, was that someone loved them, and that they could keep their dreams alive.

Maggie and Fernando had safely made their way back to Los Angeles—stopping briefly in San Bernadino and visiting Maggie's friends, Marsden and Lynette Blanch, who were presiding over a Church mission there. Maggie saw that visiting with them seemed to be a further softening experience for Fernando.

The entire trip was therapeutic for both Fernando and Maggie, as each in their own way needed to come to grips with Don Hugo's heart attack and his passing while at the Rocking "R" Ranch. They also needed to deepen their marriage vows and to express their growing love for each other. In each case, emotions were compelling and very near the surface. By the time they arrived back in Los Angeles at Maggie's apartment—which was now to be their new home—Maggie and Fernando found themselves more deeply in love than either could have possibly hoped for.

The day following their return, Fernando moved his few belongings from the polo stables, and together they re-acquainted themselves with Fernando's records and the tango, and also with the early exquisite and joy-filled memories of their courtship. Those were moments never to be forgotten, and they only served to further cement the couple's feelings for each other.

Two days later, the newlyweds enjoyed a surprise reception in their honor—hosted jointly by the British consulate's office and Roscoe. Both Lord Jockham and Douglas Boyton attended—as did university officials and faculty, and many of their former friends and classmates.

The evening was spent at the newly built Beverly Hilton Hotel, and even several of the movie executives attended. Fernando used the microphone to announce Don Hugo's tragic and untimely passing. He had privately shared the experience with Roscoe but felt that the others also needed to know.

The guests were supportive, as Fernando had expected, and both he and Maggie appreciated the expressions of sorrow and condolences shared with them. Fernando felt comforted and confident that he could now savor his father's memory, while getting on with his life.

The following morning, as Maggie and Fernando were driving to Roscoe's office at the airport, Fernando surprised Maggie with a thought that had been bouncing around inside his mind for several days.

""I've been thinking, honey," he began, "and I have an idea."

"Will it knock my shoes off?"

"No, although this kiss might . . . ."

Fernando put his right arm around Maggie, kissing her softly, while keeping his left eye somewhat on the road ahead. He was not used to driving and kissing, but he appreciated the practice such opportunities afforded.

"Oh, oh," Maggie exclaimed excitedly. "There they go." She held her feet in pretense of her shoes being knocked off, then laughed and nestled even more closely to Fernando.

"What I've been thinking, Maggie," Fernando continued, not even responding to her playfulness, "is that you and I ought to become partners with Roscoe."

"Partners?"

"Of course! I've been trying to think of how we could help Roscoe with his business, while at the same time purchase a plane that met with his approval. If we simply loaned Roscoe the necessary money to strengthen his business, that might change our relationship. I would not want to place him in an uncomfortable position where he felt subordinate to us. However, if we formed a partnership—or bought into his corporation—we could capitalize on what we would each be bringing to the table. Then, regardless of where we might live, or what we might be doing after the race, we will have ties to California—California and Roscoe."

"You have been thinking of this, haven't you, darling?" Maggie smiled, and her voice let Fernando know that she was amenable to the idea, and that he had handled the proposition correctly.

"What do you think?"

"I can't think of any reason not to do it, Fernando . . . Besides, Roscoe has become a big brother to both of us—if you know what I mean—and I would love to have his attention and support during the race."

"Then it's settled?"

"Well, it is as far as I'm concerned. But perhaps we'd better ask Roscoe. He may not want to associate on that level with the likes of us."

Fernando squeezed Maggie's shoulder; she placed her head on his chest, and the two newlyweds sped down the road toward the airport.

An hour later, after enjoying chitchat with Roscoe's crew, Maggie and Fernando made the proposal to Roscoe. Their timing was perfect, as the three of them were alone in his office, and he was just sipping a large glass of freshly squeezed orange juice.

"You what?" he exclaimed, not sure that he had heard Fernando correctly.

"Just this," Maggie responded, gleefully. "You be the managing partner, we'll purchase two new planes and infuse enough capital to put the business on solid ground, and then we'll all live happily ever after."

Her words were so sincere, yet so businesslike, that Roscoe was stunned anew.

"What do you think, old boy?" Fernando added, enjoying the unexpected effect their proposal had had on Roscoe.

"What I think is that we'd better find an attorney fast. You know, get the papers drawn up, that sort of thing. I wouldn't want you to renege and back out on me."

They all laughed, Fernando and Roscoe shook hands, and Maggie gave Roscoe a giant hug. "Roscoe" Maggie said, "I know you'll find someone someday soon. You deserve what Fernando and I have . . . but not 'til after the race! For now," she smiled as she spoke and at her words, the two men smiled as well, "we need you to concentrate on finding just the right planes. The race is in six weeks, and filming begins in just eight days. There's not a minute to lose."

"Well, then, you folks had better get going. I know you have things to do, and I've got a meeting with the movie director. To us—" he added, raising his half-filled glass of juice as though in toast.

"To us," Maggie and Fernando chorused, raising their own glasses. Things were falling rapidly into place, although in ways neither of the three had anticipated only a month earlier. Each sensed the urgency of tasks as they mentally geared up for the weeks ahead.

"Actually," Fernando stated, looking at his watch, "we don't have to leave for a half hour, so perhaps we could listen in on your conversation."

"Oh, yes," Maggie agreed excitedly.

With the arrival of the director, George Seagull, his assistant, and the two screenwriters, Fernando and Maggie listened as he spoke.

"It's great to see you folks again and to learn of the marriage."

"Thank you, Mr. Seagull," Fernando answered, appreciating the personal touch the famous director had begun with.

"Please call me George," he replied. "Everyone does, and that makes for a good working relationship."

"Then it's Fernando and Maggie on our end," Maggie smiled.

"Fair enough, Maggie. Now let's move on. Our meeting today is intended to simply be a short work session to get some more specifics on interesting incidents that have transpired in past races. Also, we need to actually reenact a couple of crashes that occurred in prior years, then work these segments into the story line."

"By the way," Maggie interrupted gleefully, "I've gotten my sponsor, and I will be flying in the race."

"Marvelous," the director replied enthusiastically. "That may complicate things a bit for us, but I'm sure things will fall into place very nicely.

"Anyway," he continued, attempting to refocus on his previous thought. "You contestants will be taking enormous risks, to be sure, and we'll have to become adept at working the script into what actually transpires. The historical reality of the race will be the ultimate box office appeal, so we need to develop the script of the race as it actually unfolds.

"We also need to show some humor and some frustration," he added, "and some engineering details to make it sound technical enough to appeal to the flying public. It must also appeal to the millions who read flying novels, and the fans of great war flying stories. What do you think, Roscoe?"

"Oh, to be sure," Roscoe replied. "But, gentlemen, we need to start with the basic philosophy of the pilots, and the people who build planes for these races. You should have heard the speaker at Maggie and Fernando's graduation. He explained how aviation science progressed rapidly in the last war. In peacetime, however, only air racing seems to push science ahead. It is not the prize money that drives the pilots and the engineers, but rather it is simply an inborn love of flying and the desire to be part of progress.

"In fact," Roscoe continued, deep in thought, "the competitive spirit between pilots and builders is there, but it takes second place to the cooperation with each other. We are all seeking the same goal or philosophy: to achieve more speed, more load carrying ability, more dependability, and more safety. We are both scientists and sportsmen." Roscoe then looked at Maggie, cleared his throat, and quickly added, " . . . and sportswomen."

Everyone, including Maggie, laughed, knowing that there was also an element of friendly competition between the men and the women—particularly in this coming race.

Roscoe took a deep breath and continued.

"Every race causes us to stretch our imaginations and our inspiration to the limit. In so doing, we run some risks because we venture out into the unknowns of our science. Even so, we take those risks because we have escaped in the past. Some of our friends have paid a sad price. We honor them and remember their contributions. Even a mistake, once identified, is a contribution to the rest of us. In a way, we are ready to be martyrs if needed, but hope that we do not disgrace ourselves or our profession with unnecessary risks. Now, let me tell you about a few specific situations."

The writers were listening attentively with notebooks opened, pens flying across the pages as fast as hands could write. Roscoe, seeing this, began to educate his audience.

"First, let me talk about the dependability of engines. Inside the racing engine, the explosions inside each cylinder exact a tremendous punishment on each part. Millions of high-temperature, high pressure explosions cause parts to break.

"For example," he continued, "here is a situation you might want to film, and if so, we can simulate this very easily for the movie. The famous pilot, Jimmy Doolittle, whom you all know, was leading a race. He was doing great in a little biplane that was very fast. At full power, no one could touch him. Even so, in this 1932 race, Doolittle's engine suddenly threw out a plume of black smoke and flame from the exhaust, causing the plane to shake uncontrollably. The plane chasing Doolittle saw this unfold and dodged to one side as Doolittle's plane lost speed. The engine, in that case, continued to produce some power from the other cylinders, but the broken piston chewed up things inside terribly. He got it back on the ground okay, but that misfortune is very typical.

"Also," he added, "valves burn up in the hot flames of the explosions. The exhaust flame exits the combustion chamber around the slender valve-stem, sometimes burning it all the way through. When that happens, we speak of the cylinder swallowing a valve. That puts out a trail of black smoke, visible flame, and vibration."

"What happens then?" Fernando asked, interrupting the narrative.

"Well," Roscoe replied, "with this problem, the engine scientists go back to the drawing board and try to come up with more exotic and harder metals that will withstand the punishment longer. Our engines are getting better and better. We used to have problems with an entire cylinder blowing off. Some of those were spectacular explosions with flame, oil, and parts flying out through the cowl.

"To simulate this kind of a situation, we could destroy an old engine on a test stand, with a camera standing by to film it, and then switch to the plane in the air with the smoke and fire coming out."

One of the writers interrupted with a suggestion. "We want that kind of thing, and then the pilot trying to get his stricken plane back on the ground while he, or she, looks out the cockpit through the smoke and flames. The pilot's face gets oil smeared and blackened—that sort of thing.

"But," he asked, turning to Roscoe, "what is most scary to you pilots?"

Roscoe was serious with his answer. "Each pilot would have his or her own fears that might be different from mine, but my greatest fears are structural failure where the wing comes off, or where the engine breaks loose from the fuselage. In this case, of course, the pilot has to get out fast—use the chute, if he is to survive."

The conversation continued, and shortly Roscoe interrupted a dialogue between the screenwriters. "Let me share an experience I had with an onboard fire, and then I'd like Maggie to tell about Ruth's wing-spar failure.

"I was doing about 250 miles an hour," he began, "when my fuel line ruptured close to the exhaust manifold. The gasoline-fed fire exploded, blowing pieces off the front of the plane. Immediately, the cockpit was filled with flames and became a real inferno. I tore open the canopy and ejected it; then I unfastened my safety belts, but couldn't seem to get out of the cockpit. The flames were reaching toward my face and hands, so I pulled myself up right into the wind that was forcing the flames back toward me.

"As a last resort, I rolled upside down and kicked myself out through the fire. I was then able to pull the ripcord, just as the tail flashed past me. The tail almost hit me, too. Then, believe it or not, my chute delayed in opening. I was trying to put the fire out on parts of my flying suit, so I may not have pulled the cord as fast as I thought. It opened just about treetop level. In fact, I hit the ground before the plane did, which came boring down on me like a flaming meteor and landed not more than fifty yards away from me.

"I lost my eyebrows and moustache," he said, concluding, "and the tips of my fingers were badly burned. And I still have those scars to prove it. From that frightening experience, we learned to run the gas lines far away from the exhaust stacks—and I personally learned to wear fireproof gloves and a fireproof flying suit."

The audience sat spellbound through Roscoe's story. When he finished, he turned to Maggie and said, "Your turn, girl."

"Roscoe is right," Maggie began, "about fire being the scariest of all. I've had some in-flight fires, but nothing as frightening as Roscoe's. Of course, mine were dangerous, but I was able to put them out by turning the fuel valve off. In one instance, I dove to get speed to blow out the fire, then landed in a field with a dead engine and a smoke-blackened plane."

The writers nodded understandingly. They could easily visualize filming this kind of accident.

The conversation continued and then Maggie and Fernando excused themselves and left Roscoe's hanger. Minutes later, they were scooting down the dirt road, leaving a cloud of dust behind them. As they drove along, they both realized—and discussed—that the next weeks of their lives were going to leave little time for their relationship. Somehow the meeting they had just attended shocked them into acknowledging this and caused them to resolve not to allow the stresses of the movie and the race to detract from the closeness they had shared up to that time.

Chapter Twenty

The next several days were hectic. While each performed their tasks for the motion-picture crew with professional fervor, neither Fernando nor Maggie could believe that so many scenes could be set up and filmed in such a short time. Then, almost before they could believe it, the prerace scenes were finished, and Fernando and Maggie were in a stately pullman of the Denver and Rio Grande Railroad on their way to the race. They would pick up Maggie's new plane in Wichita, Kansas, then meet a second film crew on Long Island—a crew that was already shooting air shots of some of the other contestants.

Winding their way up out of California, they soon reached the growing settlement of Las Vegas, Nevada. However, since it was in the middle of the night and both were asleep, each was oblivious of the stop.

By midmorning, the train began to slow down, and they came to a stop at the newly finished depot in Salt Lake City, Utah. They had been awake now for several hours, and had spent the time speaking of the Rocking "R" Ranch, which was just a few hundred miles to the south. Wilford and Doris were assuredly a very perplexed, yet deliriously happy couple on this day, who should be mulling over the events of the past few days. Their mortgage had been unexpectedly paid, a receipt of which had been sent to them.

In addition, Maggie's family would likely have received a promised cablegram from Buenos Aires, notifying them of Dame

Helen and Ricardo's safe arrival. That would have brought great relief to the family, and a sense of finality to Don Hugo's tragic and untimely passing.

With an almost two-hour layover, Maggie seized the opportunity and suggested they walk the five or six blocks east, to what she told Fernando was the famous Temple Square. Arriving on the square, Fernando was dumbfounded to see the majestic, awe-inspiring temple, as it stretched toward the heavens.

"Want to know the difference between the LDS faith, and other Christian denominations?"

"This may surprise you, Maggie, but I really would. Just what do you believe?"

"Well, our temple here is actually the embodiment of our faith. In essence, we believe that a family is meant to remain together throughout the eternities, and such a marriage—an eternal sealing—takes place within those walls."

Quick to assimilate Maggie's words, Fernando queried, "You mean to say that our marriage, performed by your Mormon bishop . . . uh, Dennis Barney, was a marriage for eternity?"

"No, darling. But, with the same power, or priesthood, that Bishop Barney has, if he had sealed us in the Holy Temple, he could have used different words—and we would truly have been bonded together for the eternities."

"Does this mean that we could have traveled up to Salt Lake, and our marriage would have been different?"

"Well, if you were a member of the Church, it would have. And if you had been ordained to the priesthood, yourself. It is all done for worthy members of the Church, and with God's power."

"Tell me more of your Church's history, Maggie. I mean, how in the world can something like this be sitting here in the middle of nowhere? You've told me a little, and you've told me of your Christian beliefs, but I need to know about the heart and soul of your faith."

Sitting down, and inviting Fernando to sit on the grass next to her, Maggie began from the beginning—telling Fernando of

Joseph Smith, of his first vision, of how the Book of Mormon was miraculously translated in just over two months, and of course of the pioneer treks across the plains.

While Maggie spoke, Fernando listened quietly. He had no idea this was the Mormon heritage and could hardly believe that he had actually married someone with such a background of loyalty and hardship.

"Do you remember, Fernando, when I told you I would give you my heart forever?"

"Of course I do. That was the night I asked you to marry me."

Maggie's eyes glowed as she spoke. "Now you know how that is possible, sweetheart."

Hers words were spoken softly, yet with a spark of excitement that totally captivated Fernando's mind. *Where did this girl come from?* he wondered, not for the first time. And almost as soon as he had asked himself the question, he knew the answer.

"Maggie," he smiled, "do you know the difference between your beliefs and mine? Before you answer, let me tell you. I've thought a lot about it . . . especially since we spent the week with your family. While the Catholic church has beliefs that are good and character building, the religion itself is more of a tradition and social commitment. You Mormons, on the other hand, have found something that . . . that takes you way deeper. You learn of faith, of honest-to-goodness prayers, and you look at life through the Savior's lens."

"Well, darling, I couldn't have said it any better. The Latter-day Saint faith and my personal relationship with Jesus Christ are my most prized possessions."

"And me? Where do I fit on your priority ladder?"

"Right at the very top, Fernando. You see, I love you so deeply that I don't want you just for this life. Nor do I want to end my mothering role with our children the day I die. I really do want you for all eternity—otherwise, why would I invest so much in our relationship in this life?"

Maggie's words were softly spoken, yet firm; and somehow,

although he sensed that his understanding was embryonic, at best, Fernando knew she was speaking truth.

"Well," he suddenly looked at his watch, "you won't have me for the summer, let alone for eternity, if we don't get back to the depot in time to catch our train. We've only got fifteen minutes until it leaves."

Grabbing Maggie by the hand, Fernando started pulling her toward the nearby gate. But Maggie, having a mind of her own, drew him back to her. Extending her arms around his waist, she looked up into his eyes and said, "Fernando, you'll never know what this hour has meant to me. I was here many years ago, when I was a little girl, and I have lived my entire life to one day walk into that temple with the man of my dreams. Just let me know when you are ready to learn more. I have forever, you know . . . ."

"That I will, Maggie," Fernando promised.

After arriving safely back to their seats in the train, Maggie and Fernando felt the train jerk back as it worked its way out past the Great Salt Lake. It stopped briefly at the much larger depot in Ogden, just thirty miles to the north, then headed east toward the Rockies and the plains.

For them both, silence came naturally, as each with their own thoughts and emotions somehow didn't want the feeling of oneness and belonging to end. For Fernando, the emotion was new, and somewhat awkward to deal with. For Maggie the emotion was a fulfillment of weeks of planning—of carrying on their very conversation literally hundreds of times in her mind. She was not disappointed, either; and as she took Fernando's hand, she somehow sensed that she would enjoy her husband's nearness through the eternities.

The grandeur of the Utah mountains did not disappoint either Fernando or Maggie, and several times in the next hours they spotted large herds of deer and elk grazing peacefully in the untamed lands around them. One day, they promised, they would return to Salt Lake City—to spend a second honeymoon in these spectacularly rugged mountains.

Before long, the mountains abruptly ended, and they were moving at a speed that approached sixty miles per hour. Maggie and Fernando's second stop, made in the famous cowboy town of Cheyenne, came sooner than either had anticipated. Once here, they checked into the most credible hotel they could find, then spent the evening relaxing and getting the train's vibrations out of their systems.

Following dinner, they took a stroll along the unmarked street facing the small depot. The night was hot and dry, although with a steady breeze coming in from the southwest.

"Oh, Maggie," Fernando spoke, breaking into the silence of the night. "Can life get any better than this?"

"Only if we win the race."

"You really have confidence in your chances, don't you, Maggie?"

"Well, someone has to win it. Actually, darling, I'm psyching myself up is all. Way down deep, I feel so overwhelmed and fortunate to even be entered in the race that I will have no disappointment, even if I don't win."

"To be truthful," Fernando paused, "given the fact that the Wright Brothers just did their thing a little over three decades ago, I'd say just finishing a race like this would be a monumental accomplishment."

"We really do live in the age of wonder, don't we, Fernando? And to think that this year, thanks especially to Amelia Erhardt, woman are allowed to participate. Why, that's an even greater wonder."

"Charles Lindbergh's wife, Anne, felt the same way," Fernando responded, enjoying Maggie's all-too-true humor. "She's an amazingly articulate and insightful person, you know."

"Did you know that Anne didn't even meet Charles until '28, a full year after he flew *The Spirit of St. Louis* nonstop across the Atlantic?"

"Has it been that long since he broke that record?" Fernando asked pensively.

"Not only that, but I was reading not long ago that it has been four years now since their eldest son was kidnapped and murdered. I can't even imagine going through a nightmare like that."

"It surely became an international tragedy. Thank goodness the man who did it was finally convicted last year. His actions changed the Lindbergh's lives forever."

"Do you think Lindberg will fly his new Miles Mohawk single-engine in the race?" Maggie asked.

"No, although I understand it's a beauty. From what I've heard, he moved his family to Wales, southwest of London, just to get away from the limelight. He's so busy being an ambassador for the various airlines that I doubt he's thought much about racing."

"I'm sure you're right, Fernando. Still, his heroic flight has given the rest of us courage to do things in the sky that will pave the way to even greater air achievements."

"Like flying clear into outer space?"

"Well, I won't go that far," Maggie laughed. "But I do think flying will become the transportation wave of the future, and I'm just thrilled to be a part of it."

"And I'm sure that my father, wherever he is, is pleased to be your sponsor, mi amor."

Back at their hotel, Fernando caught Maggie off-guard by stating emphatically, "Speaking of men and women pilots, darling, I've been observing the human species very closely lately, and I've come to appreciate that the male gender is the weaker sex. Our physical strength is superior, of course, but when it comes to giving birth and rearing children—why, that would be the greatest challenge of all."

"My goodness, Mister Realist," Maggie added, surprised by his comment, "if I didn't know better, I'd think that you're making an announcement in my behalf."

"Now, how could that happen, Maggie? You're the one who

would make such an announcement to me. I will admit, however, that spending so many hours in that train has caused me to consider what it would be like to be an actual father."

"You used that word again, darling. One day soon . . . and then we can both celebrate. Now, Mister Realist, why don't you become Mister Romantic for the evening and sweep me away in your arms."

Even as Maggie concluded her sentence, Fernando picked her up, pushed the hotel door wide open, and turned sideways as he admitted the two into the foyer. To the night clerk's surprise, he marched right past the main desk and into the elevator.

Two days passed, and Maggie was ecstatic. Other than on her wedding day, she was more excited than she could ever remember. Here she was, in Wichita, Kansas, at the actual manufacturing and assembly plant of the Staggerwing plane she would fly in the race. It was not a very large factory, but they had been in business for a full five years and had manufactured and sold enough planes to stay alive through those very difficult years of what had come to be called The Great Depression. Their facilities were on the outskirts of town and were surrounded by seemingly endless miles of ripening corn. The plant, itself, had been set up in several old dilapidated hangars.

Maggie wore her favorite dress, a blue-checked dress with full petticoat. The director had allowed her to use her own wardrobe, including jeans, for most of the scenes, with the philosophy that such a unique difference would enhance the imagery on screen. She also wore a bright blue silk neckerchief and a star-shaped rhinestone pin her father had given her the previous Christmas. This attire, coupled with her lengthy naturally curly blonde hair, set her apart from the others, although she was completely oblivious of the heads she turned.

Fernando, however, standing at Maggie's side, was not oblivious of this fact, and he found it odd that he was experiencing a tinge of jealousy for those who were enjoying his bride's beauty. Pushing these emotions aside, he allowed himself to relax and to simply enjoy Maggie's beauty and presence for himself.

Fernando was getting used to wearing western gear, American style. He wore a complete outfit that had been purchased by his brother, Ricardo, while they were in Arizona, then given to him as a wedding present. On the third finger of his right hand was a large red ruby-crested gold ring. It had been Don Hugo's ring, and at Ricardo's insistence, Fernando had retrieved it immediately following his father's passing. Using his thumb, he now rolled it back and forth on his finger, feeling very close to his father's spirit.

In the brief weeks since Don Hugo's death, Fernando had sensed his father's nearness on more than one occasion. Each of these incidents, although not preconceived, caused goosebumps to appear on his flesh. In his mind, there was no mistaking the source of these new emotions, and each time Fernando quietly, yet audibly, thanked his father for his love and support, they again appeared. It was an unexpected bonding emotion that grew more stable and meaningful each time it took place.

Now, as he and Maggie waited near the front gate of the compound, Maggie broke into Fernando's mental reflections by fiercely squeezing his arm. She then exclaimed, "Oh, Fernando, I can hardly wait."

"Nor I," Fernando replied, pulling her tight to him. "The train ride from California was much too long. I just wish Roscoe could have accompanied us to pick up the plane. After all, it was his selection. But, as he told us before he left for New York, we're on our own. Besides, he's flying a single-pilot plane in the race, and he wanted to log as many miles as he could before arriving in Long Island. Although he is pleased with our partnership, he has that competitor's heart, and I believe doesn't want to become too emotionally involved in what we're doing."

Roscoe had surprised them a week earlier by informing them that he had found Maggie the perfect racer. It was a factory demonstration plane, actually, located in Wichita, Kansas. It was an executive cabin aircraft and had logged enough air hours to be adequately tested. Now here they were, ready to spend the day in flight instruction, and then pilot it on to New York.

After what seemed like a lifetime of waiting, Maggie and Fernando were welcomed by Alan Layton, the company president, then escorted to the tarmac and introduced to their checkout pilot, Craig Nelson.

"Wish my wife, Leslie, could have been here to meet you folks," Mr. Layton began. "She's been pretty excited, thinking that one of our planes will be in the cinemas."

"And in the race," Maggie added, wanting to keep the plane's usage in proper perspective.

"You'll love how she looks," Mr. Nelson exclaimed, speaking in a mid-western twang that both Maggie and Fernando found appealing. It was obvious to both that their instructor loved his work since he exuded a little-boy excitement that they found contagious.

"Let's open the hangar, boys."

Mr. Layton's booming voice was heard by the two men who had been standing by, and within seconds the doors were drawn open, and the most beautiful plane Maggie had ever seen was rolled out into the morning sun. Deliriously happy, Maggie hugged Fernando's arm and let out a suppressed squeal. Her hopes were high, and her dreams of flying the great cross-country race in a real racer were now passing quickly through her mind. In fact, if the truth were known, she felt like jumping up and down—just as she had done when her father had given her her first colt.

From the dark, shadowy interior of the hangar, men pushed a large shape toward the light. Maggie knew it was her plane coming out onto the cement pad in the bright sun, and she squinted her eyes, peering into the shadows before them. Slowly the nose of the plane came out of the darkness and into the light. The early morning rays of sunlight reflected off the shiny chrome nose spinner like sparks of fire.

At that instant, the equally polished propeller blades likewise hit the rays of sun. The coal-black cylinders of the huge, radial engine followed, looking mean, ominous, and powerful—almost like a thing alive. The thin tubes of the valve push-rods had been chromed, making delicate accents against the black-finned fat cylinders.

Coming next into view was the streamlined cowling covering the engine. It was blue—definitely not the usual airplane-silver color—but a stunning powder blue with a thin white speed-stripe extending along each side from the point of the nose to the end of the tail.

Maggie and Fernando were enthralled with the magnificent piece of metal and fabric art appearing before them—the sharply raked windscreen, the leading lower wing. By the time the sun line had moved all the way to the top of the windscreen, the top wing was visible. The negative staggered wings, looking faster than lightening with the lower one ahead of the top one, created a swept-back rakish appearance for the aircraft.

"Just look at the small front area of that cabin," Fernando said. "This baby is designed for speed."

Maggie was thrilled beyond words with what she saw, and she was equally excited about Fernando's response. It was a magnificent plane, and the generosity of Fernando's father had made it all possible.

As the craft came to a stop, Mr. Layton cleared his throat, "We understand you're in a hurry to get to New York for your prerace preparation. Your flight east will be the first extended break-in period for the engine, but I know she'll perform just fine and dandy.

"When you arrive at Bennett Field on Long Island," he added, "do a complete oil change. Make sure the mechanics check for metal flakes in the oil. You must also make sure that the first leg of your race—getting back here—will be at controlled speeds, even though you will have already flown the plane from here to

New York. Sorry to slow you down, but after you touch down here for refueling and a thorough engine inspection, the second leg can be at full power. From what I've heard, the other participants will also be flying new planes, so they'll be under the same restrictions."

"Let's take a closer look," Maggie stated, appearing oblivious to Mr. Layton's instructions.

Fernando nodded, smiling, then followed her as she quickly walked to the nearest wing tip and then around the plane. When they reached the far side, Maggie experienced an unexpected shiver of excitement; for there, below the pilot's left window, were the words, *The Don Hugo.*

"Oh, darling," Maggie gasped, "you did it! I had totally forgotten."

Maggie's words were spoken in wonder, as Fernando simply squeezed her around the waist and said, "Father told you he would be with you during the race, so this makes it official."

"Thank you, sweetheart. Thank you so very much."

Fernando leaned down and kissed Maggie on her cheek.

This plane is an anachronism, thought Fernando. *A biplane should not look modern and swift, but this one does. A fabric covering should not look modern and new, but this one does. Not only that, but it looks as sleek and racy as any plane I've seen.*

Maggie patted the lower wing as she walked towards the engine compartment. She then stroked the cowling surrounding the huge, powerful engine that was just begging to be cranked up. After absently lifting her right foot and scratching her ankle, she rubbed the knife-edge of the propeller blade, visually examining the heart of the engine at the large cylinders and chromed push-rods.

Almost oblivious to Fernando's presence, Maggie knelt down on the cement and peered up into the pockets where the wheels would enter on retraction. Slowly and lovingly her hands caressed the silver flying wires that were like dew-covered cobwebs in the sun, stretched between the upper and lower wing. *It's a magnificent machine,* she marveled silently, *and one that I'll cherish for the rest of my life.*

As Fernando simply watched in admiration, Maggie thumped the fabric skin carrying twenty coats of dope that had been hand-rubbed to a mirror finish. She drank in every line and curve of artistic beauty, admiring every stitch in the fabric and rivet in the metal.

Following Mr. Nelson's lead, the two walked all the way around the plane toward the tail. Maggie, totally absorbed, looked past the rudder and elevators. The graceful, flowing wasp-like waist expanded to the width of the cabin before flattening out into two upper-wing panels.

After completing the perfunctory walk-around, Mr. Nelson stepped forward and presented Maggie with the key to the cabin door. He gave Fernando a small booklet. "Here," he smiled, winking, "is the handbook of instructions. It outlines our best estimates of performance with the new engine. In addition, it charts out different fuel flows at various power settings—manifold pressure versus r.p.m.'s—at various altitudes showing speed and fuel consumption and range. Your wife will need only this and a whole lot of petrol—then nothing can stop her."

"Well, folks," Mr. Layton said, smiling broadly as he walked up behind them, "why don't you put the pedal to the metal and see how this baby flies?"

"We're ready and waiting," Maggie said, rubbing her gloved hands together in anticipation.

Thanking Mr. Layton for his personal attention and for having the plane ready for them, Maggie and Fernando followed the instructor up the stairs and into the cabin. Once inside the craft, Maggie took the copilot's seat, while Fernando stood to the side and allowed the amiable Craig Nelson to take his seat at the controls.

"I've flown another model of this plane," Mr. Nelson began matter-of-factly. "In fact, it was our first prototype with fixed gear. We added a larger-than-prescribed engine to make the plane fly faster, and it really did."

"Is it still in operation?" Fernando asked, leaning over the back of Maggie's seat as he spoke.

"Actually, the engine blew a jug at only 100 hours, so we changed to the smaller Pratt and Whitney. In contrast, that engine has been totally reliable.

"This beauty," he continued, patting the control panel, "has the best of both worlds. It has a newer and larger Pratt and Whitney, which is supposed to be the finest engine on the market. Just make sure you don't use full power on takeoff."

"Why is that?" Maggie asked.

"Well, ma'am, at full power the torque is so high it will twist you toward the side of the runway. There won't be enough airflow over the rudder to keep it rolling straight—even if you use the brake. So, just make sure you don't firewall it for takeoff.

"Oh, I almost forgot," he added, "there is one more caution. When you come in for a landing, there are times when you won't be able to land but will have to go around again. Whether you come in too low or too high, or whether some person or animal is on the runway, don't suddenly firewall the throttle, or the torque will roll you upside down. Just make the conservative decision, and you'll be fine."

Both Maggie and Fernando nodded silently, each recalling times that such a decision had been made. They weren't sure why Mr. Nelson had made specific mention of this concern, but they tucked his cautionary statement away in their minds and appreciated his thorough nature.

"But," he continued, now changing the subject, "this ship is a beauty, and will serve you well. I believe you will get up to 250 miles per hour at the ideal 11,000 feet, and we've installed larger gas tanks for your race. We honestly think you can make it from coast to coast with only the one stop here in Wichita."

"Really!" Maggie exclaimed, almost in disbelief. "I've never considered making only one stop."

"We've been working that out with both the race officials and the filming crew in Hollywood. They'll be here ahead of you, as they've given their stamp of approval of our plan.

"Now," he pressed, as though he hadn't heard her reply, "don't tell any of your competitors what this thing will do—that is, until after the race. We think you can beat any of the other women, and maybe some of the men, if you handle your navigation and keep your weather flying in check."

"My plan is to win the race, Mr. Nelson, not just place ahead of some of the contestants."

Again Fernando remained silent, smiling inwardly that he had married such an unusually assertive woman. He wouldn't put it past her to win it all, even though the odds certainly weren't in her favor.

After forty-five minutes of on-the-ground instructions, Mr. Nelson gave Maggie the first shot at takeoff, and within seconds they were airborne—Maggie responding perfectly to his meticulous words.

For an hour they flew, performing every conceivable maneuver. Fernando likewise took his turn, and finally, after landing for a tedious third time, Fernando taxied the plane to the edge of the runway where several mechanics were awaiting them. The plane was refueled, and with remarkable precision, the engine was examined and cleared for their flight east.

Bidding their new friend and instructor farewell, Maggie and Fernando once again took to the air. This time they were on their own, and although each felt confident that they had mastered the aircraft, they were both nervous with the responsibility they had assumed. Fernando was especially anxious, realizing that Maggie would not only pilot the plane the rest of the way across the states with him at her side, but would then enter a race, the magnitude of which he really didn't think she understood. But then again, that was part of Maggie's makeup that intrigued Fernando most. She simply wasn't afraid to risk, and with a childlike faith appeared confident in everything she did.

That's my Maggie, he thought, closing his eyes while inhaling the almost intoxicating whine of the engine. *She's in her element, for sure; and somehow I suspect that if I just hang on, this race will be but an omen of things to come.*

Leaning over toward his very own pilot, Fernando opened his eyes. Making contact with her eyes, he kissed her tenderly. Then, without saying a word, he sat back in his seat, adjusted his safety belt, and closed his eyelids for the second time. Life . . . and love, he thought peacefully, could never be more glorious.

Maggie, accurately assessing that Fernando was basking in serenity, simply set her jaw and smiled. Pulling back on the wheel, she climbed even higher, experiencing an exhilaration that only a pilot would understand. She was definitely in her environment, and come what may, no one could ever take that away from her.

Chapter Twenty-One

Two days later, after arriving at Floyd Bennett Field on Long Island, New York, Maggie and Fernando met up with Roscoe in the pilot's lounge. Roscoe had only experienced minor mechanical problems on his flight east, and he assured his new business associates that these bugs had been ironed out.

Sensing a need to not be competing directly with their dearest friend and partner, they agreed that regardless of which one—if either—earned prize money, they would place the proceeds in a contingency fund for their business and use it to give strength to their financial statement.

The main objective, as Roscoe repeatedly stressed, was the safety factor. Aviation was still in its infancy, and neither he or Maggie could afford to take unnecessary chances in such a lengthy endurance race.

Now, as they sat leisurely in the pilot's lounge, Maggie listened absently as Fernando and Roscoe discussed Fernando's role in the filming process. The lounge, she noticed, had a worn, but practical look to it. The furniture consisted of functional, leather-covered sofas and chairs, with several low coffee tables. There were maps and an abundance of framed pictures of famous pilots and airplanes on the walls. The room had the atmosphere of a very exclusive club—but a club without much money.

Off to one side, Maggie noticed a lunch counter providing whatever food a pilot might request, and two men were visiting quietly while eating their sandwiches. Other pilots wandered about the room, greeting each other, eating, and examining maps and flight papers. While Maggie thought that each was in some way connected to the race, some were actually commercial airline pilots wearing their uniforms. Others wore soiled jumpsuits and looked like they might have just finished changing their own engine's oil.

Maggie was the only woman in the room, and the men entering stole long, curious glances at her. Trying to ignore them, she entered into Roscoe and Fernando's conversation.

"Roscoe," she began, "that Staggerwing is a dreamboat. It is so well-balanced on the controls, and as Fernando will attest, the new engine is as smooth as silk. We didn't have an engine cough on the entire trip from Kansas." Since Fernando had insisted that she practice blind-flying, he had strapped a device Roscoe had given them to her head. It had completely blocked her vision, except for the instrument panel before her. Using the radio ranges only, she flew all the way in.

"Fernando even insisted that I practice the full instrument procedure let-down and landing, just as though the field was socked in with a low ceiling," Maggie concluded.

"She was great, too," Fernando added, "although I am concerned that the directional gyro-compass is not working correctly. During our flight, we had to reset it too often, and that troubles me. I think it's processing too fast. The solution would be to find a new gyro. It would be insane for Maggie to be flying alone and have that instrument drift like it does. Do you know where we can get a new one and have it installed before the race?"

Roscoe knew that a malfunctioning gyro, or "d.g." as it was called, could slowly change, causing the pilot to drift off course—unless, that is, the pilot regularly checked to see if the gyro-compass agreed with the magnetic compass. But that meant a pilot must take his or her eyes off the instrument panel to look at the magnetic compass, then reset the directional gyro-compass. It was a distraction that a pilot did not need when concentrating on the gauges while flying blind.

When Roscoe didn't answer, Maggie added, "Fernando did the resetting while I concentrated on instruments, but in the race I won't have a co-pilot to assist me. I'll have to do everything by myself."

Roscoe's face lit up with a smile. "Amelia always has a spare of almost everything. She even has two sets of instruments in her plane—one for the pilot's side of the panel, and one for the copilot's side. I saw her over at the hangar a little while ago, so I'll check with her and see if we can locate another one."

Roscoe stood to leave, but before he did, he turned to Fernando. "Could your problem have been the vacuum? Maybe instead of the gyro being worn out, it might not be getting enough suction."

Fernando shook his head. "I think the problem is the instrument itself, but we could only determine that by measuring the suction. In any case, I feel it best to both replace the instrument and check the suction—just to be sure. The weather forecast indicates that Maggie will have one and possibly two storms to contend with. I'm confident she can handle being on instruments, if needed, but not with anything defective."

Roscoe agreed, then quickly exited the lounge. For a long time afterward, Maggie and Fernando pensively visited, each more aware than ever before of the dangers Maggie faced as she prepared for what was fast becoming the race of a lifetime.

Fernando and Maggie were practically oblivious to anyone else in the room, engrossed as they were in their conversation about the race. "Darling," Maggie said, "I forgot to tell you about one of the movie scenes we shot that made Roscoe very angry. It isn't even a flying sequence, but still he took it wrong."

"And I wasn't there?"

"No, you were at the bank, arranging the mortgage payoff for my folks. Anyway, Roscoe thought he was being insulted, and I have no idea if the director will include the footage in the movie. Roscoe said that he would sue them if they decide to use it, but that may have just been a reaction. Douglas Boynton is doing a fabulous job of playing the kind of character Roscoe is, and he made this scene look good—I mean *really* good."

The two pilots eating at the bar overheard Maggie's statement and moved over to where they were visiting. One of them, a dark-haired man who looked like Clark Gable, spoke first. "We just saw Colonel Roscoe Turner leave and couldn't help over-hearing you speak about the movie you're filming. Mind if we join you?"

Maggie was used to the straightforwardness of members of the flying fraternity, and she invited them to pull up a chair. "I was just telling my husband, Fernando, about a scene we did before leaving Los Angeles. Everyone knows how generous Roscoe is—with money or anything else—so they filmed a segment that's true, and that reflects this human interest part of Roscoe's personality.

"So, this is a true story that someone dug up and is going to possibly be included in the movie. Roscoe, however, is unhappy about it. The movie director and the writers want to use it to show the camaraderie that is common between race pilots, even though they are competitors out to beat each other to the finish line.

"Well," she continued, feeling at ease in speaking with the two strangers after they had introduced themselves, "two years ago, just before leaving California for his first Bendix Cup race, Roscoe incurred some unexpected expenses and was unable to repay them before leaving for the east coast. And so, hoping to earn some prize money that would bring his bills current, he flew here to Long Island and prepared for the race. When the race finally began—only minutes before Roscoe's takeoff, actually—one of his creditors came after him. The man was a very hard-hearted man, and decided to press him for full payment on the purchase of a double-barreled Stromberg-Carlson carburetor.

"Anyway, Roscoe was doing a last-minute check on his plane in the hangar, when a sheriff came to serve him with a summons. However, the sheriff made the mistake of asking another pilot where Roscoe was, stating that he would have to remove Roscoe from the race, then impound his plane until he paid the debt.

"The other pilot thought it terribly unfair to have a competitor grounded, especially after so much had been done in preparation; so the pilot indicated that he thought Roscoe had already taken off. He sent the sheriff to the other side of the airport to check with the officials in the tower.

"As soon as the sheriff climbed back into his car, the pilot ran out to warn Roscoe of the problem. Roscoe realized that he had no choice but to avoid the man. The other pilot helped him, and Roscoe quickly rolled his plane out to the runway. While Roscoe and his crew were starting and warming up the engine, the other pilot convinced the official in charge to move Roscoe into the next take-off position."

"You've never told me this story," Fernando exclaimed.

"I really didn't know about it until the shoot, darling. And, if the truth were known, I suspect Roscoe would have preferred it that way. Anyway, the sheriff was just entering the race office at the base of the tower, when he heard Roscoe's name announced for take-off. The sheriff missed his opportunity, Roscoe completed the race, and finished high enough in the rankings to pay the debt in full."

Maggie had been asked to play the part of the pilot who saves Roscoe's plane in the movie scene since the screenwriters had changed the *him* to a *her.* Douglas Boynton had played Roscoe's part.

"And Roscoe wasn't on hand to defend himself?" Fernando asked.

"He didn't find out about it until that evening when they were reviewing the takes for the day," Maggie answered. "I'm not sure I've ever seen Roscoe respond like that. I just hope I can convince him to let the director use the scene. It's no disgrace to be struggling in business, especially in this new field of aeronautics."

The second man, a ruddy-complexioned fellow named Zach, spoke. "Say, ma'am, aren't you the new girl who is going to fly in the race?"

Before Maggie could answer, Fernando proudly introduced her. "She sure is, and although she might shoot me for telling you this, she is the same girl who did the stunt in the movie *Saga of the West*. She was the blonde who jumped from the galloping horse to a ladder dangling from a plane. Roscoe was towing the ladder past her."

Fernando's uncharacteristic disclosure opened up a lot of questions about Maggie, and about what part Fernando was to play in the filming of the race. By the time Roscoe returned with a gyro container under his arm, the entire lounge full of pilots had joined in the conversation.

Maggie explained that her husband of just one month, Fernando, would not be participating in the race. "He's a much more experienced pilot than I am," she told the other pilots while Fernando blushed at her declaration. She explained that Fernando would fly out the next day, one day ahead of the race, with a friend. They would fly to Wichita, Kansas, with a camera crew of two, plus their equipment, and assist in her refueling filming sequence there.

"Why do you want to go through Kansas?" one person asked. Isn't that kind of out in the middle of nowhere?"

Maggie looked toward Fernando who was happy to explain that he had set up the camera crews in New York to do some takeoff shots. Maggie had enlisted the cooperation of the women entrants, who agreed to allow the film crew to shoot their prerace preparations as well as their actual takeoffs. The director had already enlisted the cooperation of the male entrants.

"I am flying ahead to Wichita," Fernando continued, "in a Gull Wing Stinson. Each plane will have to determine their own fuel stops, of course, depending upon the weather, the headwinds, how their fuel is holding up, and so forth. So, there will be several crews strategically waiting at two other air terminals—Kansas City to the north, and Oklahoma City to the south. There will also be contingency crews at three other locations—Dallas, Denver, and Las Vegas—although there will be no film crews there.

"One oil company, in sponsoring the Douglas DC-2, is expecting to make a stop in Wichita, and Amelia Earhart says she can make it coast to coast, with one stop in Kansas, since it is directly in line with her expected flight course. Maggie may need to make several stops, but the first will be in Wichita, where her plane was manufactured. Unless she is driven off course by a storm, we will all be waiting there for her."

The man named Zach turned to Fernando. "How can you allow your bride to undertake such a dangerous race? This is the first year that women have even been allowed to enter the race."

"Actually," Fernando began, "I would do anything within my power to help her achieve her dream. She is an astute pilot, with an uncanny sense of perspective in the cockpit. She is very much her own person, as you can see, and I support her in her aspirations just as she does me with mine."

Maggie was moved by his statement of support and respect. He had never treated her with anything less than equality, which she thought somewhat surprising in context with his Argentine heritage. Still, she had seen a relationship of equality between Don Hugo and Dame Helen; she should have known that Fernando would have taken such a stand. She reached out to take his hand in hers.

"All of my life," she said, "I have wanted to marry a man who allowed me to fulfill my many dreams. Still, I never imagined that I would marry someone so wonderful that he made these dreams possible. In addition to being my closest friend, Fernando is my greatest fan, and I love him dearly. I'll look forward to seeing you all at the beginning of the race, and I'll thank you ahead of time for your interest and support."

With these words, the entire room erupted in unexpected applause. The almost magical spirit of love between Maggie and Fernando was not lost on the others, and instantly Maggie became a crowd favorite to win the approaching race.

Chapter Twenty-Two

While the other contestants made final mechanical adjustments to their planes, the mysterious Russian-American pilot flew into Bennett Field just twenty-four hours before the race was to begin. He taxied over to the hangar, shut down the engine, and climbed out. He then directed several heretofore unobserved assistants as they pushed his plane into a vacant hangar. For the other pilots present on the tarmac, the Russian-designed plane was the most powerful looking racer they had ever seen—with the longest radial engine to ever land in Long Island. Word had spread that the plane's pilot had referred to it as a pursuit plane, and that he was eager to match it up against the American-made racers that were entered in the race.

Sergé Grosporov, the oversized pilot, then hailed an awaiting taxi cab, and yelled in surprisingly fluid English, "Take me to Army Air Force headquarters." He appeared as angry as a Bolshevik revolutionary—yelling and gesturing wildly. He was red in the face, and veins popped boldly out on his huge neck. In short, he appeared to be out of control, and those watching inwardly grimaced in fear from his outburst.

Low-wing with retractable gear, the plane itself was made of metal and appeared sleek and menacing as it disappeared into the shadows of the hangar. It would be serviced under guard and would not reappear until the photo session. For now, even though it was a plane that had been manufactured in the United States, it would remain a troublesome mystery—an unknown quantity that brought an element of fear into each of the other contestants. That they would have to compete against their own wit and technology was one thing; it was quite another to be imposed upon by such a clandestine entity.

In contrast, the contestants were relieved to learn that the handsome and eccentric power-broker, Howard Hughes, had officially withdrawn only hours earlier. He had intended to enter his newest designed and manufactured racer. However, production and testing had apparently revealed a weakness of some sort, so he had sent notice of his withdrawal.

Late in the morning, less than twenty hours before the first contestant would be cleared for takeoff, most of the entrants gathered in the airport lounge. They visited amiably, the energy in the air so electric it could almost be cut with a knife. This scene was something of a prerace reception that was being filmed by the movie crew, and it created the intended spirit of goodwill and camaraderie among those in attendance.

After forty-five minutes of socializing and enjoying a luncheon hosted by the Bendix officials, Roscoe, Fernando, and Maggie left the lounge to make final strategic preparations of their own. They walked slowly down the flight line, looking for the instrument mechanic, and hoping that the new directional gyro had been installed in Maggie's plane. Fernando had intended to have left hours earlier for Kansas, but he couldn't bring himself to leave Maggie until he was satisfied that the gyro was correctly installed. Now, as the studio plane he would be flying in warmed up and prepared for takeoff, he enjoyed a last hour of planning strategy with Maggie and Roscoe.

Arriving at the first hangar, the three spotted Amelia Earhart and Laura Ingalls, two lovely ladies who, along with Maggie, made up three of the five female entrants in the race. According to their buildup in the press, they were supposed to be arch-rivals. In truth, they were good friends and mutual admirers of each other's accomplishments. As Maggie and Fernando approached their hangar, each of the others was busy with their own plane.

Petite Laura, whom Fernando had met several years earlier during her trip to South America, was standing on the wing, polishing some spots off the windscreen.

She hailed them cheerfully, then asked, "Roscoe, is this the lady I've been hearing so much about?"

Roscoe nodded and smiled affirmatively.

Rag in hand, the woman known to all as Petite Laura, jumped down to the hangar floor and hurried over to them. She hugged Maggie and warmly welcomed her into the sorority of race aviatrixes. This she did by allowing their cheeks to touch, while smacking her lips into the air. The unexpected spontaneous show of affection caught Maggie off-guard, but thrilled her nonetheless. *What a thrill to be part of this*, she inwardly reflected. *I can hardly believe this is happening to me.*

"Come on up and see my cockpit," Laura invited. "Hop up on the wing—two on that side and one on this." Despite her friendly manner, she did not recognize Fernando, whom she had known briefly while in Buenos Aires.

She guided the three to the handholds, then proudly showed off the instrument features inside her plane. She also described the state-of-the-art cockpit layout and explained why she had installed the many switches where she did.

Fernando coughed, a wry smile appearing at the corners of his mouth. "Perhaps I didn't make much of an impression, Miss Ingalls, but do you remember me?"

"Oh, my goodness," Laura Ingalls exclaimed, covering her mouth with her hands, "It can't be! Mr. San Martin?"

"Yes, Fernando. We met in Buenos Aires. Only in the states I go by my mother's maiden name of Underwood."

"It's so good to see you. And you're with Maggie?"

"She's my wife," Fernando shouted, as a nearby plane was revving its engines. "Maggie, honey, meet Laura Ingalls. She's one remarkable ambassador."

Maggie held out her hand, which Laura took. "I guess we're competitors," Maggie said shyly, "although I feel like I'm competing more against myself than anyone."

"You're not alone there, girl," Laura laughed genuinely. "I've looked forward to this day for years, knowing that they couldn't keep those of the 'weaker sex' out indefinitely."

"That's for sure," Fernando chuckled loudly. "And Roscoe Turner, our friend and business partner—you know Laura Ingalls. Laura, as you've seen from the list, Roscoe is also an entry in this year's race."

"Won't this be your fourth time, Roscoe?" Laura asked.

"Sure is, although I'm not sure I'm any better off this year than I was the last three."

"Well, we won't have to wait long to see, will we?" Laura replied, again smiling.

As the three partners and friends admired the facets of the newly designed aircraft, Amelia called to them from her nearby plane. She had the hatch open above her head and was standing on the pilot's seat looking in their direction. Motioning emphatically, she cupped her hands and yelled, "I've got something every woman should see."

Meeting the trio, together with Laura, at the rear cabin door of her sleek, twin-engine plane, Amelia escorted Maggie to the ladies' powder room that had been installed in the aft part of the spacious cabin. Laughing over this unusual facility, the two then stepped back and allowed the others to likewise take a look.

"The only problem is," Amelia added, smiling, "that during the race I'll be flying alone. I won't even be able to take advantage of the accommodations."

They all laughed at the irony and spent several more minutes looking over the rest of the cabin.

As they descended from the plane, Maggie found herself almost in awe at the size of Amelia's big twin. Suddenly, she felt chagrined at the diminutive dimensions of her own racer and wondered if she even had a chance to win, not to mention a good chance.

Maggie thanked Amelia for selling Roscoe one of her two spare directional gyros, then turned to leave, as Amelia said, "Oh, I almost forgot to tell you folks what I just picked up on my radio. I was listening to the news and heard that Howard Hughes has dropped out of the race. According to the newscast, he's having gear problems with his new craft and can't get the transmission to cycle correctly."

"We heard the same thing," Fernando replied, "only we didn't know the cause. Roscoe predicted from day one that Mr. Hughes wouldn't fly his new ship in the race. He's too much of a perfectionist."

"That's right," Roscoe yelled, nodding his head. "I felt it in my bones."

Before leaving the hangar, Maggie again thanked Amelia for the spare gyro and for being so generous.

Amelia, taken by Maggie's genuine appreciation, replied, "Anything I have is yours—except my husband, of course."

They all laughed comfortably, Laura extended her hand, and concluded by saying, "Good luck in the race, you guys. May the best pilot win."

"May the best pilot win," they chorused, then waved and exited the hangar.

The late afternoon photo lineup of the planes was a thrilling moment for Maggie. All nine racers were in a line, with each pilot standing to the left of the nose of his or her aircraft. The two twins—the one sponsored by the oil company and the one to be flown by Amelia—were on each end, and the majestic-looking Russian plane was directly in the middle. It was the first good look most of the contestants had gotten of the Russian craft, and each was nothing short of amazed at the sleek, powerful presence it exuded. Maggie's Staggerwing, on the other hand, was not the smallest of the remaining crafts; nor was it the largest. The lineup, itself, reflected the progress of the aeronautical art of the day.

As Maggie paced near her plane prior to the photo session, she looked in both directions, totally taken with the grandeur of the moment. She was especially impressed with the two all-metal twins—the huge DC-2, and the smaller, faster-looking Lockheed to be piloted by Amelia. Benny Block's DC-2 made the other planes look rather small. Next was Joe Clark's Northrop Gamma—a large aluminum plane, with a long fuselage and fixed gear enclosed in giant, outsized wheel pants designed with the intent of enhancing speed.

Next in line was Roscoe's racer—an all-aluminum plane, with retractable gear and low-wing lines. It was made distinctive by the large cowl on the engine, with teardrop bumps to streamline the rocker-arm covers.

Alongside Roscoe's plane was Maggie's powder-blue Staggerwing. Next to her craft was the rather radical racer with the in-line engine. It was to be piloted by a Susan Felt and was the smallest of all the planes.

Next in line was Petite Laura, with her oversized Lockheed Orion. The plane uncharacteristically sported a cockpit on top of the fuselage, just behind the engine. Between Laura and Amelia, on the end, was Cheri and her long-range racer. It was barrel-shaped, and likewise had a low-wing design. The cockpit of her racer sat to the rear of the fuselage, toward the tail, and seemed to be part of the rudder, itself.

A man's voice sounded loudly into a megaphone, and Maggie, together with the other contestants, moved quickly to the sides of their respective crafts. Announcements were then made, while still and movie cameras captured the moment on film.

For Maggie this moment when all time seemed to stand still, was stirring and emotional. Here she was, against all odds—a woman who, only weeks before, could barely afford to feed herself, let alone her twin palominos. Now, after marrying the most wonderful man in the world, she was actually representing his deceased father as she prepared to enter the race of a lifetime.

The wonder of it all, coupled with the fact that the entire country would be viewing her part in the race on the silver screen, was almost more than she could fathom. But she would do her best, and although she had no idea what destiny awaited, she was confident that her preparation was adequate. Now all she could do was place her safety in the Lord's hands: this was enough. For Maggie, it was enough.

Chapter Twenty-Three

Maggie's self-confidence had been high as she anticipated her lifelong dream. But now, waiting nervously in her plane's cockpit, she suddenly felt like a little girl—insecure and afraid. Was it a premonition? Would she crash on takeoff, like Roscoe's stories of overloaded planes in prior years? Would she suffer a fuel or oil line leak, throwing gas or hot oil all over her windscreen so she couldn't see out? Would she make it to her destination, or would something tragic happen to her that would bring a sudden and chilling end to the happiest month of her life? Had she seen Fernando for the last time? Could she really expect to again be in his arms after landing in Kansas?

Maggie's thoughts tumbled disjointedly in her mind. Fernando had left the previous afternoon and should be well on his way to Wichita by now. Even thinking of this fact brought chills along Maggie's spine. She was suddenly so . . . so alone. And it wasn't an alone moment sitting astride one of her palomino stallions, either. She was about to embark on the experience of a lifetime, and Fernando could not even be with her.

Her fears were unavoidably becoming as dark as the cloud-laden sky overhead. Should she drop out? No, she could not even consider it. Before boarding for his own flight the previous afternoon, Fernando had asked her if she truly wanted to go through with the race. Her answer, although in retrospect quite flippant, was a resounding "Of course not!"

Now, as she revved her engines while waiting for her turn to begin the race, she mentally replayed the exciting and nerve-racking events of the previous twenty-four hours. Maggie wished that Fernando could have attended the morning meeting for the pilots, the weather briefing, or even the promotional press conference.

But Fernando hadn't been there, and although Roscoe was attentive and sensitive to her needs, Maggie could detect that he was mentally withdrawing into himself, in preparation for the exhaustive ordeal ahead.

The most crucial moment, of course, had been the meeting with the race officials, where numbers were drawn that determined the order of takeoff for the contestants. Each pilot had drawn a number from a hat; and, depending upon which number they drew, they chose their desired takeoff time. The times were spaced a minimum of fifteen minutes apart, beginning with the first rays of dawn. The race was being separately timed for each contestant, with the winner being the one with the shortest elapsed time from takeoff in New York to the imaginary finish line 1,000 feet over the center of the air field in Los Angeles. The projected time was between twelve and thirteen hours of flight.

Maggie drew the fifth position, right in the middle of the nine racers. There were five female entries and four male, including Roscoe. Howard Hughes and one other man had withdrawn, and no unexpected last-minute entries had appeared.

The one aspect of the race that had surprised Maggie—in addition to the extremely varied types of planes—was the different charted routes. Projected weather conditions and designated refueling points were the primary considerations for the different routes, and of course, consideration to the ground crews that would service the planes throughout the race.

Laura had received the second slot, and Maggie marveled at her takeoff only thirty minutes earlier. Camera crews were buzzing the field in several rental aircraft, and it looked to Maggie like the sun caught Laura's plane at just the moment for spectacular footage in the movie. Laura with her effervescent personality, had attracted the fancy of the movie director, and Maggie was happy that he was going to include her as a real personality in the movie. Likewise, he would include the more famous Amelia Erhardt and take advantage of her recognition factor and her photogenic screen presence.

From where Maggie had stood next to her plane, she had almost *felt* Laura, as she waited for the starter's flag. She had held the brakes hard and had then wound up her engine to maximum r.p.m.'s. The engine screamed, the brakes strained, and the plane shook, dust devils whipping up like small whirlwinds. A stream of dirt, papers, and pebbles simultaneously broke loose behind her plane, as Laura had lined up at the end of the runway pavement, with only soil and grass behind her. When the starter's flag dropped, Laura was ready, and her plane literally leaped forward.

With its acceleration power, Maggie knew that Laura's plane would lift off well before it reached the end of the runway. The plane was silhouetted against the gray of the morning sky, as it rose noisily into the air. Maggie tingled with excitement. She watched the landing gear fold into the pockets on the belly of the plane and stood in awe as it lifted out over the ocean.

Susan Felt had just taken off, and Maggie was anxiously awaiting the flight of the plane ahead of her. As luck would have it, this craft was vastly different than all the rest—the Russian's racer seemed to have captured the interest of the film crew. Maggie had only briefly met the pilot, Sergé, as he was drawing his number from the hat. He had seemed stiff and spitshined, his hair combed straight back; yet when he shook her hand, he smiled warmly and said, "I will be watching for you, Maggie San Martin. If you have any problems, do not hesitate to radio to me. I will likewise be refueling in Kansas with you and your friend— my new comrade, Roscoe." Then, to Maggie's surprise, he handed her a small piece of paper, upon which was written his frequency number.

Maggie was startled with the Russian's announcement that he would be traveling their same air route. She was puzzled that the race officials in Wichita had failed to mention that fact. This information—or lack of it—seemed to add to the mystery surrounding the Russian's last minute entry in the race and caused Maggie's throat to constrict with a sudden and unexpected fear. What if he tried to sabotage her ? she now questioned. What if a much deeper meaning should be made to his handshake and gesture of friendship? How could he have known Roscoe well enough to refer to him as his comrade? Was that, too, a ploy to catch her off guard, or was it a sincere gesture of friendship? The questions were inexplicable, and try as she might, Maggie could not come to a resolution in her mind.

Maggie taxied into position and shut down her engine; she watched intently as the unusual Russian-American named Sergé pushed in the throttle and began to rush forward. His plane quickly gathered speed, then almost shot off the runway and into the skies.

Once in the air, two strategically hovering film planes followed him into the increasing light to the west. Having such a beautiful and unusually crafted racer was a bonus that even Hollywood could not have staged. Won't Fernando be surprised, she considered, when the man who asked to be called Sergé descends out of the clouds in Wichita.

Realizing that she had not made her spiritual preparations for the race, Maggie bowed her head and offered a vocal prayer for Fernando, for the other pilots, and for herself. Concluding, she said, "Thank you, Heavenly Father, for bringing Fernando into my life. He is much more than I could have ever hoped for, and I love him with all my heart. And bless him, Father, to feel the truths of Thy restored gospel—and of the Book of Mormon. Give him the desire to read its pages and to prayerfully consider the things he has now learned. He is such an honest man, Heavenly Father, and again I thank Thee for him, and for his family. Especially I ask that Thou would bless his mother, and his brother, Ricardo, in their hour of loss. And, too, bless my new father, Don Hugo, as he begins his life in the world of spirits. I love him dearly, and I am so thankful that he was preserved until he could reunite with Fernando, his son."

Concluding her prayer, Maggie had to wipe away the moisture from the corners of her eyes. She was so filled with love, and with peace, and with thanksgiving. *My life,* she thought happily, *could never be better than this.*

Just as she dried her eyes and applied a light coat of lipstick to keep her lips from chapping, Maggie observed the official with the yellow flag. He was making wide, semicircular sweeps with it, while looking in Maggie's direction. It was her moment, at last. Taking a deep breath, she tightened her right hand on the throttle and prepared to restart the engine.

Working steadily, she built up her fuel pressure with a few strokes of the hand wobble pump. She hit the primer, turned on the master switch, and flipped the starter button into the on position. One blade moved, then another, signalling for her to turn the magnetos to the designated *Both*. The spark ignited the first cylinder on compression, then fired with a *bang,* blowing smoke and flame out the exhaust. Even though the propeller began to spin, no other cylinders fired. Maggie pumped the throttle, and the other cylinders finally responded—emitting flames from the exhaust pipe. Maggie knew this engine response was normal, and so she made a further adjustment to the throttle. All cylinders then caught with a roar, causing her to back the throttle off. At that point, the radial settled down into a steady rumble.

Maggie was relieved beyond words that the engine had once again started. It was always an embarrassing possibility for an engine to be balky, to get over-primed and flooded, or to wear down the battery with the heavy drain from the starter at the moment she needed to start it. Lady Luck was with her, however, and she had a perfect start. The oil pressure immediately increased, and Maggie enjoyed the feeling of knowing exactly what the engine was doing.

As soon as the engine settled into a steady hum, she gave a

thumbs-up signal to her assigned crew chief. He and his assistant ducked down, then ran behind the propeller to retrieve the wheel chocks. Each of the two men held up a wooden chock by a rope handle, letting Maggie know that she was free to roll.

She added an inch of throttle, the engine growled a little more loudly, and she began to roll forward. As she moved ahead, Maggie hit her right wheel brake, pivoted sharply, releasing the brake only when the nose was pointed to the run-up spot.

Maggie turned onto the paved circle, pointed her nose into the wind for better cooling, and braked to a full stop. She was at last ready for her final takeoff protocol. She first brought the engine up to 1,800 r.p.m., or about 60 percent of full power, and cycled the constant speed propeller to make sure it was functioning properly. At that point, she checked both magneto systems—first the left and then the right—before returning the switch to both.

It's a shame, she considered silently, that so few nonpilots know that aircraft engines have two spark plugs per cylinder rather than just one like a car has—each part of an independent circuit—in case of electricity failure in one.

Both of the plane's systems checked out perfectly. Maggie tried the carburetor heat to make sure the early morning humidity had not allowed some ice to restrict the throat of the big Stromberg-Carlson carburetor. Immediately, the r.p.m.'s dropped. She turned the heat off and watched as they returned to a normal level.

After examining the cabin to make one final determination that everything was secured, Maggie rolled out to the very end of the runway. She pivoted the plane, finding that she was looking straight down the center line of the longest paved strip at the airport. She had positioned herself so that her tailwheel was in the dirt, while her propeller was extending out over the pavement. That way she could use every inch of the runway, while not allowing the prop to get any nicks by stirring up rocks from the ground.

Because the race official had left his flag in the hangar, which was now too far away to retrieve, he pulled his handkerchief out of his pocket and dropped it in place of the flag.

Maggie released her hard-set brakes, laughing to herself about the irony of a handkerchief start, and the plane jumped instantly forward. As the craft began to move, the polished prop blades grabbed buckets of air, flinging them behind as it clawed its way forward.

The crowd edged closer to the runway in order to take pictures of Maggie, whom they had affectionately labeled as the "Rookie Blonde."

As the plane picked up speed, Maggie's back pressed magnetically into her seat. In spite of having full right rudder all the way forward, she immediately saw that the plane was drifting to the left. Then she remembered why—she was not supposed to use full power on takeoff. Thinking quickly, she pulled back on the throttle, causing a lessening in pitch inside the screaming, thundering engine. The spectators gawked intently, fully expecting her to abort her flight. Instead of doing this, however, she kept flying straight ahead.

Sensing that she was regaining control, Maggie wrestled her overpowered plane past the onlookers, then brought the tail up when she had enough slipstream over the rudder to hold it straight. Almost as though her heavy, fuel-ladened craft breathed a sigh of relief, she eased it slowly into the air.

The Staggerwing gradually gathered momentum. Within seconds, Maggie disappeared from view above the race officials and ground crew cameramen below. Her knuckles white with pressure on the steering wheel and throttle, she felt the plane shudder and was suddenly leveling out. It was only then that she noticed the two film crew planes. The first craft, a single-engine, single-wing craft that she couldn't identify, had swooped down and was flying directly to her left. The other, a beautiful red biplane, was above her and to her right. While neither was in the camera view of the other, both filmed steadily as she continued to rise.

While Maggie noticed the crowd disappearing below and behind her, she immediately focused on the tasks at hand. As she first retracted the landing gear into the wheel wells, those on the ground noticed that the plane went through a metamorphosis. With its wheels down, it had looked very old-fashioned and awkward. Now, however, as the landing gear disappeared up into the belly, it took on a totally new look. It now appeared modern and streamlined and seemed to be more in its own element. In short, it took on a sleekness that was enhanced by the mirror polish on its fabric exterior.

"The next item of business," Maggie said out loud, "is to reset the power." She thus came back on the manifold pressure by pulling the throttle back, and she twisted the propeller control to reduce the r.p.m.'s.

As Maggie made the necessary adjustments, she knew intuitively that she had to do things in that exact order—thus avoiding any excess buildup of pressure in the cylinders. She then turned off the electric fuel pump that had been used in takeoff. She also had a hand wobble-pump, in case both the engine-driven fuel pump and the electrical, standby pump failed. Finally, she turned the fuel selector valve to the right tank—the one that would be drawn upon during the next hour.

Banking the plane toward her climb course, Maggie began to fly a straight route, just as Fernando and Roscoe had instructed her to do. Now fully into the climb, her eyes scanned from instrument to instrument as she monitored her power settings, then back to her navigation instruments.

Maggie's instincts told her that the vibration from the engine and the propeller were normal, and this fact brought great relief. Without question, she had bonded with this plane when she piloted it from the factory with Fernando. The controls were balanced, and the plane responded quickly to her slightest touch. In addition, the engine growled harmlessly along, pulling them higher and higher toward the altitude she desired.

The sky was overcast, although rays of sunshine peeked intermittently through the clouds, illuminating the ground and the city below. New York was awake and bustling, but since this was Labor Day, the traffic was not as heavy as on the day they had flown in.

Long Island Sound and the Hudson River looked inviting in the last days of summer, and Maggie noticed several pleasure boats plowing the water, leaving long streaks of frothy wake etched in the textured moisture behind.

Her heart racing wildly, Maggie could not remember being so keyed up—not even when her friend, Bishop Barney, was about to pronounce Fernando and her man and wife. It was as though all of her emotions had been safely stored within her, only to be released now.

Thirty seconds into the race, Maggie turned the wheel and banked sharply to the right. She was reassured to find that she had climbed to an altitude of one thousand feet, and that she could now settle in and enjoy the spectacular view of Long Island and New York as it passed silently beneath her.

Maggie was thankful that Fernando had insisted a supercharger be installed so that she could ascend quickly above the cloud layer. It had accompanied the new engine and would prove invaluable in climbing, then leveling off in the thin air at eleven thousand feet. Maggie knew that the headwinds were potentially stronger the higher she went, but she also knew that she must fly at this altitude if she had any chance at all of winning.

As she continued her ascent, Maggie suddenly thought of Roscoe, who was still two contestants behind her, on the tarmac. She smiled as she recalled his announcement to the press earlier that morning. When a reporter had asked him what he called his plane, Roscoe had kept a straight face as he replied, "A D.G.A." Naturally the reporter followed up with wanting to know what the initials meant. Without hesitation Roscoe replied, "Damn good airplane!" That quip was sure to be repeated in all the newspapers, and Maggie smiled again, thinking how fortunate she was in having such a lighthearted and trusted friend as Roscoe following her in the skies.

The Russian Sergé's plane was directly ahead of Maggie, although above the clouds and out of sight. According to Maggie's watch, it had a fifteen-minute headstart, and she doubted that she would see it until refueling in Kansas.

Cheri Green, in her racer, would follow Maggie, although along a more northerly route. Roscoe would follow Cheri into the sky, and with his ability to respond to wind conditions, would likely catch them both along the way.

The DC-2, scheduled in the eighth position and piloted by Benny Block, did not really seem to be a threat in the race. The other pilots had contended that it would be the slowest of all. It was scheduled to make three stops, each in a large and growing city. It was thought that the transport's entry into the race was primarily for the benefit of these five local dealers who wanted publicity photos of them with the crew in front of the company's race plane. And Maggie agreed. It seemed to be more of a promotional project than anything else for the transport to even be in the race.

Taking up the rear, in almost an earned position of trust, was Amelia Erhardt. Although she had drawn the second position, she knew that Laura Ingalls was anxious to begin, and so she deferred to her friend. Besides, she had discretely mentioned to Maggie that she wanted to know that each of her competitors was safely in the air, and so taking up the rear position was in no way disconcerting to her.

It was a celebrated and high profile group that had entered the race, and from Maggie's mind-set, she was the least experienced and least likely to win. Still, these odds strangely agreed with Maggie, and she knew that anything she did would provide a lifetime of memories. She was, at last, fulfilling her dream; and that, coupled with Fernando's unique part in it all, added even greater drama to the event.

Chapter Twenty-Four

Three hours into the race, and clearly halfway to Wichita, Maggie was becoming increasingly comfortable. She had created a routine of stretching her muscles, especially her legs, and she was pleased that the headwinds had died down. She and Fernando had spent a full day with one of the university professors, analyzing the expected wind patterns according to their latest techniques.

Maggie's only concern was whether she had chosen the best route for the race. She knew that Roscoe would swing farther north than she would, taking a straight-line path the other pilots had affectionately labeled, the Roscoe Route. There was one dip in his route, and that was in New Mexico. Roscoe had insisted on dropping down to Albuquerque and making a third stop there. Although he had strongly encouraged Maggie to follow suit, she had quietly resolved to follow her original plans, and see how her instincts guided her at that point in the race.

As she now flew along, she remembered Roscoe's words, almost as though he was in the cockpit speaking them to her. "Maggie," he had told her, "the route over northern New Mexico is over the Sangre de Cristo mountains. This is some of the most barren country you can imagine. If anything goes wrong, it could take days to find you. And, if you do get over the rough New Mexico country, your line of flight to Los Angeles would still take you across northern Arizona, between the San Francisco peaks and the Grand Canyon."

Reflecting now, Maggie could mentally visualize the route Roscoe had described. She had flown over that area many times, taking off from nearby Kanab, Utah, and skirting around the unusually treacherous air turbulence over the Grand Canyon. The only time she had ventured over the canyon itself was one spring morning, well before sunrise. The heat from the canyon had been almost nonexistent, and the view was simply spectacular.

"It's beautiful country," she remembered Roscoe continuing with his caution. "But, again, there are several problems to be aware of. There are no emergency airports. You'll have rough country below and big cloud buildups at the time of day you'll be crossing. You must dodge around those big babies because they can tear the wings off racers like ours. As you know, a desert cumulonimbus storm has vertical winds of up to 200 miles per hour, so stay clear of them."

As Roscoe's detailed warnings resounded loudly in Maggie's mind, she was suddenly overwhelmed with emotion. She was hardly aware of the Appalachians beneath her, as she reflected on the love she felt for Roscoe. In ways, he had become as much a brother as Will was, and during the past four years, he had become her protector and advocate. Even with her marriage, he had continued to be concerned for her. Perhaps Maggie's greatest relief was Fernando's acceptance of Roscoe, and their mutual respect for each other. Now, as Roscoe's words played across her mind, Maggie appreciated Fernando's final advice the afternoon before. "Just keep your senses," he had said, taking her into his arms. "Your faith, and your uncanny intuition, will be your best compass."

Your faith, and your uncanny intuition, Maggie repeated silently. Fernando had always shown trust in her actions. She knew she truly was his equal by the way he treated her, and Maggie appreciated that fact as much as any other. Their marriage, although taking place much more quickly than they had planned, exceeded her greatest expectations. Don Hugo had been right—they were meant for each other, and—

Don Hugo? At the thought of her father-in-law, Maggie could almost visualize him sitting beside her, encouraging her on. *He was such a sweet man*, she reflected, smiling. *And I'll never forget the love in his eyes, as he gazed into Dame Helen's heart for the very last time.* Maggie, herself, had been standing behind Fernando, weeping quietly. Now, in quiet remembrance, she thrilled with the blessing of knowing this great man, and of feeling the love that existed between him and his lifelong companion.

Chapter Twenty-Five

As Maggie entered the fifth hour of her race, averaging a full 200 miles per hour, the pilot Joe Clark flew approximately 185 miles ahead, toward the airport in Wichita. Unbeknownst to Maggie, Joe was beginning his descent to refuel when his luck turned sour. First, there was a vibration in his plane that only a seasoned pilot would detect. The vibration occurred again, only this time it was worse. Something was going on, but what was it? Fuel? Magneto spark? A crack in a spark plug perhaps?

At that instant, a flash of flame exploded out of the engine, whipping back toward him as part of the slipstream. Quickly and completely, the fire enveloped the plane in flames.

Terrified, but in control, Joe immediately switched the fuel tank to off, eliminating the ability of further fuel getting into the engine compartment. That was the good news. The bad news— this act immediately stopped the engine. Even so, the explosion had apparently ruptured an oil line, because the fire continued to burn.

Thinking his way through the emergency, Joe knew that he had a reserve oil tank located where the flames seemed to originate. That tank would feed the fire, then perhaps blow the entire plane to smithereens. If this didn't happen, he feared the fire might travel to a fuel tank, or to the carburetor. In either case, another explosion was imminent.

Instinctively, Joe tightened his chute belts, unstrapped his lap and shoulder belts from the seat, then plummeted downward in an effort to blow the fire out. He did not succeed, and within seconds the smoke and heat were entering the cockpit.

Reasoning as best he could, Joe knew that his only choice was to jump. He knew there were no other options, but to save himself, he needed to hit the silk.

Opening the cockpit cover, he pulled the nose of the plane up, rolled it over, then dropped out. As the tail flashed by, he pulled his ripcord. Silently thanking Maggie for insisting he take her spare chute, he felt a flood of relief as the canopy blossomed open. At that instant, while he gazed in horror, the plane blew up in a ball of fire. Joe had never experienced such relief, as he knew that he had escaped certain death by only seconds.

The explosion, however, caught the attention of spectators on the ground. The authorities were notified, and the command center in Wichita was alerted. They came to see the accident site and to interview the heroic survivor of the mid-air explosion—a man they were surprised to learn had been in the well-publicized Bendix Cup air race.

Fifteen minutes behind Joe and several miles to the north, the second accident of the race was about to take place. Laura Ingalls, flying in a less direct line than her friend, Joe, was about to experience her own brush with death.

Laura had years of flying experience, but never had she experienced a storm like the one she was about to enter. As she flew into the foreboding cumulonimbus clouds, she felt confident that the plane's advanced navigation radio would see her through without mishap. She had assumed incorrectly as almost immediately, the radio went dead. It had never before failed her, and somehow she reasoned that precipitation must have leaked into the system, shorting it out. With zero visibility, Laura immediately switched to instrument flying. It was the only way she could determine if she was upright. Even so, she had no way of knowing if her navigation was close to the course she intended to fly.

Laura was not initially nervous about the radio failure, as she considered it to be merely a temporary inconvenience. After droning along in the soup for an indeterminate distance, she calculated from the maps that she must be somewhere east of St. Louis. The terrain was such that she felt it safe to try to descend through the clouds so she could see the ground and get her bearings. After all, she reasoned, the storm she was flying in might have winds from a different direction, and of a greater force than she had calculated.

She broke through the lower cloud level at a safe altitude, then searched for landmarks in which to locate her position. She could see a set of railroad tracks below, but that was not enough. Nor was a highway extending to her right enough.

At last, after almost giving up, Laura spotted a lake and river adjacent to the railroad and highway. Those landmarks pinpointed her position, and she was relieved beyond words. To her dismay, she had been slowed down by unexpected headwinds. In addition, her plane had consumed more fuel than expected.

Laura determined to stop for fuel in what had to be St. Louis, Missouri. She had made no arrangements, of course, but assumed that a city of that size should have the necessary accommodations.

By using full power in her descent, Laura made up several minutes of the time she had now lost. She could tell from the ground below that there had been a great deal of rain during the storm, and even now the water seemed to float over the saturated ponds.

Spotting what she knew had to be the airport, Laura aimed her plane toward it. But, when she was almost there, she could see that the tarmac was under construction, and that the runway was nothing more than a large grassy field. Two aircraft hangars were built side-by-side, yet with doors closed and no activity evident.

Suddenly concerned that the holiday, or perhaps the construction, had closed the airport down, Laura panicked. Instead of bringing her plane in gradually, as she knew to do, she over-compensated, and leveled off and stalled out too high. The plane dropped hard. The wheels dug into the rain-softened turf. Laura, white with fear, froze as the plane catapulted end-over-end, shearing off the right wing as it ground the cockpit into the water-soaked grass below it.

Laura, strapped securely in her seat, felt the top of the cockpit press against her padded leather helmet. Fearing the worst, she waited for her neck to snap—sensing that death was just seconds away. But the worst had already happened, taking its toll only on the plane and Laura's hopes for winning the race. As the crushed and decapitated craft came slowly to a halt, Laura suddenly understood that, unless the plane ignited, she was going to live. *Thank goodness,* she mentally pressed, *the fuel tanks are nearly empty. Now, if only I can—*

Directly outside the shattered cockpit window, Laura could see two trousered legs. Instantly, the person approaching the plane knelt down and yelled, "I'll get ye out, ma'am . . . jist hol' yer hosses an' keep sayin' yer pray'ers."

Feeling suddenly nauseous, Laura could only stare at the kindly gentleman, while slightly nodding from her upside-down position.

"Now . . ." he spit, clearing his mouth of what Laura imagined was a plug of tobacco, "my name's Benny McDowell, an' I'll do ye no harm. Le's see whar yer strap buckle is . . . ."

Reaching inside, the man quickly found the buckle, snapped it open, then cradled Laura in his arms as he slowly drew her out through the window. Scooping her up as though she were a sack of grain, he literally ran away from the smoldering plane.

Seconds later, as the man gently lay Laura's body in the safety of the uncut wheat at the edge of the uncompleted runway, he knelt on one knee, gasping for breath.

"Don't want thet thar plane o' yourn takin' ye under . . . not after yer mir'cle-like landin', I don't."

"Th- thank you, sir," Laura managed, barely in a whisper. "I-

I'll be all right, thanks to you."

The two became quiet, waiting for the plane to explode. Only the craft didn't explode, but simply continued to smolder, somehow seeming to sense that it had made its final flight.

Laura lay in a prone position with the man's shirt tucked securely beneath her head. Her rescuer—a huge, bearded, colored man—simply sat on his haunches, his hands clasped in front of his legs. He had done himself proud, and as the airport security watchman, he would now telephone the police station. Help would be on its way, and with good fortune, the woman lying beside him would be fine.

Laura, meanwhile, was entering a clear state of shock. She knew she was alive, and although she could feel no specific pain, she had survived an impossible crash. Closing her eyes, she took a deep breath, and slipped silently into a state of semiconsciousness.

Fernando was worried, and it showed. His brow deepened by the minute as the storm clouds continued to gather. Maggie, who was now ten full minutes behind her forecasted schedule, was nowhere in sight. Although Fernando had not left the airport upon hearing of Joe Clark's accident, he had learned of the man's safe parachute escape, and he was relieved. Petite Laura, the number two contestant, was also unaccounted for; but with her inclination to do the unpredictable, he released her from his mind.

Circling slowly around the airport with one of the two airborne filming crews, he realized more than ever before just how extremely treacherous the transcontinental race was for his relatively inexperienced pilot-bride. Twelve hours of gut-wrenching anxiety—not to mention the feeling of floating alone through the skies, helplessly praying that the weather and the mechanics of the plane would not fail her.

Susan Felt, the number three entrant, had just taken off, and Sergé, the Russian, was taxiing down the runway for the second half of his flight. While there was no word as yet about the other contestants, they had all safely begun the race, and other than Roscoe, only Benny Block, with the huge DC-2, were scheduled to refuel in Wichita.

Just as Fernando's plane was beginning a further loop around the airport, a plane broke through the clouds and headed straight for the runway. Fernando immediately recognized the powder-blue color of Maggie's plane, and his heart leaped within him. It was Maggie, and she was now being filmed as she descended well below the clouds and onto the runway.

Five minutes later, with the strong urgings of Fernando, the plane he was in also taxied toward the hangar, hunting out Maggie's Staggerwing, as it was now being lined up for fuel.

As his plane stopped, Fernando stepped quickly down onto the tarmac. Glancing toward Maggie's plane, he was surprised not to see her running toward him. Then, he saw out of the corner of his eye, his sweetheart coming out of the lady's room.

"Fernando, darling," she shouted, as she broke into a full run toward him. "I've missed you terribly."

"Maggie, oh my beautiful Maggie," Fernando exclaimed, sweeping his bride into his arms. "I was afraid something had happened to you."

"Oh, you worry-wart, why? Other than a bit of a rocky descent out of the clouds, I've had a perfect flight."

"Have you had enough to eat?"

"Actually, darling, I can't remember eating so many sandwiches. It's more lonely up there than I could have imagined, and I think I'm eating just to keep myself company."

"Maybe I could stow away in the rear of your plane," Fernando said, jokingly, "then the last half of the flight will be as close to heaven as you could get."

"Oh, ho!" Maggie laughed, "And risk being disqualified if you're found out? Not on your life, buster."

Tickling Fernando as she spoke, the two newlyweds embraced silently, basking in the warmth of their love. They knew that, within minutes, Maggie would again be into the sky, heading toward Los Angeles.

Several hours later, after crossing the imaginary line into eastern Arizona, Maggie began to experience a gnawing discomfort that she was unable to explain. Her Staggerwing, performing to perfection, purred along mile after mile, and her workout routine kept her blood circulating while she maintained her seat in front of the controls.

But there was something askew—something invisible and impending—that would simply not go away.

"Perhaps," she said aloud, "it's just the cloud cover in the distance."

But the cloud formation, creeping menacingly in and around the peaks west of Flagstaff, did not seem to offer a squall-like wind potential. Instead, they seemed localized and could be flown through if she but maintained her present altitude of 11,500 feet. She could not easily fly over them, and it would take a half hour to change her course either to the north or to the south.

"Then again," she said wistfully, "if I flew north, I could skirt the north end of the Grand Canyon, and buzz my folks at the ranch. If only they could see me now."

Just thinking that she was flying over the state in which her family lived, brought tears to Maggie's eyes. She was so humbled to think that, without expectation or pretense, she had married into a family of almost inconceivable wealth. At times, given the fact that this condition provided an almost too easy solution for rescuing her family's homestead, she had even experienced guilt. Still, the pervading emotion had been one of deep gratitude and appreciation, and just seeing how money could be manipulated to ease suffering and pain, brought a resolve to Maggie's mind to always look outward, as Fernando called it, to see how they could bless the lives of others.

Fernando was almost too good to be real, she now reasoned, yet given the remarkable genetic inheritance he had received from his parents, Dame Helen and Don Hugo, his disposition was not accidental. His greatest attributes, she now knew—in addition to his blatant quest for honesty—included the unlikely twin sisters of modesty and strength. He really did consider his family position to be one of trust and responsibility, rather than one of selfish aggrandizement.

Suddenly, there was an interruption to Maggie's thoughts—the staccato sound against the windshield that she immediately recognized as large, splattering rain drops. The clouds had grown around her almost without her being aware and were thicker and darker than she had expected.

"Well then, so be it," she whispered with a deep, long sigh.

The clatter on the plane grew louder and heavier, almost as though a spicket had been turned on in the heavens. At first the raindrops were being whipped into a fine spray by the propeller. Now, however, they were so heavy they were getting through and hitting the windshield with a wilder sound. The big drops seemed like lead shot being thrown at the plexiglass in front of Maggie's eyes. Instinctively, she reached for her old flying helmet and goggles—an insurance against the possibility that if the plexiglass broke, her face and head would be protected.

Within what seemed like only seconds, Maggie could see the rain streaking past her like tracer bullets zipping past from an unseen machine gun. The sound was growing so deafening that it was drowning out the roar of the engine. Maggie, peering into the sudden storm before her, suddenly realized that she could no longer see the ground. She was engulfed in the clouds and must begin to fly exclusively by instrument—making every effort to gain altitude and work her way above the storm. Although Fernando had made her do this in the flight to Long Island, at this time it seemed eery to do so, and not at all comforting. She had never before flown in such heavy rain, and suddenly she felt a constricting in her throat.

At that instant, Maggie began to ask herself one question after another. Would the Staggerwing's engine run in the rain? Would the moisture drown out the carburetor? Would swallowing so much water hurt the engine in any way? Would the water short out the two magneto systems? Would the water get into the fuel system?

In the midst of Maggie's increasing anxiety about the engine stability, leaks started to develop in the cabin, with water first dripping through the ventilation system. Although she needed fresh air, she immediately shut the system off so that her maps wouldn't continue to get wet. Water began seeping through cracks around the wind screen. The seams were supposed to have been caulked and made watertight, but water was nevertheless coming through.

Just then, Maggie saw lightning flash to her left. "An embedded thunderstorm." she exclaimed loudly. "I'd better turn thirty degrees to the right, and fly around it."

Her plan did not work, however. Almost immediately after she changed course to avoid turbulence, she spotted more lightning in the darkest area to her right.

"Better come back ten degrees, then fly between the two cells," she directed herself. The din was so deafening that she couldn't even hear her voice.

Suddenly, Maggie's composure was put to the acid test.

Lightning flashed again, with a crash of sound and blinding light, shaking the plane violently. The turbulence seemed to be wrenching the wings from the sides of the plane. An unseen force catapulted the craft upward with a jolt, dropping Maggie's head to her chest. Fighting to keep the wings level and the nose boring straight ahead, she realized that the rate of climb indicator was pegged at the maximum vertical on the dial—over 3,000 feet per minute. Her altimeter had gone haywire and showed her moving upward, although she was flying with her nose level.

Then, just as suddenly, the little plane—still enmeshed in roaring rain and hail—dropped like a car driving off a vertical cliff. The wings twisted and creaked, and the fuselage bucked like a wild horse groaning under the extreme stress. Maggie's head was being thrown back and forth, preventing her from maintaining a visual bead on the instrument panel. She was now flying more by sheer instinct than by instrument readings, although her head was confused and spinning wildly.

For what seemed forever, Maggie felt as though she were inside a cement mixer with a million hammers beating on the sides. Just as she thought it couldn't possibly get worse, her hair stood on end—not from fright, but from static electricity. The wings of the plane took on an eerie luminescence, and the struts and chrome brace wires glowed weirdly. She was blinded, and because of the torrential downpour, she couldn't see so much as the cowling in front of her.

The instrument was pegged at a power dive of three thousand feet per minute. In reality, it was probably worse. The engine was not screaming as loudly as it would in a normal dive, and the air speed was uncharacteristically decreasing. What was happening? she questioned groggily. Was she losing control of the plane? Being torn by the violent up and downdrafts?

Be calm, and you will fly through it . . . .

The words, spoken into Maggie's mind, caught her completely off-guard.

"Who? Wha—?"

Maggie, my daughter, be calm, and you will fly through it. The light is for you.

Suddenly recognizing the accent and spinning her head to her right, Maggie fully expected to see someone—Don Hugo—sitting next to her. It was the second time during the flight that she had felt his presence, and now she was hearing his voice.

Sensing the need to not over-control in regaining mastery over the plane, Maggie felt a renewed strength enter her hands as they clasped the wheel and the throttle. Just as quickly as her mind regained clarity, she felt her eyes rolling upward. Her head then began to spin, and she found herself losing consciousness. She had wanted so badly to finish the race and to win it for Fernando. But now, as blackness closed in around her, she somehow sensed that it was forever too late. She was floating in a sea of darkness and, try as she might, she couldn't bring herself back to reality. The darkness was strangely peaceful, and the last thing Maggie knew, she was drawing a cool breath of air into her lungs.

Chapter Twenty-Six

The remaining six contestants were having their own problems, mostly mechanical. Number nine, Amelia Earhart, had gained several minutes on the field, and flying in last position, she had been able to get an update on the others when refueling in Wichita. Word had been received from Kansas City about Laura Ingall's misfortune, but she had wired her reassurances of being alive and uninjured. Thus, she joined Joe Clark in the ranks of the contestants now out of the race.

Susan Felt and Cheri Green, although both continuing unhampered in the race, were slowed down by flying around the great desert storm.

The huge DC-2 Transport, piloted by the eighth contestant, Benny Block, had indeed landed safely in Wichita. Benny knew that his slower time thus far, coupled with the first two stops, had taken him out of serious contending in the race. Besides, the objective of his sponsor was to give the plane public exposure, and he was accomplishing that goal to perfection.

While Benny was refueling the transport in Wichita, Fernando had convinced Joe that it would be okay for him to hitch a ride aboard and fly as a passenger to Los Angeles. While Fernando would likely not arrive prior to Maggie's completion of the race, he should be there within the hour, and thus enjoy the celebration with her.

But will it be a celebration? he questioned silently. For some inexplicable reason he had been worried for the past hour and found himself offering one silent prayer after another, hoping that Maggie would not encounter difficulties. Prayer was such a different experience for him, but since his father's untimely passing, he had felt an unexplainable closeness to the heavens above.

While Sergé headed straight into the storm ahead of Maggie, Roscoe chose to skirt it to the south and was enjoying the grandeur of the Arizona desert.

The blinking red light was annoying. Why couldn't they shut it off, and allow her to sleep.

Sleep? Light? It simply didn't make sense.

Struggling with all of the energy she could muster, Maggie opened first one eye, then the other. Focusing as much as she was able, she could see that the blinking red light had not disappeared. Rather, it was bleeping on and off, and was perched atop an airplane.

"An airplane?" Maggie shouted, not understanding. Then slowly, and with great mental effort, she came to the realization that flying directly ahead of her, and at the same altitude was Sergé. She was not dead, she had not crashed, but was flying at a registered 5,500 feet. *My seat belt! It was too loose. I must have hit my head against the roof and been knocked out.*

Maggie felt the top of her head, and sure enough, there was a large and painful bump protruding from the top of her skull. She reasoned that, after going unconscious, the plane had dropped a full 6,000 feet—over one mile—before she had regained her senses.

The storm, now raining only lightly, was quickly disappearing. In its place, breaking through the mid-afternoon skies to the west, was the sun—the most beautiful sight she had ever seen—which allowed its first rays to enter the cockpit.

What was the Russian doing? He had maintained his lead

when he left Wichita; yet now here he was, flying directly in front of her.

Pushing in on the throttle, Maggie increased the engine revolutions and pulled to the right to overtake him. She came broadside to the charismatic Sergé. Looking over to her left, she could not help being surprised looking him squarely in the eyes. He smiled brightly, gave her an emphatic thumbs-up, then moved ahead at what had to be 100 percent throttle.

Following suit, Maggie felt her plane climb. The Russian plane was likewise gaining altitude, only much more quickly; and within minutes, he had pulled ahead and above Maggie's craft. He continued to ascend to what had to now be 13,000 feet, until, almost forty minutes later, he disappeared completely from view.

"Well, that decides it," Maggie breathed softly. "He had a seventeen minute lead on me when we left Long Island, and I'm sure he'll lengthen that in the final stretch."

Resigning herself to simply completing the race, and relieved beyond words that her accidental blackout had resulted in such unusual good fortune, Maggie's flight then settled into boredom. No flying by instruments, no tuning the temperamental radio, and no bad weather. Only the radio and direction finder of her plane had gone out during the storm in Arizona, and now she must rely upon her own devices and judgment as she settled in for the final 300 plus miles of the race.

The big question, for Maggie, was not how she could complete the race on her own. Rather, it was the source of the voice— Don Hugo's voice—that had filled the cockpit during the darkest moment of the storm. That, and the unexplainable manner in which she stayed aloft while totally unaware and unconscious. That was the biggest mystery of all, and as Maggie considered it, goosebumps spread up and down her arms. It was a moment to savor, to be sure, yet still the questions remained, and Maggie resigned herself to solving them one at a time after the completion of the race.

As she entered the final hour of flight, Maggie suddenly felt deeply exhausted and spent. Although she had reopened the circulation vents, she was perspiring heavily, her metabolism seemingly out of kilter.

Looking down, and recognizing the newly populated resort and lake called Big Bear, Maggie fondly remembered her Santa Monica friends, Tom and Kit Myers, who, with their skilled son, Rick, were presently developing a ski resort there. Passing by this lake and Lake Arrowhead, Maggie marveled at the vastly different terrain over which she had flown. Sighing wistfully, she could hardly wait to fly again with Fernando, enjoying his marvelous wit and wisdom, as they traversed the shrinking globe together.

Maggie remembered a statement Fernando had made just prior to her departure from Wichita. "Flying cross country, Maggie, is nothing short of hour after hour of sheer boredom—punctuated from time to time with moments of stark terror." He had been right, of course, beyond his wildest imaginations, yet would assuredly believe her as she related her miraculous conquest of the storm in Arizona. She was glad that Sergé had been there for her, even though she was sure his presence was purely accidental. She couldn't wait to speak with him and to thank him for his silent encouragement. He had likely landed by now and would win the race.

For Maggie, the final hour passed quickly. As she began her final descent through the vast cloud cover, she was surprised to look out to her right and see another plane. Thinking it was a plane from the studio, she turned her eyes back toward the instrument panel. *But, wait! It couldn't have been a filming crew, for it was a lone pilot.*

Taking a hard second look, Maggie was surprised, yet elated, to see the plane flown by Susan Felt. Susan had flown in the number-two position, and so should have landed much earlier; but she was safe and was now waving excitedly in Maggie's direction.

Waving back, Maggie adjusted her controls, as she continued her descent. She was now at 2,000 feet and needed to drop another 1,000 feet before reaching the airfield that marked the end of the race.

Almost like two tandem racehorses, Maggie and Susan surprised the waiting crowd below by simultaneously crossing the imaginary finish line. They had done it. They had traveled the 2,800 miles, and according to her watch, she had personally accomplished the feat in just over 12 hours.

Signalling to Susan, Maggie motioned for her to land first. Then, banking hard to the right, she herself made a large loop, circling the field while she silently reveled in the feat she had just accomplished. Her right fuel tank was empty, yet her left tank still showed a quarter of a tank. Roscoe and Fernando had judged correctly, and she could afford to remain aloft while Susan landed, and while the film crew continued to film footage for the movie.

Maggie had no idea how her time compared with those who had finished the race, but she did know that she had done her very best, and her audible sigh of relief reflected the sentiment of the moment. Now to land, to meet with Sergé and Susan, and any others who may have completed the race. Maggie had known elation before, many times, but never had she experienced the flood of varying emotions that were in her heart at this time.

Chapter Twenty-Seven

Maggie hit first on the right wheel, then bounced to the left. Finally, after twelve hours and eighteen minutes in the air, including five minutes of circling after passing the finish line, both wheels settled on the tarmac, and she was safely on California soil. A brief taxi to the waiting throng of well-wishers and officials and her magnificent powder-blue Staggerwing came slowly to a stop—its engine coughing, then sputtering, and finally growing silent.

Climbing down from the plane, she was immediately surrounded by dignitaries and celebrities. Douglas Boynton reached her first. Pumping her hand up and down enthusiastically, he shouted, "You did it, Maggie! What's more, your time is the best so far."

Allowing the actor's words to sink in, Maggie just blinked and smiled. "How many have finished?" was all she could manage.

"Only Miss Felt and the Russian," Lord Jockham, who was also nearby, answered. "So far as we know, only two racers— Laura Ingalls and Joe Clark—have been unable to finish the race; although both are quite alright. But, by jove . . . you flew a right jolly flight, and we're all terribly proud of you."

"Thank you, sir," Maggie sighed genuinely. "I'm just relieved for Laura and Joe. But, how about Roscoe? Have you heard from Roscoe?"

"Not yet," an official broke in, "although we expect to hear from him soon. There's been no word of problems. For now, however," he added, motioning for Maggie to sit down in a nearby chair, "the press would like a statement. It will be filmed by radio and newspaper reporters, and, of course, cameramen from the film studio—so make a good impression."

Almost two hours later, after Cheri Green, then Roscoe, and finally Benny Block in his large DC-2, had landed, the mood was ecstatic. Roscoe, unfortunately, had experienced an oil leak that had covered his windshield, and so had been forced to make an extra landing at Las Vegas.

That left only Amelia Earhart to arrive, and radio contact had just been made with her, so it wouldn't be long until she appeared below the blanket of low-hanging clouds.

Benny's huge transport was turning around at the end of the tarmac, then beginning its taxi back to the terminal. Five minutes later, after the pilot had descended from the plane, Maggie was surprised beyond words to look up and see Fernando standing in the doorway.

"Darling!"

Maggie's salutation was being observed by everyone present, as they had kept Fernando's flight from Kansas a well-kept secret. Now, as his identity was made known, Fernando waved while the entire crowd whistled and shouted their applause.

Stepping quickly down from the plane, Fernando had barely gotten a firm grip on his duffle bag, when Maggie ran into his waiting arms. Staggering back, then regaining his balance, Fernando threw his arms around her and kissed her passionately. Their safety had been preserved, their reunion was complete, and now they had but to wait for Amelia to appear from the east, to bring an end to the race.

Amelia did arrive, minutes later, and the emotion in the crowd was electric. Maggie's time of 12 hours and 13 minutes had placed her almost a full minute ahead of the Russian. That surprised both Maggie and Fernando, and they now held their breath as Amelia flew past the finish-line, officially concluding her race.

The timekeepers whispered amongst themselves, allowing Amelia time to land and taxi to where they were standing. Then, as she climbed out of her plane and descended into the arms of her well-wishers, the officials asked for quiet.

Maggie and Fernando, having congratulated Amelia on her flight, stood silent, waiting. Fernando gently pressed his hand on the bump on Maggie's head and allowed his eyes to tell her of his concern.

Sergé chatted with them briefly, then quieted for the announcement—

"Ladies and gentlemen," the senior official shouted, his voice booming through the megaphone, "we have an official winner. However, taking second place, a full 55 seconds behind the winner, is a very special lady who is loved by us all . . . Amelia Earhart. We can all be thankful, that even though she had the hatch blow off her cockpit causing a forced landing for repairs, she completed the race in fine form."

As the official's unusual announcement continued, Maggie found herself unable to breathe.

"And the winner, also a lady we have come to love and admire, is none other . . . than . . . Mrs. Maggie Rockwell Underwood."

As the man's words echoed in her ears, Maggie threw her hands over her mouth and let out a gasp of air. Tears of recognition spilled over her eyelids and she flushed, letting out a cheer that would have made all of Arizona proud. Fernando, who had his arms around her, simply smiled with justified pride. They both waved excitedly, and then lightly kissed.

"Give her another one," someone shouted from the crowd. "We need a picture."

Kissing Maggie again, only this time more passionately, Fernando whispered, "You did it, *mi amor* . . . you just flew the race of your life, and you won."

"The race of my life, darling, was when I caught you. Today's race, although most gratifying, will always be my second greatest race."

As Maggie's words of poetic humor escaped her lips, Fernando simply squeezed her tightly, closing his eyes as he rocked her back and forth. This moment was one to be savored for all time, and somehow neither wanted it to end.

Later in the evening, after Fernando and Maggie had returned to their apartment, they received an unexpected guest. As Maggie answered the door, she was totally surprised to see Sergé the Russian holding his hat in his hand.

"May I please come in?"

Sergé's polite nature again surprised Maggie, yet still in shock over winning the race, she smiled and said, "But, of course. Fernando, darling, we have a special guest."

For the next half hour, after each of the two contestants related their separate experiences to each other and to Fernando, Maggie was dumbfounded.

"You say, Sergé, that you were flying above the storm when your engine cut out on you? I . . . I don't really know what to say."

"I am not sure, madam, there is anything to say. It is unexplainable. All I know is that, after slowing down and being tossed mercilessly around in the storm, the engine started back up and I continued my flight. By then, though, I had lost most of my altitude, and I stabilized just meters in front of you."

"But did you know she was there?" Fernando asked, unbelieving.

"Not at first," admitted the Russian. "But as if I were being spoken to, I felt the urge to turn and look to my rear. There, not more than 50 meters behind me, was your Maggie's Staggerwing. I was so taken back, I allowed her to come to my side."

"And you signalled that all was okay."

"Yes, to be sure. I don't know why I did that, really," he mused, pushing his lower lip up against his moustache. "I could see that we were coming out of the storm, though, and I needed to regain my altitude and get back in the race. It was really quite ironic."

"To say the least," Maggie whispered honestly. But she had another explanation, one she would reserve for just Fernando. She could share it later, after Sergé had gone. For now, however, she wanted to savor the moment with this giant, gentle man from Russia. He had become a true friend, and somehow the moment they had shared over the skies of central Arizona would be etched forever in her mind.

Ten days later, after completing their employment with the movie, and after enjoying the festivities and accolades given in Maggie's honor, she and Fernando climbed aboard the Staggerwing. It was only the second time for either to be aboard the craft since completing the race. The first had been to load what belongings they could take with them to Buenos Aires. Fernando, settling in the pilot's chair in the cockpit, strapped himself in and then assisted Maggie in doing the same. As they lifted into the air and banked toward the east, Fernando spoke, "Thank you, Maggie, for understanding our urgency to return to Buenos Aires. I feel just terrible about the death of our foreman in the labor dispute. Roberto's cablegram yesterday has shaken me to the core. I really believe I can have a calming influence on the unions once I get there, and now this will make that possible."

"You know," Maggie replied honestly, "I support you one hundred percent."

"Well," Fernando added, "we're on our way to a world you won't believe—the *pampas* of Argentina. I would have loved to have taken you over for a brief visit with your family, but that will have to come later."

"We have no other choice, Fernando. Besides, this will give us a great excuse to invite my family down to spend some time in Argentina."

"The very moment they can come," Fernando stated excitedly.

They were both silent, basking in the peace and quiet that engulfed them. At last, looking over to Fernando, Maggie asked, "Penny for your thoughts, darling?"

Maggie's request, as always, was simple and to the point. It was also made when Fernando was having a difficult time seeing clearly.

"Actually, Maggie," he smiled, his heart heaving with unexpected emotion, "I think . . . I *know* that my father loves you."

Fernando's voice broke when he said the words, and Maggie allowed them to linger briefly in the cabin of the plane.

"He also loves you, Fernando, or else why would he want me to stay here in this life, while he basks in the serenity of the world of spirits?"

"Point well taken, my love . . . point well taken . . . . But, do you know what else? I love your book."

"My book?" Maggie questioned honestly.

"Yes, your infamous Book of Mormon. I finished it last night, and although I want to proceed with caution, I think the most beautiful pool in the world—in our front yard—would be the perfect place for me to be baptized—if we can find some Alma-like fellow who can baptize me. I know it's not the Waters of Mormon, Honey, but—"

"Fernando! I didn't even know you were *reading* the Book of Mormon."

"Of course not . . . that was my plan. I just needed to do it quietly and learn for myself whether or not it is true. Before Father died, he mentioned that he had never felt what he felt in your parents' home, and his words stuck. I think he was referring to an embuing of the Spirit of the Lord, Maggie, although I may not be saying it right . . . ."

Fernando's words came out so softly, and so genuinely, that Maggie was caught completely off guard. "And you want to be *baptized?!*"

270

"Well, of course. How else are you going to get me into that temple of yours?"

"Oh, darling, I don't know what to say, I—"

Without completing her thought, Maggie released her shoulderstrap, removed her leather helmet and goggles, then twisted around. Pulling herself over next to Fernando, she pressed her lips against his, fully oblivious to the fact that the plane was flying without a pilot. But that didn't seem to matter. What did matter was that the two newlyweds were locked in each other's arms, enjoying the warmth of one another's emotions.

"Fernando, darling, I have a surprise of my own, if you are stable enough to handle it. I—"

"Well, then spill the beans, Maggie. What is it?"

"Oh, I don't know. Perhaps nothing that's important . . . ."

"Maggie, *pleeaase!!*"

"Very well, my handsome husband, I will. You, my gaucho prince, are going to be a daddy!"

Maggie's announcement took several seconds to sink in, but when it did, Fernando let out with a booming "WAA-HOOOO!!!! We're going to have a son!!!!"

"Who says it's going to be a son?"

"Why, I don't know. I just assumed that—"

"That your ego demands it?"

Maggie's question was stated in jest, and both laughed. It was a moment of discovery, and a moment to give thanks.

Maggie, her mind spinning wildly as she listened as Fernando offered a simple prayer of gratitude, considered the announcement she had just made. She closed both eyes and focused her entire energies in expressing her gratitude for her husband's faith, and his humility.

Fernando—in the ambiance of love—finished praying, then closed his left eye while they kissed. His right eye, however, in the spirit of caution, continued its bead on the panel ahead. It was a marvelous feat; and he smiled inwardly, proud of his newly discovered capability.

The plane, seemingly aware of the moment, droned on. Then, gaining altitude, it began to feel very much like it had a mind of its own. They were approaching the Mexican border over the horizon, and an entire life of adventure awaited them.